PRAISE FOR
THE NIGHT GWEN STACY DIED

"Bruni drops us into a dreamy world where comic book characters and psychic visions are as real as teenage boredom and young love. Strange, funny, sexy, and full of insights you'll want to revisit, Bruni's debut is a magical story, a white-knuckle thrill ride."

— DIANA SPECHLER, author of *Who by Fire*

"A brave and bold new voice. This thrilling novel is as wise and intelligent as it is young at heart. With humor and grace, Bruni takes us on an unexpected adventure of love and loss, of beginnings and ends, all the while showing us what it really means to be a hero."

— ALISON ESPACH, author of *The Adults*

"The perspective shifts, slippery identities, and lurking weirdness in this book recall the peak moments of Kurosawa, Hitchcock, and Lynch; Sarah Bruni even choreographs her production with the easy verve and keen eye of a great director. But to describe *The Night Gwen Stacy Died* in cinematic terms would risk slighting the patience and generosity and grace of Bruni's language, and it's that bighearted, sneakily exhilarating voice that can finally be only the work of a masterful writer."

— SEAN HOWE, author of
Marvel Comics: The Untold Story

"Bruni's fiercely smart and delectably unpredictable first novel delivers again and again that most sought-after shiver up the spine, the chill that comes when you realize the world you thought you knew and understood is newer and stranger than you ever dared imagine. *The Night Gwen Stacy Died* is a genuine page-turner."
— KATHRYN DAVIS, author of *The Thin Place*

"Mixed into this novel's blustery atmosphere are gusts of contemporary masters, like Joy Williams, Lorrie Moore, Kelly Link, and Michael Chabon. But, like the heroes of her story, Bruni is too spirited to be confined by the voices and tales of others. The magic in the air, it turns out, is Bruni's singular voice, a spell that so easily carried me away. Bruni's debut novel gave me the sort of reading experience I always hope for but almost never find: a world that somehow both resembles the one in which I live and is also unlike any other I've ever seen or read."
— STEFAN MERRILL BLOCK, author of
The Story of Forgetting

"In this sterling debut, a pseudo Bonnie and Clyde with Peter Parker and Gwen Stacy delusions go on the lam in Iowa and hide out in Chicago, but the pleasures here go far beyond the propulsive narrative. The prose is blade-sharp, the eerie love story is leavened with moments of unforced wit, and the nuanced observations are utterly idiosyncratic. It's as if Lorrie Moore wrote a taut thriller — not an updated Western, but a modern Midwestern."
— TEDDY WAYNE, author of
The Love Song of Jonny Valentine

THE NIGHT GWEN STACY DIED

GWEN DIED

SARAH BRUNI

A MARINER ORIGINAL

MARINER BOOKS

HOUGHTON MIFFLIN HARCOURT

Boston   New York   2013

For information about permission to reproduce selections from this book,
write to Permissions, Houghton Mifflin Harcourt Publishing Company,
215 Park Avenue South, New York, New York 10003.

WWW.HMHBOOKS.COM

Library of Congress Cataloging-in-Publication Data
Bruni, Sarah.
The Night Gwen Stacy Died / Sarah Bruni.
pages cm
"A Mariner Original."
ISBN 978-0-547-89816-2
1. Young women — Psychology — Fiction. 2. Self-realization in
women — Fiction. 3. Iowa — Fiction. I. Title.
PS3602.R848N54 2013
813'.6 — dc23 2012040352

Book design by Patrick Barry

Printed in the United States of America
DOC 10 9 8 7 6 5 4 3 2 1

For my parents
and for my brothers

PART ONE

SEASONAL CHANGE WAS descending in its temperamental, plague-like way in fits and spurts on the middle of the country. There was a false sense to the air, all the wrong smells. That spring, Sheila bought herself a single-speed bicycle from the outdoor auction along Interstate 80. She rode it down the Coralville strip to work. She pedaled fast, as if to keep up with traffic — an exercise in futility — and swallowed the air in gulps. When she reached the Sinclair station, Sheila felt faintly dazed, like someone about to pass out. Sometimes she saw black spots where the white line of road was supposed to be. "You all right? Miss?" Motorists would lean their heads out windows when Sheila stopped on the shoulder of the highway to catch her breath. Or sometimes: "Lady, get out of the road!" This was Iowa; no one rode bikes along the highway. Bicycling was a nice hobby for children but not a reliable mode of transportation. For Sheila, this was the most exhilarating part of the day. This was the only exhilarating part of the day.

It was the spring of the year that coyote sightings started garnering national attention. The headlines sounded like a string of bad jokes: COYOTE WALKS INTO A BAR. COYOTE CAUGHT SLEEP-

ING IN MATTRESS SHOP. PACK OF COYOTES CAUSES DELAYS AT O'HARE. The scientific community insisted there was nothing to worry about, that the species was extremely adaptable, that they mostly traveled at night, that they rarely ate domestic animals without provocation. Yet, people couldn't help but notice how stealthily the coyotes seemed to be infiltrating the small towns and cities. Morning joggers complained of coyotes crouched behind trees along public parks. The presence of the animals often wasn't witnessed firsthand by more than a few early risers. But hearing of such sightings was enough — also knowing they were out there at night, outsmarting the rats, sleeping in the alleys.

It felt as if entire ecosystems had become confused. That fall, two whales had dragged their giant bellies onto dry land. The whales seemed determined to beach themselves despite rescuers' efforts to return them to the water. Strange symbiotic relationships were popping up everywhere, often involving the abandoned offspring of one species adopting an unlikely surrogate parent. A lion cub might choose a lizard as its mother and receive a five-minute slot on the evening news, curbing coverage of the latest political corruption scandal or plane crash.

There were other things too. Even in the Midwest, anyone could tell that the whole planet was out of whack. It had been too warm for snow until well after New Year's. The salt-truck drivers were mad as hell. Shovel sales were way down. It was months later that all that hovering precipitation finally found its way to street level. March came in like a lion, went out like a lamb being devoured by a coyote. Which is to say that it warmed up, but in a sneaky, violent way that made everyone slow to pull out their lighter clothes, so as not to look gullible at a time when everything felt like a fluke.

You could feel all this in the air, riding to work each day. Sheila was a gas station attendant, and she was a model employee. Four days a week she biked along the strip, straight from school to the station. She never missed a shift. She never called in sick. She was saving up. She had a year's worth of deposits in the bank — all from working at the Sinclair station — and when that growing fund hit a certain number, she was leaving the country for an undetermined length of time. She was buying a plane ticket to Paris, and anyone who had a problem with that could shove it. "France?" her father said when Sheila told him her destination. When he said it, the whole country sounded like an adolescent stunt, a dog in a plaid coat and socks. "Remind me again what's wrong with your own country? Are you hearing this?" he'd ask Sheila's mother, who would shake her head or shrug. Her sister, Andrea, and her sister's fiancé, Donny, thought it was a frivolous way to spend money. They were saving to open a restaurant. Andrea was watching prices for lots on the west side of town. There was a business plan. It was going to be called Donny's Grill.

"But you do all the cooking," Sheila had protested.

"Yeah, well, it's a team thing. We're a team, okay? Teamwork? Does that mean anything to you?" asked Andrea. "Think about it. Would you eat at a place called Donny and Andrea's Grill?"

"No," said Sheila.

"No, you wouldn't. And you know why? 'Cause it's too friggin' long. Besides," she said, "we're going to try doing all the cooking together."

Andrea had moved out of the house two years ago, which was about how long she had been engaged. She started wearing acrylic fingernails so that the hand with her ring didn't look so otherwise lonely and unadorned. She favored shades of salmon. As a girl Andrea had been overweight and eager to fall in love. Sheila wanted, of course, to fall in love, but not with someone like Donny. Not with someone from Iowa.

Sleeping in her parents' house, Sheila would sometimes wake

to the wheels of jeeps screeching around the corner. As they turned near the street, several boys would shout, "Iowa Hawkeye football!" Then, they would make animal noises. The real animals that lived nearby were quiet, frantic things that made no sounds. Squirrels that scattered and little sparrows that hopped between the cracks in the sidewalk, scouting out crumbs with an awkward deference. Most of the animals that had been indigenous to the land before the college moved in had been preserved in the Iowa Museum of Natural History on the third floor of Macbride Hall. There, they were stuffed and arranged before paintings of their natural habitats, interacting with predators, feeding their young. Several prairie dog pups curled up close beside their sleeping mother; rabbits and ground birds were positioned as if scurrying at the feet of an elk. A single coyote in a large case did nothing but stare straight ahead, sitting off to the side of the other animals, as if it were too proud to act alive. The plaque outside its case said, "Mountain coyote. Genus and species: *Canis latrans lestes*. Indigenous to Nevada and California, the species can be found from the Rocky Mountains westward, as far north as British Columbia and as far south as Arizona and New Mexico."

The coyote, the sign explained, takes its name from the Spanish word *coyote* — *coyote* from *coyote!* This redundancy struck Sheila as hilarious — but the scientific name was derived from the Latin: barking dog. Coyotes were wilder, noisier cousins of dogs: kept later hours, spanned greater territories. Their hunting was marked by extraordinarily relentless patience. Coyotes were stubborn, though also oddly adaptable. Their communication, described as howls and yips, was most often heard in the spring, but also in the fall, the time of year when young pups leave their families to establish new territories. "You idiot, you could have gone anywhere," she wanted to say to the coyote in the case, "and you came to Iowa?" But the coyote still seemed young; clearly, it either was the progeny of transients, or it migrated straight to Iowa only to be promptly shot and stuffed.

The coyote that Sheila visited always regarded her with a look that seemed to say, Well, it's just you and me here, isn't it? We might as well say everything. Sheila liked how isolated the coyote seemed to be in the middle of its glass case, staring straight forward as if about to address her, mixed-up in a survival narrative that had nothing to do with other coyotes, a transplant from some other territory. At least once a week Sheila rode her bike to Macbride Hall, pressed her nose to the smooth glass of the display case, and spilled her heart out.

Sometimes she would ask the coyote questions that she never had the guts to ask anyone alive. The coyote regarded Sheila stiff lipped from inside its case. The last time she had visited, Sheila had pushed her forehead flat against the glass and asked, "How am I ever going to get out of here?"

The coyote knew things. You could just tell. Sheila wasn't stupid enough to expect a straight answer to a question posed like this, but she knew how to interpret signs. This was how things were in the middle of the country. People believed in waiting for signs. People believed that things happened for a reason, and Sheila was not above this logic. She fixed her eyes on the still glass eyes of the coyote. The coyote was past the point of escape, but in its eyes was something fleeting that belied a former familiarity with the concept.

When you work in a gas station, people love to assume there's something wrong with you. That you're not driven, or you're lazy, or you didn't have the grades in high school, or you're not all there. It makes them feel better about their own lives. This was just a theory that Sheila was harboring. But it was a theory based on research and observation. Behind the counter, she performed sociological experiments. Sometimes, still red faced from her ride in, she'd sit behind the counter, out of breath, and stare into space, sneak an occasional cigarette, or put quarters into the M&M's dispenser and listen to the stale candy turning around in her mouth like gravel under a wheel. When customers would enter the station and find her gnawing on hard candy by the handful, Sheila would receive cold, disapproving looks, especially from women, many of whom were not that much older than Sheila. "Really?" their looks said, "Isn't there something sort of pathetic about this?"

Other times, Sheila would place her French vocabulary workbook on the counter. She wouldn't even open it, just let it sit there between herself and whomever she was helping. The effect was remarkable. "What a great job for a student!" the same women would shout. "You must get all your homework done here." As she counted their change, Sheila would smile in a demure, hard-working way and let them go ahead and think whatever they liked. She was a student; she was a gas station attendant. Student. Gas station attendant. A young woman with promise. A burnout at seventeen. She had observed women around here long enough to see the way they sized one another up like that, always a series of calculations to determine who would amount to something, who would amount to nothing. So she liked to move the French book around and screw up their calculations. She thought the whole town could go to hell.

Sheila was a decent student, actually. Not great — probably good enough to get herself in to some college, but not enough to get scholarship money. Her father had told her that he could help her out a little, but if she wanted to do college, she was going to need to take out loans. The thing was, Sheila felt like she had a pretty good idea of what college entailed; she had grown up in a town that bordered one of the more modestly sized Big Ten universities in the Midwest. The boys wore white hats, backward, and called each other *fag* as a term of endearment. The girls carried handbags to class in lieu of backpacks and did not seem to own winter coats. On weekends during snowy weather, girls could be seen in tight black pants and multicolored leotardlike tops, floundering between bars in hordes to keep warm while buying gyros, safety in numbers against frostbite. By the time she was about eleven, Sheila felt she had already been to college, and she really hadn't thought much of the experience. Instead, she was saving all her money, and she was going somewhere she hadn't lived her entire life.

Most of the teachers in her high school — themselves the products of a liberal arts education — endlessly praised the benefits of applying to college straightaway, but her French teacher was the exception to this rule. "Yes, let's all rush off to school and waste thousands of dollars before we even know what we care to study or do with our lives!" Ms. Lawrence mocked the conventional wisdom that the guidance counselors were doling out. When speaking in English, Ms. Lawrence had a habit of using the first person plural like this and engaging in arguments with herself. She wore complicated patterned scarves in her hair and had immaculate posture. She had been sighted kissing a man — through the window of a car in the school parking lot — who looked about ten years her junior and whom she referred to as her "boyfriend." She would come to class on Mondays and say things like, "Did anyone make it to the opening of *Mother Courage* this weekend at Hancher? My boyfriend and I went on Friday, and it was really exceptional — well, if you're in the mood for Brecht." Ms. Lawrence had come to Iowa from Delaware, a place far away enough that it might as well have been France. A humble state, modest in size, that Sheila imagined to be full of lanky women with hairstyles and handwriting as deliberate and meaningful as Ms. Lawrence's.

Très bien! Ms. Lawrence would write in the margins of Sheila's homework. *Fantastique.* And staring into the neat, narrow letters that Ms. Lawrence's pen had produced, Sheila felt a temporary relief pass over her like finally here was someone with whom she could communicate.

At the station, Sheila had a few consistent patrons. Ned, a Vietnam vet, came in daily to purchase a pack of Pall Malls with change that he accumulated from bottle returns. Five cents for empties in Iowa. He'd stuff his hands deep into the pockets of his jeans and pull out fistfuls of change — he started with the pennies and stacked them up in tidy piles of ten on the counter. Sometimes Sheila would tire of counting and say, "Ned, they're on the house today," but Ned didn't want her charity.

There was a guy who bought gas sometimes, or sometimes a pack of Camel straights. The first time Sheila checked his ID — state law for anyone who appeared under twenty-seven, although he hardly did — she barely registered that his name was Peter Parker, but she wondered about it later. Peter Parker didn't talk much. The first couple of times she offered him the wrong pack of cigarettes he looked away and said, "Straights, no filter." So she thought he was a bit stuck-up. Once she started getting it right, she'd have the pack waiting on the counter for him before he asked for it; sometimes she'd give him the cigarettes for free. She could tell Peter appreciated her generosity, but he never let on. He wouldn't even say thank you, just sort of tip his head.

The gas station was on the same highway as the exit for one of the biggest malls in Iowa. Cars would pull off Interstate 80, cars from all over the state. There were vans and minivans and pickup trucks. They were filled with people, kids with faces pressed against the windows in the back seats. The men all came into the station and bought a pack of gum or a soda and asked her how much farther to the mall, just straight ahead, was it? Was it true that the mall had a carousel inside? A movie theater? An ice-skating rink?

They would pile their families into the truck and start driving blindly. When they reached the gas station they knew they were on the right track, but the kids had become restless, they needed gum to quiet their running mouths. Their mothers needed a fresh pack of Ultra Light 100s, their fathers needed confirmation that they were almost there.

"I hear this mall's got twenty restaurants inside," they'd say.

"At least," said Sheila. "There's a whole food court."

"Just straight ahead, then?"

"Yep."

Peter Parker stood in line once behind one of these families, smirking. When he reached her register he put on a voice. He made his eyes all big and pushed his dark hair off his brow. He said, "I hear this here mall's got a full casino on a riverboat floating in the basement, and the parking lot is paved with gold." He leaned into her across the counter, and Sheila felt her stomach rise in her chest as the distance closed between them.

"Absolutely right," she said. It was the first time they had spoken more than the few words necessary to exchange money for cigarettes or gasoline.

"So what time do you get off?" Peter said. "Sit at the blackjack table with me and we'll throw some cards around. What do you say? We'll make a killing."

"I get off at eight," Sheila heard herself say.

In her mind, the slot machines glittered. Coins spilled from them to the floor. People threw up their hands. People raised their glasses. When she closed up the station and started to ride her bike home, she was a little hurt that he never showed, though obviously he had no intention of doing so from the start. She had to reason with herself on the ride home — that casinos were desperate and lonely places, that she wasn't even old enough to gamble, and that anyway, the place didn't exist! — to stop conjuring an image of Peter playing slots alone, to stop thinking of the fact that he hadn't come back for her.

But after this day he rarely missed one of her shifts. Peter made it a point to sit with her for a few minutes in the station, long enough for a cigarette and a conversation. After he'd been coming in for a while, Sheila asked Donny if he knew of any Peter Parkers. "Sure I do," Donny said. "Spider-Man." No, not Spider-Man, Sheila had explained patiently. Just some guy. "Some guy who thinks he's fucking Spider-Man," Donny said. But Peter Parker was just a guy who drove a cab at night and who would stay for five or ten minutes when he came into the gas station if he was between fares. Sheila was supposed to discourage patrons from loitering like this — there were some shady characters who drove up and down the Coralville strip after nine — but she liked Peter Parker. He had nice hair, dark, overgrown, with strange waves that fell into his eyes if he leaned in to look at something closely, like if he was spilling the contents of his pockets on the counter, searching for a five. There was always dirt under his fingernails when he rested his hands on the counter, and his hands were broad and calloused, like maybe they served him in a particular way that had nothing to do with gesticulation or the exchange of money. Donny was probably wrong about Peter Parker. It was a common enough name. Anyone could have it. But it gave Sheila a welcome diversion to reroute her brain in the direction of secret identities and second lives. It seemed a fine way to pass the time to imagine that the dirt under his fingernails was residue from saving the world.

"I'm home!" Sheila called through the house after slamming the door behind her. She walked into the kitchen, and her mother appeared, standing over the sink with a sponge in her hand, Sheila's father beside her with a towel. After thirty years of marriage, they still washed the dishes together every night. They took turns being the one to wash, the one to dry.

"Hi honey," her mother said. "We're just cleaning up from dinner."

Sometimes they waited for her to eat on the evenings she worked in the station, but if she got off too late, they'd save a plate of whatever dinner had been for her to heat up in the microwave.

Her parents hadn't wanted her to take the job at the Sinclair station. Her mother thought it was a job for a man — the tire grease, the cigarettes. Her father thought gas stations on the strip weren't safe at night.

"Some crazy idiot could come in and rob the place," her father had said. "And then what are you going to do, a girl alone in a gas station?"

"I'd give them the money," she had said. "And I'd call the cops. Same as you would."

"You just better hope that's all you'd have to give," her father said, "in a situation like that."

"Like what else?" Sheila had asked, but her father said nothing. Was the implication that she would be sexually accosted or attacked? Was this why it was irresponsible for a teenage girl to take an evening job at a gas station? Because the possibility existed that certain men couldn't resist whipping out their genitals and making demands of other people? One always needed to suspect! One needed to be steadfast, vigilant! Especially girls like Sheila who were charged with *applying* themselves. For example: the option of college was made available to girls like Sheila by generations of struggle, and now she wasn't even going to *apply*? She was going to work in a crappy gas station to save money for some ambiguous plan?

"Good thing I'm almost eighteen," Sheila had insisted. "Old enough to make some of my own decisions, I'd guess."

But of course she was living at home. Her father was always quick to bring up that fact. She was living in his house. None of it mattered anyway, Sheila had liked to tell everyone, because by the end of the year she'd be fluent in a completely foreign language, and living in another country as well.

"This country's not good enough for you?" her father had asked recently. He had caught her making French vowel sounds in the hallway while carrying a basket of laundry up to her room.

"That's right," said Sheila. "Too many rules."

"Because the French don't have any rules," her father said.

Sheila shrugged her shoulders. "Je ne sais pas."

She didn't know, not really. That was why it was so difficult to have an argument about her plans. When posed the question of what exactly she would be doing in France, Sheila was hard-pressed to generate a response that sounded acceptable to most of her adversaries. The truth was that her goals were somewhat modest. She imagined she would have a job in a shop or behind a counter somewhere. She imagined she would rent a room with a window that opened onto a street with traffic. Maybe there would be friends, some sort of community, but mostly she saw herself negotiating the city streets with a bicycle, its basket filled with the vegetables whose names she knew how to pronounce. The point was only that this place existed, and she could get to it. The point was only that for a time she would be there, and *there* was not here.

Her father had studied her hard around the eyes. He said, "You can't start a life in a language you don't understand, Sheila." Sheila had been ready to say more, to defend the fact that she already understood loads of conjugations and vocabulary, but her father hadn't taken his eyes off hers. He held her stare until she looked down at her fingernails. Historically, in the family hierarchy, her father was the parent with whom Sheila could have a reasonable dialogue, a good argument. When things became heated, her mother got a breathless look and went to fold laundry in the other room. But lately, her father was the quiet one, as if defeated by the thought of competing with a foreign country for his daughter's affection. It was Sheila's mother these days who would say things like, "Honey, we just don't understand why you feel you need to do this." As if Sheila had announced that she was going off to war, as if she were proposing to irrevocably disown them all.

"I mean, how will that work, exactly?" her mom had asked. "Are you going to come home for Christmas, or are you just going to start celebrating holidays with a bunch of foreigners instead of with your family?"

Now Sheila opened the fridge and found a plate of some kind of meat and mashed potatoes. Her parents finished washing the dishes and hovered around her briefly, like insects, like hummingbirds.

"How was your day?" her mother asked.

"Fine," Sheila said. She peeled back the plastic wrap and set the microwave for two minutes.

"Learn anything at school?" her father asked like some dad on television.

Sheila thought for a second. She thought, a scalene triangle has no equal sides, no equal angles. She thought, je veuille, tu veuilles, elle veuille. Also, something about the Ancient Mariner and his albatross necklace.

"Not really," she said.

Her father nodded and folded his towel on the counter. Her mother kissed her forehead.

"Turn off all the lights before you come up, sweetie," her mom said.

Sheila sat at the kitchen table with her plate. There was a time when her parents would sit with her and keep her company while she finished eating, but that time seemed to have passed. There was a time when there were things to say to these people — her parents — things to explain, to ask, to offer, and it made her bottom lip tremble in the start of what could be, but was not, a sob, to watch her father fold his towel and take the stairs slowly up to his bedroom, the weight of his hand on the banister, because maybe it was her fault that in seventeen years she had already exhausted the possibilities for communicating with the people who had produced her.

Sheila sat under the cool light over the kitchen table, raking her fork through her mashed potatoes, flattening and raking, flattening, then raking, conjuring a white field on her plate, an alien terrain that required her attention, a plot of land that required nothing so much as her specific and ardent and immediate care.

IN THE MIDDLE of the night, it was always the same. The dreams told the dreamer, pay attention. The dreams told the dreamer, consider *this* and consider *that*, and for the most part, it was fine to consider these things, to engage the subconscious in the exercise of willful consideration.

Always the dreams told the dreamer, Let's pretend the world is this way for a few minutes, I mean, no big deal, no commitment, just something to do until you wake up.

Come on, say the dreams, it'll be fun.

Imagine: A stairway. A city map. A girl in her underwear. A lion lives in your basement. A migratory bird explains microclimates in the Pacific Northwest. A train runs on the output of your mental energies.

Hypothetically speaking, none of these dreams would present a problem. The dreamer actually thought of these dreams as enjoyable. But there were other dreams, too. The other kind started the same way, with a directive — pay attention. But this time it wasn't a suggestion; it was more like a demand. It was more like a threat. These dreams felt more like lived events that would happen somewhere to someone if the dreamer didn't intercept them in time.

Here's one: You are driving to Chicago. Why Chicago? It's difficult to say, but every fifteen to twenty miles the signs on the road are counting down to that city, so in the logic of dreams, this word, *Chicago*, becomes synonymous with *destination*. A beautiful girl sits beside you in the car. A gun rests in the glove compartment. The gun is small and cold; you know this because before it was in the glove compartment, it was in your hand, pointed toward the girl. The girl you know from somewhere, she's been in your dreams before, but you can't place her, you can't name her in the same way you can name this place where you're going.

There is a sense of urgency. The windows are open and the breeze picks up your hair and slaps at your cheeks and chin. The mile markers count down: fifty miles, then fifteen, then the unknown skyscrapers are a visible glow ahead in the distance. You hear a radio playing softly somewhere. You see a parking lot, a pigeon flap one wing helplessly, crushed metal floating in stacks down the surface of a narrow river. An entire scrap yard of flattened cars, half of them inching downstream, the sun catching the light off a resilient fender. The other half stacked on top of one another in an empty lot, their true colors muted by all the dust that has settled. The dust is the residue from nearby explosions. Sometimes there are explosions, the dream advises. You try to pay attention.

Then there is the cramped apartment you don't recognize. What happens next is the thing you can't shake. You see a man walk into the room. His eyes are clear and slightly familiar. The rest you see in fragments, flashes that blur and fade around the corners. You see him walk into the bathroom with a clenched fist, open his fist above his mouth, and invite the small trail of white pills into his body. They stick in the man's throat, and you see him start to cough, to choke. You see the man start to moan, and everything that follows. By now it is impossible to stop watching, to turn it off.

He reminds you of someone you know. In the terror logic of the dream, the vision, the threat, the premonition, you understand that you are the only one who can save him from himself.

AS SHEILA DISMOUNTED in the school parking lot, she always inhaled as much of the outside air as she could before heeding the last warning bell, locking up her bike, and submitting herself to the eight-period day. She caught her breath with her hands resting on her knees while she watched the rest of the student body — her peers — disengage from cars, embraces, conversations, and wander, group by group, into the building. It was senior year. Everyone had already become whatever they were going to be to one another for the rest of their time together. Alliances had been formed, rivalries established, and now the name of the game was hang on like hell to what you had worked to get, and hope for the best. Reinvention was futile; deliverance was not up for discussion.

She walked into first-period English and took her seat.

"Okay, people," Mrs. Gavin was saying, "announcements. Listen up."

Good morning, said the voice over the PA. Can I have your attention please? Annual blood drive starts tomorrow. As always, type O, we're depending on you! The votes are in and the theme for Spring Fling, as decided by popular demand, will be Girls Just

Wanna Have Fun! The voice over the PA reminded the students that it was Spirit Week and said they should feel comfortable expressing their school spirit by creatively incorporating the colors of the Cougar — blue and orange — into their manner of dress. The students were reminded that hats, bandannas, head-coverings of any kind were not permitted. T-shirts with offensive language or T-shirts bearing explicit product insignia, also unacceptable. The students were encouraged, as always, to use good taste when selecting socially appropriate ways to show their school enthusiasm during Spirit Week. There would be a pep rally the following Friday in anticipation of Spring Fling, which was something everyone could look forward to, but, of course, the antics that ensued during the last school-wide pep rally would not be repeated.

The announcements droned on. Sheila made a pillow of her crossed arms on her desk and placed her head there. No matter what was said over the PA on a given morning, Sheila could rest assured that it did not apply to her. She had been fairly successful up until this point of her high school career existing just on the periphery of whatever was going on.

She knew how to give a straight answer to a question. She knew how to make eye contact. She had decent grades, mostly Bs. She had two physical assets: wide eyes, long legs. This physical evaluation was not Sheila's own. These were only the facts; these were the parts of her body that boys' eyes rested on when they glanced in her direction. Otherwise, everything about her was expected. She was on the skinny side, and tallish — but not so tall that her height summoned attention — with long, light brown hair. Light brown, dirty blond — the same hair everyone had.

She had one ally in the cafeteria: Anthony Pignatelli. Anthony was the only real friend she had hung on to since the start of high school. She knew some people assumed they were a couple, and as far as Sheila was concerned, people could say whatever they wanted about her and Anthony Pignatelli. He was a normal kid, and he made her laugh. Which was more than you could say about most people.

To the untrained eye, the cafeteria might appear to be simply a place for students to eat, but in fact, it was composed of two disparate social spheres, universally referred to by their relative size: Small Caf and Large Caf. Small Caf was crowded — skinny girls shared metal folding chairs at the most populated tables — because it was preferable to squeeze together than to surrender one of their own to Large Caf. Large Caf, by contrast, was underpopulated. Empty chairs abounded. Much in the way that a deserted city with formerly big ambitions might feature large parks and grand, sweeping avenues but a few too many boarded-up windows as a result of its waning population, the space in Large Caf made it quite easy to detect who was eating alone; who had shimmied a folding chair up to the end of a table to seem a part of it but was, in fact, not; who clearly must be recognized — even by the residents of that respective Large Caf table — as extraneous.

Freshman year, before Sheila had understood all of this, she'd sat at a Small Caf table while half its residents were still in the lunch line — a table of girls. The girls did not make any attempt to remove her, but when the table had reached capacity and Jessica Reynolds had to pull up a folding chair from another table, someone finally leaned in and made contact. "Who are you?" the girl asked.

"Sheila," Sheila said.

"Sheila," the girl repeated slowly amid laughter, nodding as if homing in on some shared truth.

Sheila took a bite of her sandwich. This had been back before she completely gave up on the entire student body. This had been back when she still cared about things like what other people thought.

"To Sheila," someone raised a Pepsi in the air, and the table drank to her.

Sheila forced a smile.

Then someone else raised her drink, and it happened again. It happened six times during the lunch period. Sheila finished her sandwich and never stepped into Small Caf again.

She was wary of groups. There was an impenetrable exchange of glances, an unspoken etiquette to which she had never felt privy, and tables in Small Caf obviously operated by these same unknowable rules. Sheila had always preferred the company of intense and loyal outsiders. If there were only two people in a given conversation, there was not as much room for error, margin for misinterpretation. As a child, her only friend had been a reclusive raven-haired girl in the neighborhood named Amelia. Amelia's father was perpetually away on business, and her mother had a habit of sleeping until noon and spending the day pacing around the kitchen in lacy pajama shirts, refilling her glass from an endless supply of a blended drink. Amelia's family was from Miami, and the way that Sheila's own mother pronounced the word *Miami*, Sheila had the impression it was an untrustworthy landscape: polluted and dangerous. She had always thought Amelia's mother very glamorous, but Amelia did not agree. Amelia was not allowed to come out of the house and play until her mother woke up, so Sheila would often spend the long late morning hours camped outside of Amelia's bedroom window with a folding chair and a notebook, and together, through the screen, the girls would write plays with titles like *Amelia and Sheila Save the Day* and *Amelia and Sheila Save the Day Again*. On summer nights, they gave performances on the concrete patio of Amelia's yard and all the adults would line up folding lawn chairs in the grass: clapping awkwardly, making stiff chitchat during intermission. When Amelia was eleven, her family moved back to Miami. "Well, that's the way it goes, honey," Sheila's father had said. "That's life." This had seemed an unnecessarily heartless assessment of the situation, but it was true. She and Amelia wrote letters for the first few months, but before long, they fell out of the habit.

It was only after a week of eating lunch in front of her locker freshman year, dodging hall monitors, that Sheila attempted to stake out a more modest seat in the cafeteria. She had sat down at the other end of a safe-looking, half-populated Large Caf table and busied herself taking her sandwich and drink out of her paper bag, looking as extraordinarily preoccupied with it all as possible, when she heard the boy at the other end of the table say, "It's Sheila Gower, right?"

Sheila looked up from her sandwich slowly. It was always a shock to hear people you didn't know say your name. It made you wonder what else they knew.

"Yes," Sheila admitted.

"You're in my English class," the boy said.

He looked familiar. For a moment the words *pig* and *toenail* inexplicably flashed into her brain; she heard the words in tandem as a half-chant, a whisper. "Second period, Mr. Clemmont?" she asked.

"That's the one," said the boy. "I'm Anthony."

"Anthony what?"

"Pignatelli."

Pig Toenail. *Tony Pig Toenail.* That's how some of the other boys in her English class referred to him. But the name sounded different the way he said it.

Anthony seemed to see that this is what she was thinking because he said, "The 'G' is silent."

"Okay," Sheila said. "Is that like Spanish?"

"Italian," he said. "The 'G' is fucking silent anytime it comes before an 'N.'"

"Sure," Sheila said. "Cool." She nodded, but in her brain a neat row of pink toes persisted, nails pointed uniformly, dangerously in one direction. She stabbed her straw into the mouth of her juice box and gulped furiously.

"Wait," said Anthony, "Didn't you used to sit in the Small Caf?"

"Briefly," said Sheila. "But it turns out I don't have an eating disorder, so it's not really my crowd."

Anthony smiled. "You like the stuff we're reading in English?"

There had been a lot about disembodied hearts all that year. The hideous telltale variety, noisily thumping through the floorboards of a murderer's home. Then, there was the way some poet's heart was stolen during the cremation of his drowned body, and how his wife wrapped the damaged organ in a poem, like a piece of meat in butcher paper, and placed it in a drawer of her desk for thirty years. The point of everything they read — even freshman year — seemed to be about how life was short and everyone should just sleep together before they all died.

"You mean all that gather-ye-rosebuds crap?" Sheila asked.

It wasn't crap, not really. It was fascinating to conjure one's death and imagine life to be so brief a glint of a thing that all it made sense to do was grab hold of the closest breathing body and not let go. "I think Mr. Clemmont is maybe a little too invested in this unit," Sheila said finally.

Anthony was laughing. "Definitely," he said. "The guy is like obsessed with sex. If I have to 'unpack' one more metaphor about virgins and coy mistresses this semester I'm going to vomit."

"Second period is way too early for unpacking virgins," Sheila agreed.

This is how their friendship began. One of them would make observations about stupid people or stupid metaphors, and the other would laugh. For a while it seemed like she and Anthony weren't simply clinging to one another out of desperation, but actually had something in common. It wasn't until her senior year when she was enrolled in Mrs. Gavin's English class that Sheila considered the possibility that Mr. Clemmont had not been sex-obsessed at all. All of English literature was obsessed with sex. When she shared this observation with Anthony at lunch, Anthony seemed to agree wholeheartedly with this as well. After a while, it seemed there was little she could say that was disagreeable to him.

Today, Anthony was already sitting at their table, halfway through his sandwich, by the time Sheila got through the line and sat down.

"Didn't bring your lunch today?" he asked.

Sheila shook her head. "I didn't have time to pack one. I was at the station until late."

"That's so cool that you have this whole other life."

"Not really," Sheila said. "It's a gas station."

"Still," Anthony said. "Maybe some night I'll borrow a car and come and visit you. We could steal a pack of cigarettes and smoke them and make fun of all the people who come in."

"That's against the law," Sheila said. She could feel all the hairs standing up at the back of her neck. Her reaction surprised her. The thought of Anthony walking into the station made her uneasy. "I mean, you don't even smoke," she said.

"Yeah, but you do."

"Not really," Sheila said. "Only every once in a while to pass the time."

"Whatever," said Anthony. He took a bite from his apple. "Are you going to this pep rally thing next Friday?"

"No," said Sheila. "Are you?"

"I don't know," Anthony said. "Maybe. You're not even a little curious who'll get nominated?"

"Nominated?"

"Jesus, Sheila," Anthony chided her. "Spring Fling? They're nominating the court at the pep rally. They've only been talking about it over the PA for the last three weeks."

Sheila looked up at Anthony from her side of the table as if from the other side of the room, past the lunch line and panes of glass. He was wearing his favorite blue jeans and a faded T-shirt with a vintage ad for Orange Crush soda. It wasn't immediately obvious that these were the school colors, but there was no denying that that's what they were. It made her feel a little sad for him, and for an instant she wanted to grab ahold of Anthony's hand and save him from some obscure threat. She had been kissed by two boys in her entire life — once by a college boy she met swimming at the reservoir, once by a boy in the fluorescent-lit parking lot of a movie theater the summer after eighth grade — and both times the transition from talking to having his tongue in her mouth had felt non-existent in a way that made her wonder what had been going on in the boys' brains up until that moment. Was there something specific she had said, some obscure invitation, that made them think touching their tongues to hers was the obvious course of action? The thought occurred to her that this was happening all over the country. There were kids in every cafeteria draping themselves in the representative colors of cougars and falcons and mythological animals, pushing their tongues into one another's mouths, chanting things, casting votes for the kings and queens who would represent them. *But so what?* Sheila had to remind herself. This was high school.

It was a regular thing. It was no cause for alarm. It was nothing to be depressed about.

Pickup trucks were always pulling into the station. They had bumper stickers at eye level that said things like AMERICA: LOVE IT OR LEAVE, not even LEAVE IT, which at least would have been a parallel construction. Sheila knew all about parallel construction. She knew all about past participles and all about subjunctive tenses because she was teaching herself a whole new goddamn language. Her father's critique seemed to place her knowledge of French around that of a traveler with a well-read phrase book, but by her own assessment she had to give herself more credit. She had studied vocabulary for a wide range of social situations and predicaments, chapters with titles like "At the Library," "A Doctor's Visit," and "Accepting and Declining Invitations." She knew how to borrow rare books, blow off important social engagements, and describe obscure sources of pain in her body — vocabulary clearly way beyond the grasp of the prudent traveler. Behind the counter she had her English to French dictionary and a CD and workbook set. Sheila could play whatever she wanted over the speakers at the Sinclair station, so sometimes she played the workbook CD, and she'd join in conversations between ringing people up. Today she and the French CD woman had met at a museum.

"Ça va?" said the French woman on the CD.

"Ça va," said Sheila.

"Tu as de la chance d'être à Paris pour cette exposition."

"Pump four, sixteen dollars," said Sheila.

Ned never mistook her for one of the college girls, but if her French CDs were playing in the station when Sheila paused in her lesson to count out his payment, he'd solemnly repeat the foreign phrases along with the woman on the CD, as if he were taking the responsibility for saying the things that needed saying.

Truckers who walked into the station to buy a box of condoms or a bag of Doritos would stare at Sheila's lesson speechlessly for the eternity it took for their tanks to fill with diesel before saying something like, "You ever heard the French invented the threesome?" Sometimes they winked. With this particular kind of customer, Sheila played ignorant to her native language completely.

"Je suis désolée! Je ne comprends pas!"

Peter Parker usually let the lessons go without comment, but today he entered the station especially riled by something.

"What's that you just said?" Peter asked.

"Oh nothing," said Sheila. "There was a demonstration in the street, and one of the organizers was trying to give me a leaflet to read."

Peter snickered. "Did you take it?"

"Oh no, I refused to take it because I was practicing being furious over how this student demonstration has created a huge traffic jam in the street," said Sheila. "But the next time I practice this dialogue I will take the leaflet and practice being sympathetic to his cause."

"Lots of opportunities to speak French with student organizers around here?"

"For your information," Sheila said, "I'm getting the hell out of this town."

"Let me guess," said Peter. He raised his finger in the air as if it were an antenna picking up signals from Sheila's brain. "You're moving to Paris." He continued to hold his finger in the air and the smile persisted — knowing, accusing.

Sheila started to ring up Peter's pack of cigarettes. She said, "You owe me $6.25."

Peter made no attempt to reach for his wallet. He closed the distance between Sheila and himself and leaned in across the counter. "Tell me if I guessed wrong," he said.

Sheila placed a hand on her hip. "You're right," Sheila said. "I'm glad that amuses you. Now take your cigarettes and get out of my station."

"I'm not the least bit amused," said Peter. He didn't take his eyes off her. "I just don't quite understand what you're waiting for. If you want to leave, leave."

"It doesn't work that way," said Sheila.

"Says who?" said Peter.

"I'm saving money."

"How much money is in the register when you close out the books?" asked Peter.

"It doesn't work that way," Sheila repeated. "That's not how the world works."

"If you say so, sweetheart," said Peter, and he threw seven dollars on the counter and left before she could make change.

Sheila sat behind the counter of the station and continued to watch the doorway he had walked through. Peter was wrong. Still, she felt a kind of electricity coursing through her, some kind of foreign energy she didn't know what to do with, and when it was time to go her hands shook as she counted down the register and turned off the pumps for the night.

"Bring me to the bar with you?" Sheila asked her sister.

She had ridden straight to Andrea and Donny's from the station. Why ride home to her parents' to eat microwaved mashed potatoes alone in an empty kitchen, when Andrea and Donny would be eating tamales and popcorn out of greasy paper-lined baskets, splitting pitchers? She and Donny were friends with most of the bartenders, so it shouldn't be that hard for Sheila just to walk in with them. Her sister wouldn't deny her; Andrea liked to feel older, more experienced, showing Sheila how the adult world operated. Usually Sheila resented this attitude, but sometimes she saw how useful it could be.

"Sure," said Andrea. "Okay."

Sheila would turn eighteen in a few weeks, so it seemed conceivable that she could pass for twenty-one in a college town inundated with fake IDs. She had never wanted to try it before. Donny dropped Andrea and Sheila off at the door and parked around the corner. Sheila felt nervous for only a second before following her sister inside. Immediately, she was impressed with how many people were clearly trying to get away with the same subterfuge, unsuccessfully. There were two college girls up to the bar, fluttering their eyelashes, who asked the bartender for a vodka tonic and for a Cape Cod, and when they were asked for identification the girls shrugged and giggled and said they had forgotten their wallets in the car. As the girls turned to leave, the men at the bar's eyes fell to the words ironed into the asses of the girls' sweatpants: "princess" and "volleyball."

"I'll take 'princess'?" one suggested to the other. "You take 'volleyball.'"

"Sure," said another man, "I'd do 'volleyball.'"

"Gentlemen." Andrea nodded in their direction, and they greeted her as she made her way toward the bar. "Hey Carlos," she said to the bartender, "What does a girl have to do to get a drink around here?" Andrea ordered a drink for herself and then turned to Sheila. She was impressed by the way her sister commanded the attention of the men in the bar. She never would have guessed her capable.

Sheila tried to think of the least likely drink an underage girl would ask for. She heard one of the men sitting at the bar order a Maker's and Coke. Sheila asked for the same. The bartender didn't even look up. He just started making the drinks Andrea ordered.

"Damn," Donny came up behind Andrea and wrapped his arms around her shoulders, "Your sister doesn't mess around with her liquor!"

When the drinks arrived, Donny threw down enough to pay for all of them, and they made their way to the far side of the room. Donny and his friends added their names to a list on the chalkboard by the pool table, started placing bets on games. Sheila sat with her sister in the wooden booth and watched the ice bob and twirl in her drink. The first few sips felt like fire, but then the taste turned sweet, like the fire was responsible for caramelizing everything as it passed her tongue. There was this heat expanding throughout her body; there was Pasty Cline on the jukebox correcting some jerk who had done her wrong; even Donny didn't seem so bad when Sheila was watching him calculate shots on the pool table. In the corner by the bathrooms, a couple was dancing.

"Sheila," Andrea said, and her name sounded far away. Sheila smiled up at her sister and for no reason at all remembered this time when they were kids Sheila had become lost in a Hy-Vee supermarket, and Andrea had called her name down each of the aisles. Sheila had heard her sister's voice leading her and had followed it from the chaos of the cereal aisle all the way back to produce, where her family was waiting. And for a moment, she wanted to reach out and seize her sister's hand and say, *let's get out of here, Andy, you and me, we could just go.*

"So are you?" Andrea said.

Sheila's smile faded. She swirled around the ice in her glass that signified the end of the drink. "Am I what?" she asked.

"Sleeping with anyone!" Andrea said. "Hello? Are you in this conversation or not?"

"No and not," Sheila said. But she smiled.

"But you'll tell me when you are, right?" Andrea said.

"I wouldn't hold your breath or anything."

"You should do it in high school," Andrea said wistfully. "That's when it's the best, sneaking around behind lockers, and those dark storage rooms near the gym."

"I'll probably do it when I'm in France," Sheila said. "By the river or something."

"Ugh, gross," Andrea said. "That sounds like a great way to get a disease. The river is probably where women go to get molested."

"The Seine? The fucking Seine, Andrea, really?"

Her sister rolled her eyes. She opened her mouth as if in rebuttal, but then shut it just as quickly.

"What?" said Sheila.

"Nothing," said Andrea. "Forget it."

"Say it," said Sheila.

Andrea shrugged. "Just that the whole thing's weird."

"Maybe to you."

"Not just to me. I think Mom and Dad sort of thought you would go to college next year."

"You didn't go to college," said Sheila.

"It's different," said Andrea. "I have Donny. And we have a business plan."

"So if I was having sex with someone who I was starting a business with, I wouldn't have to go to college either."

"Touché," said Andrea rolling her eyes.

"French!" Sheila shouted. "Ha-ha!" She waved her finger in her sister's face, as if she'd caught Andrea in the act of something, as if this usage were evidence Sheila was winning the argument they were always perpetually having on some level. "Vive la

France!" she growled in the direction the pool table. She laughed until she hiccupped, until her body shook, and when she looked up again, she saw that Andrea was regarding her with a look of slight concern from the other side of the table.

Sheila felt uneasy. The fire that had felt warm under her tongue had moved into her stomach. She wanted to feel as she had before, as the drink was still going down. Patsy Cline had given way to Peggy Lee, who was angry in a different way, demanding to know whether or not *that* was all there *is*. Sheila looked at her sister, five years her senior, who obviously had figured out some way to live in the world, and wanted to ask of her something similar. But she held her tongue. "I'm going up for another one," Sheila said. She was looking through the money in her purse to go up and ask for the drink herself. But just as she was getting ready to leave the booth, she froze.

Peter Parker walked in and sat at the bar. She watched him take a roll of bills out of his pocket and lay a few of them down on the counter. He counted the money flippantly, as if it were irrelevant how many dollars were there, and how many needed to be laid down to pay for his drink. When he looked up and met Sheila's gaze, she looked away.

"Who is that guy?" Andrea asked.

"Oh, just this guy."

"Well he's looking at you like some kind of pervert."

"Let him," said Sheila.

She needed to stand up now, to signal to him somehow. But she felt scared of walking straight up to the bar. It didn't seem right to run into him this way, with Andrea and Donny. Peter belonged to another part of her life that had nothing to do with this one. Sheila got up to go to the bathroom.

The bathrooms were at the far end of the bar, with a sink just to the right of the back door that led to the alley. Sheila felt sure that Peter Parker would be on the other side of the door when she finished. She fantasized about slipping out the back door with him without even washing her hands. She imagined how his taxi would be waiting just in the side lot and how he would gesture toward it, silently opening the passenger-side door for her, how she would get in, how he would close the door, run around to the driver's seat, and then: they would drive. Where didn't matter. Anywhere really. She pressed her hands to the bathroom door in anticipation of him being there, the way that she'd been taught in grammar school to touch her bedroom door to detect if there was a fire in the house at night.

Sheila's family had always slept with their doors open. If a door was closed, her father said, something fishy was likely going on behind it.

"I demand an open door policy in this family," he said, as if their bedrooms were foreign countries resistant to trade.

Sheila checked her face in the bathroom's dirty mirror and it was pretty much what she expected: limp brown-blond ponytail, smudged eyeliner, thin smile. She opened the door slowly. Peter Parker was not there. She washed her hands and turned the corner, but he wasn't even in the bar.

"Looks like your buddy took off," Andrea said.

"Who?" said Sheila.

Andrea shook her head. "Just be careful. He's way older and he was looking at you like a piece of meat. I wouldn't get into that if I were you."

"I met a boy," Sheila told the coyote in Macbride Hall.

The mountain coyote gazed at Sheila, eager for her to go on.

A *piece of meat!* Had he really looked at her that way? Sheila knew she was supposed to feel objectified, but she felt fantastic. She could feel every muscle in her leg, every tendon expand and contract, as she pedaled her bike to the museum.

"It's stupid," she said to the coyote. "He's not even really my age."

But the coyote did not seem bothered by this detail. It stared straight ahead as if to suggest that relative age was the most insignificant factor in the world to a coyote that had lived in a glass case for over a century.

"There's a chance he thinks he's a superhero," Sheila admitted.

This too barely fazed the coyote. For all Sheila knew the mountain coyote was also susceptible to delusions of grandeur, what with the plaques and glass around it.

"I might say something."

Silence.

"I must be an idiot," Sheila told the coyote, "I must be crazy," but the coyote didn't give any indication that there was any reason for her to hesitate in approaching the boy.

She couldn't sleep that night after her conversation with the coyote. She couldn't explain the endless flicker of her thoughts or how they continued to route toward Peter: the outline of his shoulder under the sleeve of his T-shirt, the flat surface of his fingernails moving quickly as they counted though dollar bills, the way he had looked at her in the bar, the way he had looked away from her. She slipped on a sweatshirt over her pajamas, tiptoed downstairs, and turned on the computer that sat idle on her father's desk in the corner of the room. She typed "Spider-Man" and "Peter Parker" into the empty search engine box that was waiting for her there. She had never bothered to see any of the blockbuster Spider-Man movies, because — well, why would she? She generally didn't waste her time with films marketed to prepubescent boys.

"Sheila?" her father called down the stairs. "Is that you?"

"Yeah, I'm on the computer," she paused, "looking up some stuff for school." Was there something devious about researching Spider-Man in the same way that there was something devious about learning French? She wasn't sure what would create worry in the minds of her parents anymore, what would signal that she was in some way not living a normal life or healthy life. Her own father could probably tell her as much about Spider-Man as the Internet, but she wasn't about to ask him.

A pause, and then nothing. The creak of the stairs that signified her father had retreated back into his bedroom.

First there was the expected stuff, the stuff everyone knew: spider bite, spider sense, great power, great responsibility, blah blah blah. Sheila scrolled down the page. Most of the stuff she read had to do with villains and superpowers, not the kind of thing that interested Sheila. But the more she researched, the more the varied facets of Peter Parker's character seemed to gesture in directions that were completely contradictory. By some accounts, Parker was a hopeless recluse, a school nerd who was ridiculed by everyone; by others, outside of his school work, he was a part-time photojournalist who drove a motorcycle through the school parking lot and revved the engine around pretty girls, asked them out for sodas.

He was a chameleon, and not just because of the whole secret identity thing. The other people in Peter's life sometimes seemed baffled by his actions. Sheila clicked on a reproduction of a short spread from one of the early comic books. Peter Parker peeling around the school parking lot on his motorcycle. A blond girl named Gwendolyn Stacy gasps, clearly impressed, *Actually I never thought of you as the motorcycle type before, Pete!*

Peter Parker smiles in a satisfied way and looks the girl straight in the eye.

Lady, there's a LOT you don't know about me! But stick around — I'm planning to educate you!

Sheila sat back. She blinked at the screen. This is not the way science nerds spoke to pretty girls. Some things were not adding up here; some things were going to require further investigation.

The next time she was near the college, Sheila walked into a store that sold comic books.

"Can you please direct me to your Spider-Man section?" she asked the boy behind the counter.

"Huh?" said the boy.

"Spider-Man," said Sheila.

"Depends on the title. And the year. Back issues in the boxes, more recent on the walls. Alphabetical order," he said.

Sheila found a few relevant comic books in plastic sleeves along the walls. She brought them back up to the counter.

"Could I look through these?" she asked the boy.

"Sure," he said, "if you buy them."

Sheila turned the comic books over and looked at the prices written on little white stickers on the cellophane.

"Oh, I don't really even want to read them," said Sheila, "I just want to find out about Spider-Man's life."

A few boys flipping through issues looked up from their shopping. Shuffling quieted near the front of the store.

"What for?"

"Oh, personal reasons," said Sheila. "Anyway, they're awfully expensive."

"They get much more expensive as you move up the wall there," said the boy, finally making eye contact, or perhaps just catching her eye on his way to glancing down at her selections. "These in your hand are barely controversial issues."

"Just give me the bottom line," said Sheila. "What sort of person is he really?"

The clerk sneered. "He's shy. He wears glasses. He gets bit by a spider."

"Glasses?" asked Sheila. "No, that doesn't sound right at all. I thought he rides a motorcycle to school."

She started to put her selections back on the shelf, but in the back of the store she cornered a customer who looked about twelve and who set everything straight. Peter Parker didn't really *need* eyeglasses; he wore them despite 20/20 vision. The motorcycle he bought with money from working as a photographer for the local newspaper, which was just a part-time gig he worked on the side of high school. The reason why he worked side jobs was to fund his life as Spider-Man; he had to pay for his web-shooter and some of the other tools hidden away in his costume. When he wasn't fighting villains, his life as a regular kid was pretty rough. His uncle Ben was killed by a criminal who broke into the house one night; he lived alone with just his aunt May. His parents, don't even ask — he doesn't have any. His first real girlfriend, Gwen Stacy, was killed by the Green Goblin, and Peter Parker, first crazy with regret at not being able to save her in time, then fell in love with Mary Jane Watson. Spider-Man had never wanted to be Spider-Man. It was just something that came up; he didn't want so much responsibility, but he did what he could with it since there was no getting out of the role once it came. It wasn't always easy for him to know what was the right thing to do.

The next day at lunch, Sheila decided to see if Anthony had any further information. He was a guy. He might know something.

"Did you ever see any of the Spider-Man movies?"

"First one," Anthony said. "Kind of sucked."

"I never saw it," Sheila said. "Would you want to maybe watch it this weekend or something?"

"Did you hear what I just said about it kind of sucking?"

Sheila stared. "Forget it," she said. "I'd rather watch it alone."

Anthony laughed. "Since when are you into Spider-Man movies?"

"I don't know," Sheila said. "I'm not."

Anthony nodded. "Okay."

"What?" asked Sheila.

"Nothing," Anthony said.

Sheila looked from the crumbs on the table and up to Anthony. She felt a prickling at the back of her ears. "Since when are you so interested in pep rallies and the court of Spring Fling?"

Anthony shook his head. "It's a dance at our school. We go to school here. It's not like some random thing I just decided to become obsessed with for no reason, like, I don't know, French or Spider-Man."

Sheila bristled. "Yeah, except you've never been to one of these dances in your life. I mean are you even going? I haven't heard you talk about asking anyone."

As soon as Sheila said it, she wished she hadn't. Anthony was looking down at the crumbs now on the table and he was biting down on the inside of his cheek. Don't say it, Sheila prayed, Please don't say anything. But it was too late.

"I guess I was kind of thinking we could go together," Anthony said. "I mean I know dances are a waste of time and everything but it's our last year."

Sheila felt all the blood rush to her face. She placed her sandwich down slowly, diplomatically, on the table. "Let me think about it," she said, and though she had tried to say it with as even a tone she could manage, she could tell that she had said the wrong thing, because Anthony shoved the rest of a half-eaten apple in his backpack and walked away.

"I saw you in the bar the other night," Sheila told Peter Parker when he came into the station between fares.

"Yes," said Peter, "I saw you too."

"Do you usually go there?"

"I don't go out that much."

"Do you think I'm pretty?" asked Sheila.

"How should I know," he said.

"Because of how you were looking at me."

A glazed look went over his face. "You had your hair pulled back that night at the bar. At first I didn't recognize you. There was something with the light: your hair, your chin, your neck, your jaw — " He reached across the counter then like he was going to touch her jaw, but he stopped himself. He shook his head. "I think you're interesting," he said finally.

"But not in a sexual way, I guess?"

Peter smiled. "How old are you?"

"Twenty-one," said Sheila. "How old are you?"

"Shouldn't you already know that? You checked my ID enough times when I first started coming in here."

"It's state law," said Sheila. "Anyway, *Mr. Parker*, I know that's a fake."

"You're a fake," said Peter.

"You think you can say whatever you want to me," Sheila said. She was playing with him, testing him. Then she felt herself lift her palm and open it. Before she'd thought the action through, she had raised her hand and pulled it back, as if she planned to strike him. She had seen a woman do this in a French movie once, and when she did, the man she was after took her to bed.

Peter raised his hand in reflex and caught her hand midair.

The force of his hand stung in her palm. She paused, rubbing her hand with her fingers. "Oww," she said.

Peter stared at her strangely. He didn't look like he wanted to take her to bed at all.

Sheila exhaled slowly and slapped a pack of Camel straights on the counter. "Was there something else you needed, sir?" she asked. "Or will that be all?"

Peter Parker looked from the cigarettes to Sheila. "That will be all," he said finally, and he laid down $6.25 before leaving, which Sheila made a point to ring into the register, though she would have given them to him for free. She felt furious. She had two hours before her shift would be over, and she could hardly stand the thought of it. She stared at the shelf of forty-ounce beers in the cooler directly opposite her counter for another five minutes before pulling open the cooler door and selecting one.

"Est-ce que vous êtes libre vendredi prochain?" the French woman on the CD asked.

"Je suis désolée," said Sheila. "C'est impossible."

"C'est toujours pareil!" the French woman gasped. "Tu n'es jamais libre!"

Someone was throwing an important birthday party in the world of the French CD, but Sheila expressed regret that she didn't feel up to attending. Sheila declined each one of the French woman's pleas until her regret for not attending the party and her general regret grew into something amorphous and inconsolable. She was sorry for everything. She was sorry that she had worried her parents. She was sorry that she couldn't seem to communicate with the only person who stirred something in her. She was sorry that she had disappointed Anthony. She wished she could be the kind of person who could want the things she was supposed to want. She sat behind the counter of the gas station and drained her forty ounces of beer and willed herself to want those things.

She stood outside of Anthony's window for a few minutes before she threw the first rock. She had been to his house a bunch of times when they were younger, but lately they had stopped hanging out when they weren't in school. His house looked smaller than she remembered, the landscaping more overgrown. Anthony's parents were sometimes away on business for stretches of a few days at a time, so when this was the case, Anthony was always helping his dad out around the house on the weekends. It seemed like he had slacked a bit lately, which probably meant he was home alone tonight, but Sheila figured she'd better not take any chances. It took the contact of three rocks for Anthony to come to his window and open it.

"What the hell are you doing?" he asked when he saw Sheila standing on the sidewalk.

"Waking your ass up," said Sheila. "Let's go for a walk."

Anthony laughed, "It's nine o'clock. I'm not sleeping. You could have rung the doorbell like a normal person."

"Oh well," said Sheila. "Are you coming down or not?"

Anthony closed his bedroom window and was downstairs with an extra hoodie in his hand within two minutes. He offered the hoodie to Sheila. "You cold?"

"I don't get cold," said Sheila. "I'm superhuman."

"Oh, not this shit again," said Anthony.

"I'm kidding," said Sheila. "I just rode my bike pretty fast over here, that's all."

There were woods close to Anthony's house, and without saying so, Sheila began navigating in that direction.

"Listen," Anthony said as soon as they had stopped in a clearing where moonlight rendered one another visible. "I'm sorry about the other day. I shouldn't have tried to push you about the dance thing."

Sheila leaned in and hesitated only a second before kissing him on the mouth. Anthony pulled away from her in surprise, only slightly, but then he started to kiss her back. Anthony was directing the kiss now, slowly, quietly, in a way that let her know that he respected her, that he wanted her to feel safe with him. As soon as he started to lead the kiss, Sheila regretted what she had started. But it was Anthony who pulled away first.

"You taste like beer," he said. He said it like a parent.

Sheila stared at him. She shrugged. "Do you want some?" she asked. "I brought another one with me." She looked at her backpack in the dirt where the other beer was waiting. Beside her backpack a tiny trampled plant was trying to wrestle its way through the soil. It was spring. Everything was trying to figure out how to come back to life, and it seemed like it should have been an easier thing to figure out.

Anthony took a step back. "Why are you doing this?" he said.

"I don't know," said Sheila slowly. "I thought it was something you wanted."

"And what do you want? Is it something you want?"

Sheila stared for a minute before she began to shake her head, slowly. She wanted to say she was sorry but the words wouldn't come. Maybe she had exhausted her capacity for regret already with the people throwing the French birthday party, because now that she really needed to produce a genuine version of the feeling, the sentiment stalled in her throat. "That's fucked up on so many levels, Sheila," Anthony said, and when still Sheila said nothing, Anthony turned and started walking back to his house alone.

* * *

She awoke with a headache. There was a pounding sound coming from somewhere, and at first she thought that it was inside her own brain, but when it started up again she realized there was someone knocking on her bedroom door. After Anthony had left her alone in the woods behind his house, she had spent another few hours sitting on a log. She had polished off a reasonable portion of the second forty-ounce beer on her own. The knocking started up again. Sheila stood and walked to her door then opened it. Behind the door, her father stood with the newspaper in one hand and his reading glasses in the other.

"It's eleven-thirty," he said.

Sheila blinked. "So?"

"So, your mother asked me to come up and check on you. We weren't sure if you were alive up here." He smiled.

"Oh, I'm alive," Sheila said. She rubbed her sore head in her hand.

"What time did you get home last night?" her dad asked. "And don't feed me any B.S."

Her father never swore when the girls were younger, but now he had started in his own way, through a self-censoring system of initials he used that let him really say what was on his mind: "What the F. is going on here?" he'd ask. "Looks like a whole lot of B.S. if you ask me."

"Not so late," said Sheila. "Before midnight?"

"And Tuesday night?"

Sheila paused. She tried to remember. "I slept at Andrea and Donny's." It had been the night they went to the bar.

"Yeah," her father said. "I know that because I talked to Andrea. But you didn't call us and let us know you weren't coming. We've barely seen you all week."

"Sorry," Sheila said. "I guess I wasn't thinking."

As a girl, Sheila had been closest to her father. He was her favorite. When the family played games or sports of any kind — badminton, Monopoly — it was always Mom and Andrea versus Sheila and Dad. They won at everything. "Ten to zip, we whip!" Sheila would taunt through the checked wires of the badminton net, and her dad didn't care at all when she threw her racket into the air to celebrate their victory, even when it got stuck in the branches of the sycamore tree, although Sheila's mother thought this behavior illustrated poor sportsmanship. But lately, when she tried to crack a rare joke with her father, even the idiotic sort of joke dads are supposed to love, Sheila's dad would give a forced snicker and look back at the television.

"Are you making it a point to spend as little time here as possible? We haven't seen you for dinner," her father said.

Sheila looked at the carpet on the floor of her room. She understood how she looked to her father — like a girl without a brain in her head, without a sense of place, of pride, of respect for her roots or thought for her actions. But she sometimes felt that she thought too much, that she considered every option too deeply, took every half-thought of a possibility too seriously. *Bloom, bloom, bloom where you're planted*, the choir from the church where Sheila's mother had taken her as a child used to sing. But what about cross-pollination? What about those shockingly colored hybrid plants you sometimes saw at the farmers' market? No one ever sang about them. She said nothing.

"I guess it's your life," her father said finally. "You're going to do what you want with it." Then he turned to walk down the stairs.

"That's right," said Sheila, and she backed away from the door and willed herself not to cry.

She sat on her bed for only a few minutes before deciding to leave the house for the day. Sheila sometimes spent her Saturdays at Andrea and Donny's, sifting through the newspaper, painting her toenails, writing out French flashcards. Today, she dressed as fast as possible and went to Andrea's without eating or brushing her teeth or hair.

"Hello?" Sheila called as she opened the door to her sister's house. She could already hear the whirring sound of early spring landscape maintenance — the neighborhood determined to take back the lawns frost had destroyed — and through the sliding back door of her sister's split-level house, she saw Donny in a sleeveless undershirt, pushing a lawnmower in slow diagonals across the yard. "Andy?"

She found her sister sitting on the couch in the living room, hovering over a needle and thread that she moved between two hands. "In here," Andrea called out, but she didn't look up from her lap. Sheila went to the kitchen and poured a glass of water. Then she sat down next to her sister.

"Hey," she said.

Her sister smiled.

Andrea had recently joined a cross-stitching circle, and she was working on a throw pillow that was going to say LOVE MAKES THIS HOUSE A HOME, but so far it just said THIS H, because you were supposed to start from the middle and work out to the ends to make sure it came out even. *Love Makes This H. a Home*, thought Sheila, *Love Makes this F-ing H. a G.D. Home.*

"What's the big difference supposed to be between a house and a home?" she asked.

"Who knows?" said Andrea. "The words are really just decorations."

The cross-stitching group that Andrea had joined called themselves the "Stitch-n-Bitch."

"I'm not going to lie," Andrea said. "The bitching is more fun than the stitching."

They met every Wednesday evening in somebody's basement.

"It's a good hobby," Andrea said. "You could use one."

"I have my own hobbies," said Sheila.

"Yeah, like what?"

Sheila cleared her throat and pulled a French flashcard out of her purse.

"Words," her sister nearly spat. "They don't mean anything. What if you needed to actually say something?"

"Like what?"

Her sister frowned at the needle and thread in her lap. "How should I know?" she said. She seemed to think about this for a second. Then she said, "Say you were in trouble. Say you needed to say, 'I demand to be released. I'm a citizen of the United States of America and I want to speak to a lawyer.' What if you needed to say something like that?" asked Andrea.

Sheila knew the verb *to want*, but not *to demand*. She knew *to leave*, but not *to release*. The limits of her skills in the language were considerable, the gaps in her knowledge more gaping than she'd realized.

Sheila exhaled and clutched at her glass of water. "I guess I couldn't say it," she said. It felt awful to admit to it.

Andrea shrugged. "Yeah," she said, "Or you could just say it in English."

The following Monday Sheila walked though the halls like a ghost. She spent the entire lunch period locked in the last stall of the girls' bathroom so as not to have to face Anthony. Following French class, Sheila lingered and approached Ms. Lawrence's desk. Ms. Lawrence was busy erasing the day's lesson and chalk dust filled the air between them. Sheila cleared her throat.

"Miss Gower," Ms. Lawrence said, straightening up, "what can I do for you?"

Ms. Lawrence's English voice was slightly higher, more nasal, than her French voice, and immediately it put Sheila on edge. In English, she sounded more like any other teacher, less like an ally.

Sheila leaned into Ms. Lawrence's desk. "I wanted to tell you that I'm going to Paris," she said. "In the fall."

Ms. Lawrence's face brightened instantly, and Sheila felt her chest open again, her breathing steady. "That's wonderful, Sheila," she said.

"I just thought you would like to know," Sheila said.

"Of course, how exciting," said Ms. Lawrence. "Just think of how much your French will improve! If you need a recommendation or anything of that sort, I'd be happy to write you one. What type of program is it?"

Sheila watched Ms. Lawrence's manicured fingernails pick a piece of lint off her sweater while she waited for her to say something.

"Oh, it's not really a program," Sheila said. "I'm just going."

"I don't understand," Ms. Lawrence said. "You mean you're going on vacation?"

"No," said Sheila, "to live. I've been saving for a while."

"You know people there? Family?"

"Not really," said Sheila.

"I see," said Ms. Lawrence. She bit her bottom lip.

It was quiet for a second.

"It's very expensive, Paris."

"I thought I could maybe get a job when I get there."

The chalk dust was settling around them. Sheila thought she could feel it drifting off the edges of things in the room.

"Have you thought about Canada?" Ms. Lawrence said finally.

"Canada," Sheila repeated. Like *Canada*-Canada? Like *Canada-north-of-Minnesota*-Canada. She felt suddenly like she was going to pass out.

"Because Paris is," Ms. Lawrence paused. "How do I put it? Well, there's '*Paris*,'" and here she extended her four fingers as if to place a quote around the word, "and then there's Paris. The Paris that our textbook talks about just doesn't exist, not really."

"What?" Sheila said. "What do you mean?"

"I mean sometimes our expectations of a thing create a kind of unreality."

Sheila wondered if Ms. Lawrence was insane.

"I mean it's a city like any city. Yes, it's wonderful, but there are Burger Kings there too, for example. There are ignorant drivers. There are thunderstorms. There are bills to pay and waiting rooms. The common cold. I mean I could keep going," Ms. Lawrence said, but she trailed off.

"So Paris is Coralville," Sheila said.

"Oh, there's a thought! How interesting!" Ms. Lawrence laughed. She shook her head. "I don't want to discourage you. But a place like Montreal is also really lovely, and it's so much cheaper too, and closer to home. If you're looking for an adventure, I mean. If that's what you're looking for."

"An adventure," Sheila repeated. She repeated it again biking down the Coralville strip to the gas station after school. As if all she had been looking for was a cheap and convenient thrill. As if she had memorized all that vocabulary and all those conjugations to move to a place where it snowed so much that underground tunnels had to be dug so the people could still get to work in the morning without using the actual streets. "Maybe give it some thought," Ms. Lawrence had said. "Just as an alternative. We could research some options together." Sheila swerved slightly across the white line of the road and was brought back to the task of pedaling by the sharp horn of a driver.

"Get on the fucking sidewalk!" the man yelled out his window at her as he sped past.

Yes, of course, Sheila thought for the instant in which problems conflate in one's brain and this seemed like the solution to everything that had steered off course in her life, *I should get on the sidewalk!* But if there had been a sidewalk, she would already be on it. SHARE THE ROAD a bright yellow sign sprouting from the concrete advised, as if it were that simple a thing to share something as open and straight and endless as a road. "There is no fucking sidewalk!" Sheila screamed back, near tears, pedaling fast, but minutes later, to no one, after the man had already driven off and was surely by now circling around the mall in pursuit of parking.

Sheila sat in the gas station and waited for Peter. She didn't know what she would say to him, but something was going to be said. She understood, irrationally, suddenly, that she needed him to walk into the station. It was toward the end of her shift, shortly after she'd decided that he would not come in at all, that she heard the sound of his engine cutting in the lot by the bathrooms, and she turned to see the headlights of his cab just as he switched them off. Sheila lifted the stack of flashcards from the counter and placed the top one — *la carotte, le céleri, la pomme de terre* — directly in front of her face.

Peter walked into the gas station and stood at the counter.

"What's going on?" Sheila asked, looking up from her flashcard. This close to her face the words on her flashcard meant nothing at all. The letters blurred. The letters made her feel uneasy. "Slow night?"

Peter reached into the pocket of his jacket and placed a shiny gun on the counter. He didn't say anything. He just took it out the way someone might take out a set of car keys and placed it up there as if it had been uncomfortable in his pocket.

"Uh, what's with the gun?"

"A proposition," said Peter.

"What is a gun doing on my counter?" Sheila clarified. Her heart beat faster, but it wasn't fear exactly that directed her blood to move like this.

"Have you ever been to Chicago?" asked Peter.

"No."

"I'm going to Chicago," said Peter. "I thought you might like to come with me."

Sheila knew she wasn't putting in twenty-plus hours a week at the Sinclair station to go to a place like that.

"I was going to leave the country soon," she said.

Peter shrugged. "So I'm heading east. It's on your way."

"What's in it for me?" asked Sheila.

"If you don't want to go," he said, "I'll go without you."

It occurred to her then that maybe this was one way to leave a place, with a boy and a gun. This was teamwork, having a plan.

"What's the plan?" she asked. "I'm assuming there is one."

Peter cleared his throat. "I will hold you at gunpoint. You will empty the cash register into my duffle bag. We will drive to Chicago. Fast," he added.

A *city is a city*, she thought, *is a city is a city*. Is that what Ms. Lawrence had been trying to tell her? She thought of her father as he had looked standing in the doorway of her bedroom. She raised her chin and looked straight into the eye of the security camera.

"I don't even know your real name," said Sheila.

"Sure you do, Gwen," he said quietly.

He looked at her queerly, smiled at her with his eyes, as if they two were in on something wonderful, some unnamed thing she wanted.

"Point the gun at me," said Sheila.

Peter Parker did as he was told.

FOR A LITTLE OVER TWO hours, Peter had been driving up and down the Coralville strip with a gun in the glove compartment. It wasn't even his glove compartment. It belonged to Yellow Cab number ninety-seven, the taxi he drove most nights. Any one of the inebriated clients he might pick up — and, working nights in a town bordering a college town, a good percentage of his clientele was inebriated — could get curious in the front seat and find the gun nestled between outdated city maps and his emergency stack of Dairy Queen napkins. Peter removed the gun from the glove compartment while stopped at a red light; he admired its petite muzzle and short black trigger, then he lay it down quietly on the passenger seat. He didn't know if it was loaded; he had been afraid to open it up and find out. Better not to know, better to allow himself to be in awe of the certain danger of it, to use this danger as backup, a motivation to walk into the gas station and say what he had seen.

What he had seen was the girl, the gas station attendant who showed up in his dreams. Often she appeared in her underwear. In these regular dreams, the girl's underwear was always white cotton with lace trim. She spoke French to him in these dreams, but not much else happened, and anyway Peter didn't understand French, so she could have been saying anything — "Nice weather we've been having," or "Can I borrow your car?" — the stuff of everyday necessity. Still, these dreams were nice. They did nothing to upset Peter.

He was on his way to the gas station now. Perhaps she would be expecting him, because it was almost eight and he hadn't yet been there. Peter pulled off onto the shoulder of Highway 6, half a mile from the station. He picked up the gun from the passenger seat. *The shotgun rides shotgun.* But it was a handgun, and he was hoping the girl would want to sit beside him.

He had been driving a cab for the past five years, but he had been coming in to visit the girl when his shifts were slow only for the past month or so now. She was nice to look at even if she sometimes acted like she didn't want him around. The first time he'd come into the station, the girl stared at his ID for maybe a full minute, but she hadn't said a word about it.

"Something wrong?" Peter had asked her.

The license he carried in his wallet was a fake he'd made some years ago on the occasion of his twentieth birthday. But everyone called him Peter anyway, so it didn't seem to make much of a difference. Unless he had to sign his name for some tax or employment purpose, this was the license he pulled from his wallet. His face was getting old and familiar enough around town not to be asked for identification much, so there seemed to be little reason for an adolescent gas station attendant to make him feel self-conscious about it. "Is there a problem?" Peter repeated.

"Not unless there's something I'm missing," the girl said, in a way that made it seem as if he were the one with the staring problem.

The next time he went in to buy cigarettes, Peter pulled off the cellophane and knocked one out from the pack. "Do you mind?" he asked, raising the freed cigarette halfway to his mouth.

"You're not allowed to smoke in here, if that's what you're asking," she said. He started to make his way toward the door when he heard her say, "Unless you've got one for me?"

Peter turned to face the girl, regarding the entire wall of cigarettes behind her, in every package and variety imaginable — hard packs, soft packs, filtered, unfiltered.

"I just want one," the girl said. "I'm not really a smoker." She reached out her hand, and Peter placed a single cigarette between her fingers.

After that, he'd made a habit of coming in. The girl would have his pack waiting for him. While Peter finished his cigarette in the station, the girl would tell him random facts about foreign countries she thought he'd appreciate. "In Paris, you can bring dogs everywhere," she'd say. "Into restaurants and everything. Nobody cares, it's just the culture."

"Hmm. Sounds like a health code violation," Peter would say.

"You're really arrogant," the girl said, smiling, "if you think your health codes are the same as everyone else's."

It was around this time the girl had started showing up in his dreams.

But more recently, there had been no French, no underwear. What Peter kept seeing in his sleep — it had happened every night this week — could not exactly be called a dream, and he knew better than to call it that. It was closer to sensing something while awake — complete with smell and taste and touch. The things Peter saw weren't always the most important things. They were often isolated and individual, not enough to affect more than a few other lives.

His mother called them nightmares. The first time it happened he was seven: he woke up coughing, a mouthful of water lodged in this throat. His mother had been sitting at his bedside, striking his back, trying to get his lungs to take in the air. She thought that he must have reached for the glass of water on his nightstand in a dream, and tried to drink. But Peter had not been the one swallowing water in his dream. It had been quiet ten-year-old Henry Macy from the neighborhood whom Peter had watched drown, and when two weeks later the Macys found Henry face-down in a flooded ditch, Peter was afraid to tell his mother that he had seen it happen exactly the same way and had done nothing to warn anyone. Most nights he would dream like any other person, but there were a handful of things he saw around this time that could not be circumscribed to his own dormant brain. He saw the grocer slip on a patch of ice and break his hip, one week before he saw him lose his balance chasing a cart in the parking lot; he dreamed his own dog running away from home and wouldn't leave the dog's side unless absolutely necessary, until one time, they were playing with a tennis ball together, and he could do nothing to stop the dog from bolting out of the yard, away from him; for the past month he had endlessly dreamed two women he didn't recognize fall asleep at the wheel of their car and slam into a highway median in the middle of the night. The women were so young. Girls. They looked barely old enough to drive, and when they crashed into the median each night Peter watched their long hair rush forward toward the dashboard as the car began to spin.

He told no one.

This week, six nights in a row, he had seen the same sequence of information each time he closed his eyes. Always, it started with the girl. Peter would feel himself giving in toward sleep when the girl from the gas station would appear there in his bedroom beside him. She would be sitting on her knees near the foot of his bed, like someone in prayer, when the warm feeling started to move around the room, when the heat got under his fingernails, and then the heat became a warm breeze from an open window in his taxi. The taxi was heading east on Interstate 80. The gun was in the glove compartment. He was driving and the girl sat beside him in the car.

Just before he woke up each night he would get as far as the strange apartment. He would watch the man swallow water. He would watch the man swallow pills.

It was the same way his brother had died.

But the girl had seen it too; she had been there in the bedroom, and somehow that had implicated her. It made Peter think she was a part of the equation. It made him think she was part of everything that would come next.

Peter lifted the gun from the passenger seat and turned it in his hand, assessing the level of threat it posed. He didn't want to scare the girl, but he wanted to encourage her to help him. It wasn't entirely clear to him what the point of the gun was, but it had been in his hand in the dream. It seemed important to use it somehow, to point it somewhere. Peter tried to think of it more as a prop than a weapon, something to keep in his hand in order to ensure he would say what he had come to say, to make certain he wouldn't deviate. He angled the rearview mirror so he could see himself, so he could watch his mouth form the lines. He understood, then, how he would appear to the girl when he entered the gas station. "I'm going to Chicago," Peter practiced, steadying the gun so his hand wouldn't shake, his best attempt to sound confident and inviting. "I'm going to Chicago. I thought you might like to come with me."

At twenty-six years old, Peter knew himself to be an expert driver, a decent pool player, reasonably good looking, but he only needed to consult the corners of his mouth in the rearview mirror of his taxi to understand what he was slowly becoming: a man nearing thirty, living alone with his mother. The arrangement had been borne of necessity and habit. They had been living like this for the past twenty years.

He never knew his father. As a child, he had been afraid that his father was both everywhere and nowhere. Any male of a certain age he encountered in the street who was not the father of another child he knew had the potential to be him. The man walking a dog in front of the movie theater? Possibly. The new assistant principal of his school? Unlikely, but maybe. Peter's mother had been of the opinion that children didn't really need to know the details of everything, only the gist, so he understood that his father and mother had met in Davenport, Iowa, that they had quarreled before he was born, that he and Peter's mother had lost contact shortly after. All the photographs had been cleared out of the house. Peter had found an old Polaroid of his father, but in the moment it captures, his father is bent over his shoe, his features largely obscured by the angle. In the photograph, his father is sitting on the living-room sofa — the same one Peter had sat on for years! — pressing his heels into a pair of loafers with a shoe horn. A shoe horn? The instrument seemed superfluous to him and slightly awkward, but his mother insisted that in those days everyone used them.

Then, there was what happened when his brother went missing. Peter had been six at the time, and his brother eighteen. For two full days, Peter and his mother searched the parks and police stations, while Jake had slept in the closet of his childhood bedroom after swallowing every pill in the house. When their mother found him, she'd had his stomach pumped clean, but two weeks after his medical release, Jake had tried it again and succeeded. Then Peter and his mother had lived alone in the house.

Sometimes his mother played the piano in the evenings, and Peter sat beside her and turned the pages of her music when she said, "Now." Sometimes they went to the movies and ordered the large popcorn with extra butter to share. But the house was too big for them. It was two stories high with enough rooms for entertaining — which they never did — and often Peter had a whole story and an attic to himself to make all the noise he wanted. But mostly he stayed quiet.

He had been playing dominos with his mother when he first understood. They did that sometimes, if he didn't have homework, and after the dishes were done. His mother would wash and Peter dried. There was a drawer in the kitchen that held the dominos and he and his mother would divvy them up face-down on the table. Every once in a while, they convinced Jake to play with them. But usually he was too busy to play with dominos.

Peter was counting dots. He was very close to winning.

"You and me, honey," his mom had said very quietly.

Peter was counting the dots on his tiles. He was trying to concentrate. Sometimes if his mom drank a little wine with dinner she talked quietly, under her breath. It was not such a strange thing. He was adding the dots on the tiles in multiples of five. Those were the rules.

"How about it?" his mom said again. "How about you and me." Her voice was so soft it sounded like it was coming from the other room.

Peter looked up at his mom.

"How about what?" he said.

His mom was running the palm of her hand slowly up and down the side of her face. She wasn't looking at him. And she wasn't looking at her tiles either.

"Honey?" his mom said after a minute.

He didn't know why he'd said something that night. His

brother sometimes didn't come home for a few days at a time. Even after his first try with the pills, it was not such a strange thing for Peter to be left alone with his mother in the evening.

"Where's Jake?"

She hadn't told him then. It was another four days of waiting before his mother would tell him Jake was gone. Still, Peter had understood then that it would be him and his mother alone for some time.

Around then Peter began spending his afternoons in his brother's old bedroom. His mom was often working late into the evening at the hospital, and after school Peter was alone in the house. His mother had kept the room exactly as he had left it, so it wasn't hard to find the milk crates filled with comic books and drag them out of his closet one at a time. At first, the sliding doors of the closet had been a place that Peter avoided. He looked at them and saw his brother slumped in the corner as they'd found him before his mother dragged him out. But eventually, he could look at the closet doors and think only of the comic books behind them.

Peter had never seen his brother read the comic books. But once Peter had watched him from the hallway sorting through issues, organizing them into the crates where they were kept.

"You're not a very good spy," Jake had called into the hallway. "I can hear you breathing."

Peter knelt on the floor next to the crate Jake was pulling from. There were hundreds of them, and Peter had the impulse to run his fingers along their stapled edges.

"Take one if you want," Jake said. "It's just a pile of trash." But he never threw them out, and when Peter found them after Jake left, each issue was still preserved in a cellophane sleeve.

"Where did you get them?" Peter had said, but then he was sorry that he asked.

"My old man," Jake replied.

Jake's father was not Peter's father, but when Jake talked about him, sometimes Peter liked to pretend he was. Jake remembered all kinds of things about his dad — his taste in music, the type of beer he liked to drink, where he used to take Jake sledding when it snowed — but Peter remembered nothing of his own father, and his mother never spoke of him.

"Can I have this one?" Peter asked.

"Any one you want," Jake said, without looking.

Peter chose a later issue, once Spider-Man had already settled down with Mary Jane, because he was attracted to the red swath of her hair, filling the empty space; but it was later — it was after Jake was gone — that he read from the beginning of the story. How Spider-Man was just a regular kid whose family kept getting killed by villains, and what it was like to be lonely for a long time before he discovered these powers that showed up out of nowhere, and then even after that, to be lonely sometimes still.

After school, during the afternoons, Peter read the comic books Jake had left behind, and he started to realize there were certain undeniable similarities. There was a long history of superheroes being lied to, men and women with superhuman strengths who only ever had been told half their own stories and had to find out the other half on their own. It also wasn't uncommon for their families to be largely absent or dead by the time they reached adulthood. These were the facts. Peter was not embellishing. He also was not suggesting that his was the life of such a hero — obviously there were certain abilities missing. For example, he couldn't move buildings. He couldn't propel off them either. He couldn't see through them. Basically, he couldn't do anything extraordinary having to do with buildings. So he wasn't superhuman. It had really been devastating to come to this realization. But when his so-called nightmares had started shortly after, Peter understood that while he wasn't *necessarily* superhuman, there was definitely something abnormal going on with him. When, at eight years old, he told his mother that he wanted her to call him a different name, a name that just happened to be the same as Spider-Man's alter ego, his mother complied. She was working under the assumption that this request was a reasonable response to childhood trauma, and at the suggestion of some child psychologist at the hospital, she went with it. But the more time that went on, the easier it was for the name to become permanent, and for neither of them to use his old name at all.

Was that all? It was habit and nothing more? Not exactly. Yes, it was habit, but even now, there was some part of Peter that felt grateful to have this story to defer to. If he actually had a friend call him out and say, "Who do you think you are, Parker? You think you're pretty goddamn special, huh?" of course Peter would punch the friend in the arm and insult him for even coming to this conclusion in jest. "Yeah, I'm a fucking superhero," he'd say. "Let's go out back and I'll teach you how to fly." He'd give the guy a real hard time, rile him up a little for the mere suggestion that he was trying to be someone he was not, trying to be something better than what he was. There would be a good laugh over that. But Peter mostly spent the evenings with his mother. There were a few guys he talked to over the CB radio or in the dispatch office, but that was it.

The thing about keeping to yourself for so long is that there's no need to defend your actions, so a lot of gray area has room to grow. It is possible for two things to be true at once in one's own mind, for one statement and its opposite to coexist, so that Peter could understand on the one hand the he is no one, that he is nothing special, and at the same time to create a private space in which he knows certain things about himself to be irrefutable.

That there is something special about him, that there is something wrong with him, that the thing that is special/wrong has to do with reading too many comic books as a kid and with the dreams that started when his brother died, that under the right conditions, in the right place and time, he could actually be the kind of person who could use his gift or curse to do something extraordinary.

The business of saving the world is tricky. The incredible difficulty of the endeavor weighed on superheroes' brains constantly. Spider-Man, for example, was overwhelmed by how to balance superheroic feats with girls and biology class. But it was tricky even to save a single living thing. The problem was that, in real life, events are always already happening all the time, and there's often little to be done in terms of interception.

This is how it happened when Peter's dog ran away.

Patch was Jake's dog first. Jake had brought him home from the shelter one afternoon with a red collar and a twenty-pound bag of food.

"Who's this?" Peter's mother had asked.

"Our new best friend," Jake said. He placed his hand on the dog's head and told Patch to sit, but the dog only scratched its ear.

"He's got all his shots?" their mother said.

"Sure," Jake said.

Peter had given the dog his hand to lick, and the dog complied. "So you're his favorite," Jake said. "Maybe you want to take him for a walk with me?"

By this time, there was little their mother could do to prevent the dog from inhabiting their home. Peter had the leash and collar in his hand and Jake was helping him fasten it around the dog's thick neck. As they walked, Jake told Peter about how dogs were really the first ones in space, but the reason no one around here ever talked about it is because it was Russian dogs, and everyone had hated the Russians so much.

"Why?" Peter said.

"Because they're communists," Jake said.

Peter nodded. "The dogs too?"

"Yeah, they're communists too," Jake said. "But they can't help it."

Peter was five. He was interested in space travel.

Jake said, "You think Patch would make a good astronaut?"

"Yeah," Peter said.

"Hell, you're probably right," Jake said, and Peter had laughed because he thought this was supposed to be a joke.

But later that night, after Peter's bedtime, when he had snuck downstairs to watch his brother smoke a cigarette on the front porch, he heard Jake talking to the dog. He heard his brother say the words *orbital velocity* and *stratosphere*. "The problem with space travel," Peter heard his brother say to the dog, "is that you always think there's going to be enough oxygen saved up to go around, but there never is." This was the first time it occurred to Peter that maybe there was something wrong with his brother.

Later — after they both were gone — it would seem sometimes as if his brother and the dog had planned it this way, that while Peter sat at home alone with his mother and dusted the piano keys with his fingers, Jake and the dog were in orbit somewhere, Jake asking the dog to give him his paw, and then feeding him some cryogenically frozen food scraps.

When Patch finally ran away, Jake had already been gone for four years. Peter was ten years old when he started dreaming of Patch standing on the cusp of a field near their house, looking both ways as if contemplating something. Within two weeks of the first occurrence of this dream, the dog was gone. For those two weeks, Patch couldn't even go out into the yard to go to the bathroom without Peter following him out the door and crouching beside him.

They had been playing fetch with a tennis ball. "Go, fetch," Peter told Patch, and Patch did. He was the sort of dog who was happy to fetch, content to bring any object back to the place from which it was launched. Peter was working on his arm. He was old enough to play baseball, but didn't, and he wanted to know what it felt like to throw.

"Patch, fetch," he yelled, and the tennis ball shot into the air with the dog trailing beneath it. Patch gathered the tennis ball between his teeth and lifted it, but then rather than bounding back with it, he paused.

"Patch, come," Peter called.

Patch sat down. As soon as he saw the dog sit, Peter knew that it had started to happen. The dog looked at Peter and then he looked the other way, beyond their property, where there was an expanse of farm land full of corn that was already half harvested, and beyond that a forest of pine and fir. Peter didn't call the dog again. He looked Patch in the eye, and under his breath he said, *please*, but it was an entreaty to no one, least of all to Patch, who clearly was already following a path he intended to keep. Patch dropped the tennis ball. He looked at Peter for maybe another four seconds before running the other way.

He couldn't save his brother. Even with warning, he couldn't keep his dog. How many nights had he watched Patch run from him? He had watched him take off at least fifteen times in his dreams. You'd think that it would make the real moment, the moment in which it truly happened, feel like just another enactment of the same scene. But it was different. It was the moment in which the possibility arrived to change the course of things. It was for this reason that he now wanted to save the man he'd seen swallowing pills in the bathroom, to finally for once separate someone from these certain fates he saw at night, and see if anyone was better off for his effort.

The house had taken on the particular state of disrepair endemic to grown men who live alone with their mothers. It was not just that there were perpetually socks in the dryer and dishes in the sink; their entire existence resembled the domestic unrest of an elderly couple at the brink of not being able to care for themselves. Except — of course — she was his mother, and he was not even thirty years old. His mother was sixty-two and retired; Peter drove his taxi at night. For most of the day they shared the house.

Despite the long shifts she'd worked when he was a child, Peter's mother had put in every effort to raise him with a modicum of normalcy. When she returned from her shifts at the hospital, she cooked dinners that represented each of the four major food groups. There was a deficit of cereals with high sugar content in the pantry. Red M&M's, containing Red Dye 40, a substance suspected to cause cancer in laboratory animals, were separated from the other colors in the pack and expelled upon opening. His mother had given him piano lessons. From the age of eight, he had sat with his mother — who had pulled a kitchen chair beside the piano bench, instructing his small hand in the preemptive posture of stretching for an octave. She taught him the way his thumb must tuck neatly beneath his middle finger to run through a handful of the major scales without impediment. It was a kind of therapy for them both. Peter knew the lessons put his mother in mind of her own childhood, in Davenport, when her marriage and children were just some looming murky things in a future she still wanted to meet. For Peter, the exercise taught him a peculiar sort of patience, to read this foreign language and begin, slowly, to comprehend its cues — it took his mind off other things. But he was never any good at it. He was sixteen when he told his mother he was through with the lessons. Though he could tell that it disappointed her, this was a routine she let go without protest.

These days, the older woman his mother had become was a departure from the mother he'd grown up with. She seemed somehow to need a mother herself. Peter would come home from driving a night shift and round the corner of the kitchen to find it empty.

"Out here," she called into the house. "I'm having breakfast on the patio."

Peter followed the sound of her voice, and found his mother propped up in a lawn chair — the first streaks of sunlight passing over the yard — staring into space with a piece of string cheese clenched in her fist.

"Hi, honey," she said.

"Where's your breakfast?" Peter said. He looked around, hoping to see a bowl of cereal stashed behind the mums, a bagel beside the birdfeeder.

His mother waived the string cheese above her head like a limp flag.

"Strings of cheese?" Peter said.

"And some almonds," his mother said.

She freed another thread from the cheese and placed it in her mouth.

"Don't you want eggs or something, Mom?" he said.

"No," she said.

Peter was still working out whether he was going to let the conversation go at that when his mother had theatrically lifted the rest of the log of string cheese and took a big bite out of it and finished it off that way.

Then there was how he'd found the gun. His mother was getting ready for her water aerobics class at the Y, and Peter was going to give her a ride. His mother was perfectly fit to drive; it was her car, but if he wasn't working himself, he drove her, and waited in a bar near the Y for her class to end. He knocked on the door of his mother's bedroom when it was time to leave.

"Come in," she said.

She was sitting on an armchair in the corner of her room, leaning over each foot to tie her shoes. It wasn't until he was halfway into the room that he noticed something off in the opposite corner. Her top drawer was open, and its contents spilled from the drawer onto the dresser — leggings, underwear, swimsuits, and some sharp, dark object that immediately contrasted itself from the soft-hued stockings and undergarments.

"Mom?" he said. The question that was supposed to come next was so evident it wasn't readily available on his tongue. The gun looked so absurd in its disorderly pile, Peter paused for a moment, as if there were a clear reason for its presence that he only needed to summon.

"Just about ready," his mother said.

Peter felt himself begin to back up, slowly. "I'll pull around the car," he said.

The bar where he drank while he waited for his mother was a local staple, the size of a trailer, with animal heads and glossy eight-by-tens signed by minor celebrities tacked to the walls at odd angles. Peter sat at the bar and began counting out singles to pay for his drink. Everyone sitting at the bar had the old haggard look of extended family, the uncles and cousins whose faces you recognize and nod amicably toward but feel no need to converse with.

Peter ordered a beer, took the first sip. He had swiveled around on his stool to lean his elbows on the bar when he saw the girl from the gas station. She sat with a small group, and it was clear she'd noticed him but she was trying not to look his way. It took him maybe thirty seconds to get her to look up. He fixed his eyes on her as he drank his beer. The girl's eyes were darting around like crazy, trying to find somewhere else to rest. Her dark blond hair was pulled back in a lopsided ponytail, slightly off center, and she was pretending to laugh at something someone said that he couldn't hear. He thought then that she was more interesting-looking than he'd realized at the gas station. He thought if she would look up, he would walk over to where she was sitting and buy her a drink.

But a moment later, when her eyes met his for an instant, Peter felt himself look away, down at some stray cat from the neighborhood that had wandered into the bar and was sitting on its tail by the pool table. "Evening, Edgar," the bartender addressed the cat, but the cat paid attention to no one. When Peter looked up again, the girl was no longer sitting in the booth with her friends. He took this as a cue to finish his pint in a single gulp and drive to the Y to wait for his mother.

When her class got out, his mother walked from the building alone, her gym bag firmly under her shoulder, and got in the car. His eyes were fixed on the road and his mother had just stopped fidgeting with the radio when he heard himself say, "So," as if casually, "there's a gun in your underwear drawer."

"Yeah," his mother said. "What about it?"

"Isn't there?" Peter said.

His mother exhaled quickly through her nose, half of someone else's laugh. "It's been there for years," his mother said. "It was your father's."

Peter felt all the muscles in his neck tense. "Have you ever used it?"

His mother laughed. "Lord no, what do you think?"

He wasn't sure what he thought, but already, before he even drove the car home or pulled it into the driveway, before he closed his bedroom door and pulled back the covers of his bed, Peter had an uneasy feeling in the bottom of his chest that had something to do with the gun in his mother's underwear drawer, and something to do with the girl. It was that evening that he first had the dream, and after that, the dream came nightly.

He tried once more, that week, to go back to the station. He wanted to see the girl, to see if she too could sense something strange between them, to see if she understood that she was showing up on the floor of his bedroom every evening, as if on schedule.

"I saw you in the bar the other night," the girl said when he walked in.

"Yes," said Peter. "I saw you too." He wanted to explain how at the bar he felt he had to look away. He wanted to say, You keep coming in my room at night and kneeling on the floor. He wanted to ask her who she was, to warn her that she was showing up in his sleep every night, and what that might mean.

"Do you think I'm pretty?" the girl asked.

"How should I know?" he said. The conversation was already derailing itself into the most vapid sort of flirtation, and Peter tried his best to set a better course for the things he'd come to say. "I think you're interesting," he said.

"But not in a sexual way, right?"

It was impossible. She wanted him to kiss her. He could feel it, and though a few weeks ago, it was exactly what he would have hoped for, he now felt annoyed.

"You're a fake," Peter heard himself say to the girl. He felt misdirected. Yes, the girl was sweet and pretty, but that was it; there was nothing more to search for there.

Everything up until this point the girl seemed to take in stride. But then she looked down at the counter, trained her eyes there.

She was staring at the keys of the cash register when she spoke again. "You think you can say what you want to me," the girl said.

Before she even lifted her hand, Peter had raised his own to catch her palm midair. The reflex at first obscured the reality that she had been about to hit him. Initially, Peter understood only that there was something too familiar about this action, something *enacted*, as if he already knew that the girl was going to try to strike him before she'd even finished speaking. He was rattled by it. He walked out of the gas station in a daze and began to drive, and it was only when he was at a stoplight two miles away that he understood the reason he knew what the girl was going to do after speaking that line was because he had read it somewhere already. He had read it in *The Amazing Spider-Man* #37.

There are moments when such slippage occurs, between the regular, everyday world and the interior worlds created, and these are the moments that fortify and support the worst delusions. Peter knew this much. He knew there was absolutely no evidence to support the conclusion that the girl in the gas station was Gwen Stacy. He knew — furthermore, because after all, he wasn't insane — that Gwen Stacy was a fictional character created by Stan Lee and Steve Ditko, who did not exist outside of a hundred and some odd number issues of comic books from the sixties and seventies. But how to reconcile the simultaneous truths that clamored for attention in his chest, one asserting that this girl, this gas station attendant, was the living incarnation of Spider-Man's first love: she had spoken a line straight out of the comic book.

In *ASM* #37, the attempted slap is a kind of physical awakening, of mutual attraction, of tension, of the hierarchy of human relationships in the world not necessarily being quite what they've always seemed. Peter offers to walk Gwen to class, but feeling snubbed by his aloofness the past few weeks, Gwen Stacy replies, "What are you doing, Mr. Parker — slumming? Usually you're too stuck up to say hello to anyone." Peter suggests that Gwen is a "temperamental female." A few more words are exchanged before Gwen accuses Peter of arrogance, and throws out her hand to slap Peter on the cheek, half-playfully, but with anger behind it as well: "You think you can say what you want to me, and then — Oww!" Peter catches her hand in his palm before it reaches his cheek. After this moment, the world shifts slightly to accommodate the reality introduced by Gwen Stacy's action. Parker seems to feel himself capable of flirting, of asking for what he wants, of calling out his adversaries at school. This quiet moment of Gwendolyn Stacy's attempted violence seems to alert to him that he is someone worth the effort of slapping, that his actions matter — that independent of any heroic acts he may perform as his alter ego — he matters. Gwen Stacy makes Peter Parker count for something besides the freakishness that he uses to save the city from villains each night.

Peter continued driving down Highway 6 until the ominous expanse of the Coralville Mall spread before him in the distance. There was a carousel in the parking lot and on it children were rotating. There was a theater where the blockbuster movies played every summer. Also an ice-skating rink. There had been a pond that sometimes froze in the back of his house where he and his brother would slip around in their sneakers in the winter, but this was long before the Coralville Mall had been built, with its assemblage of various atrocities and attractions. He parked the taxi and gazed onto the rink, thinking of Jake, of those winters when there was nothing to do but slide across the expanse of the water and hope not to fall through the thin parts. Before he had considered exactly what he was doing there, Peter approached the ticket counter. He purchased an hour on the ice, rented a pair of skates, and laced them up. He emerged on the rink and clutched the side railing as he slowly made his way around it.

In his dreams, the girl sat beside him in the taxi. What a small detail this was, her presence beside him, but what a difference it made to have someone else there, to give witness to the things he saw. It was a shock to the system to consider that the things he saw were real enough that someone could bear witness to them. The children were going around the rink quickly in pairs, and they were singing along to whatever song was playing over the loud-speakers, a song that sounded vaguely familiar, like something outdated, something kids shouldn't know.

"Mister, gotta get off the ice," one kid was saying, and it took Peter a moment to realize that the kid was speaking to him.

Peter regarded the kid who had addressed him, a boy of twelve or thirteen who was holding the hand of a girl who looked a little older. "Couple skate," the boy said. Peter nodded, not exactly sure what the boy was getting at, until he looked to the boy's companion who seemed to take amusement at Peter's unfamiliarity with the rules of the rink.

These kids had grown up with things he hadn't — ice skates, technology, different kinds of wars. They understood things that he did not. Peter mumbled in appreciation for the tip, and he started to skate toward the swinging door. When he tried to exit, he noticed a girl of about nine standing in his way. She was wearing one of those costumes, with the leggings that are the color of skin and a skirt that swirls around as she spins. Her lips were heavy with gloss, like the mouth of a doll. She held out her hand.

Peter looked behind him but there was no one there.

"Do you need a partner?" the girl asked.

"No, thanks," Peter said.

The girl rolled her eyes.

"I don't know how to skate," Peter said.

"Come on," the girl said. "The song is half over."

Precariously, Peter placed his hand in the hand of the nine-year-old girl, resisting, holding back at first, to let it be made clear to any father or legal guardian who might be watching that the girl was the one who was directing things here: Peter was simply following her lead. He was not a pedophile. He did not habitually come to the ice rink to find the hands of prepubescent girls to clutch during couple skate.

In his first solo laps, Peter had stayed very close to the outer wall, to have something to fall into should he lose his balance. But this girl was leading him out to the center of the ice where there was nothing to hold onto, nothing to guide him but her hand.

"You've never been on the ice before?" the girl asked him.

"Not like this, with skates, no," said Peter.

"You don't have to hold on so tight," she said. "It's easy."

"How long have you been doing this?" Peter asked.

"My entire life," the girl said, and she said it with such quiet dignity, it was easy to forget he was speaking to a child whose entire life was a fraction of a reasonable amount of time. It seemed incredible that she could take herself so seriously, could trust in her experience so effortlessly. Behind the child's hand, Peter could still make out the slow tingle of the place in his palm where he had caught the girl's slap in the gas station. It seemed to be couched there under the skin, auguring something. He began to skate, and as he did, he felt a slow certainty growing in his body. There were patterns carved into the ice from the laps of skaters who had passed before them, who were continuously passing, and he clutched the hand of the child, for balance, for assurance, but after a little while he felt steady; he felt that for the first time in his life, he was following signs that were meant for him to interpret. That he would find himself capable of things heretofore impossible. The song neared its climax, *Love shack, baby love shack! Love shack bay-ay-bee-ee!* A love shack seemed in those moments a sensible place, not only a place where people could get together, but a place where people could get things done, before it mutated again into an absurd place, an idiotic made-up, vaguely seedy place conjured by people on drugs — a place that didn't exist.

When he hit the ice, the girl went down with him. He tried to release his grasp from her hand, but the weight of his body was so much greater than hers, the momentum of the fall pulled her on top of him. So first there was the impact of his tailbone hitting the ground, and afterward the impact of her body hitting his. There was no blood, no breaks, no sprains, no reason for the pairs of skaters to do little more than shift their path slightly to accommodate the obstruction on the ice. But in the moment in which he began to fall, thinking back on it from his bedroom later that night, there was no fear. The drop weight of panic into the stomach, yes, but it was closer to pleasure. The throb in his tailbone was an old familiar pain, he was remembering now, there on the surface of the pond, Peter and his brother: they had tried to fall. The object of the game had been to wipe out in the most outrageous and unimaginable ways, how they had flung the weight of their sneakers into the thinnest parts of the ice, how they had hoped to fall through the ice and drag up a fish, its body squirming outside the breathable water. To be the most reckless, the most unhinged, the first to break into another dangerous world and bring back evidence of his daring achievement.

"Are you all right?" The child stood over him, or she had been standing over him for a while, a slight concern passing over her tiny brow, her toothpick legs beneath her again, the sequins on her costume glittering like some promise, close enough to touch.

Peter looked up at her. He smiled.

* * *

For the first night in seven, the dream did not come. Peter didn't wish for it, or wonder where it had gone. Even without it, he had made up his mind on what he was going to do. He stayed up late in his bedroom, composing a note that would serve to communicate his absence to his mother, until he returned.

Mom:
I'm sorry for leaving unannounced, the same as everyone. I borrowed Dad's gun, but don't worry, it's not what you think. I'm coming back — believe me.
Your son,
Peter

There was nothing about the note that felt right, but it was the best he could come up with after several hours of trying. He went to sleep with the note under his pillow, and when he read it again in the morning, he decided it would do. Then he brushed his teeth and made a pot of coffee. With every action, his joints tingled beneath his skin. He sat with his mother on the patio for half the day, and only in the late afternoon, just before his shift, did he begin to pack a small duffle bag. When it was time for work, he let himself quietly into his mother's room. He found the gun wrapped in one of her stockings as if it had been quietly waiting for him there for years. He left the note face-up on her dresser. He kissed his mother goodbye. Then he walked to the Yellow Cab lot, duffle bag in hand, and picked up taxi number ninety-seven, whose FOR HIRE sign he extinguished halfway down the Coralville strip, and continued driving to the gas station where he would collect the girl whom he had already begun to think of as Gwen Stacy, and explain to her the nature of the responsibility they shared.

PART TWO

TEN MINUTES LATER she was beside Peter in the car, heading due east on Interstate 80 in a stolen taxi. The radio in the taxi was promising a cloudless, breezy night, lows in the low sixties. The air on the interstate felt thin and bright and hydrating as a glass of water. All the windows were open, and the longest strands of Peter's hair were blowing all over the place, skirting in and out of his eyes. He didn't drive fast like he'd said they would: he was a cautious driver, using the left lane only for passing, the needle of the speedometer hovering just above sixty-five. Most of the guys that Sheila knew — Donny and his friends, mainly — were pretty reckless drivers.

The CB radio was saying, "Fifty check. Fifty check. Fifty, head out and check me at Mormon Trek. Fifty, where the hell you at?"

"Are you fifty?" asked Sheila.

He nodded.

"Can't you turn that thing off?"

"No. You'll be able to tune it out after a while."

All together, there had been $716.64 in the cash register. Usually it would have been less on a weekday, but Sheila was nearing the end of a long shift. There was a single surveillance camera in the corner of the station, which would eventually be viewed, but there was no audio feed, so the crime would perhaps look authentic — which could be a good thing or bad thing, depending on the plan. But there didn't seem to be much of a plan. Of course, if anyone viewed the tape, there would be the matter of the five minutes of calm conversation she and Peter had before he pointed the gun at her. There was the possibility it wouldn't look authentic in the least. Sheila had turned the pumps off and left a little sign on the door of the station that said BACK IN A MINUTE, which probably wasn't the right sign to leave. OUT OF ORDER may have drawn less suspicion. It didn't take her long to realize that she had left her phone on the back counter beside the radio. She could picture it ringing in the empty station. Who had called her? Her father, maybe, would have called by now. It was past nine o'clock.

"What's in Chicago?" Sheila asked when it was clear that she'd be doing most of the talking on this trip.

Peter exhaled slowly. He smiled. He said, "We make it up. Is that worth anything to you?"

Sheila thought about it for a minute.

"Yes," she said.

They drove. They drove through the night and through the state. It was pitch black and they were about fifteen miles shy of the Illinois border when Peter slowed the car along the road's shoulder. Half settled in a ditch there was a car, or part of a car, smoke pouring from where the engine would be. Peter turned off his lights and pulled up just behind it.

"An accident?" Sheila said.

It was obviously an accident, and a serious one, but Peter said nothing. Pieces of the car were scattered between the taxi and the white line of the road. Peter got out of the taxi and closed the door behind him. Sheila watched as he walked up to the driver's side door of the car. It took some effort to force it open, but he used his body as a counterweight. He dropped to his knees at the spot where the door fell open. Peter knelt on the shoulder of the road and started to rock his body back and forth.

Sheila ran from the passenger side of the taxi. She didn't want to see what Peter was seeing, but she felt her body move toward the spot independent of any will of her own.

An SUV whizzed feet away from Peter's knees on the white line of the road. The vehicle pulled off to the shoulder a little further up, and a man emerged from the driver's side.

Peter just looked at her. "I failed," he said.

"Failed what?" she yelled. The passing traffic on the other side of the median made it hard to hear. "Failed who?"

She saw them then, the people in the car. It was impossible not to see them then. There were two of them, girls, a little older than Sheila, driving home from college for the weekend, she imagined, their bodies now slumped against the dash. One of them had red hair. One of them was wearing a thin silver chain that ended in a locket near her chest. The one who had been driving had a gash on her cheek.

"They're dead?" Sheila whispered.

The man from the SUV caught up to them now and stood on the other side of Peter. "I'm a doctor," the man said, like someone on television.

Peter shook his head. "We're too late."

The man leaned into the car and reached for each girl's wrist. A moment later the ambulance pulled up and the paramedics and police took over. Sheila and the man who said he was a doctor stood to the side of the car, and Peter took a few steps back toward the taxi. The paramedics asked what they had seen, but what could they say? They had seen nothing. They could do nothing. They had come upon the car just moments before the ambulance had arrived. They shook their heads, and the police thanked them for stopping and asked them to be on their way. Then, too quickly it seemed, Sheila and Peter were back in the taxi, the drone of the road beneath them, the steady pelting of insects on the windshield, like nothing at all had happened, and this felt not right, that two girls were dead on the side of the road now, but that she and Peter could just keep driving, the highway under them impartial and unchanged.

"I feel sick," Sheila said.

Peter stared straight out the windshield. His eyes were wet.

"Hey," Sheila said. "Are you all right?"

He nodded.

"There's nothing we could have done," she said.

He shrugged. He opened his mouth but his voice shook. He tried again. "That's what I'm tired of."

"Of what?"

Peter blinked. He said nothing.

But this was something Sheila could understand. There was the way things should be and then there was the way things were, and the two rarely seemed to overlap. Peter's hand was on the gearshift and before she had given thought to what she was doing, Sheila placed her hand on top of his. She was driving away from her home with a stranger, away from her family and everything she knew. She was driving past mile markers, away from cornfields, cows, from roadside debris, from the mangled bodies of two girls who, half an hour before, like Sheila, were still making plans. She squeezed Peter's hand in that moment without knowing why, but feeling the uneven jitter of the road through his hand cradling the gearshift, Sheila felt grateful — that his hand was there, that she had thought to take it.

* * *

After four and a half hours, the skyscrapers could be detected, but only in the distance. The landscape looked as much a certifiable city as anything Sheila had ever seen. You couldn't see much of the buildings in the dark, but Sheila could see enough to be impressed by their height alone. Peter merged with the lanes of traffic headed into the city, and pulled off the expressway at Western Avenue. This was the longest street in the country, he told her, and they were heading north on it when suddenly he parallel parked the taxi and said, "We'll hail a local cab from here."

In the glove box, Peter retrieved an envelope full of his fares, unrecorded — a sum that nearly matched the Sinclair register count. Just after crossing the Mississippi, they had pulled over at a rest stop to scrape the company decals off the car doors. He had by that point already smashed the CB radio on the side of the road with the sole of his boot and thrown his own cell phone in the Mississippi as they drove over it. Sheila had gasped, "Why did you do that?" Peter shrugged. "I don't want to talk to anyone else," he said. Her phone in the station, his in the river. They were acting recklessly. They were cutting themselves off from the rest of the world. But there was a strange calm in it, a promise implicit in the risk. WELCOME TO THE PRAIRIE STATE! LAND OF LINCOLN! the signs in the grass by the bathroom had shouted. Now Peter unscrewed the license plates and grabbed the laminated sign off the dash — so aside from being the wrong color yellow, the wrong make and model of car to blend in with Chicago taxis, with the wrong type of FOR HIRE light affixed to the roof, and parked on a busy street through several rush hours, the taxi fit right in.

A Chicago cab drove them to a hotel. Peter carried the duffle bag full of money.

"Have a seat," he told her.

Sheila sat in the lobby while he checked in. It wasn't really that much money. Sheila had more saved in the bank than what they had stolen.

"What if we get caught?" Sheila asked.

"You can say you got kidnapped. If you wanted to bail on me."

"I wouldn't say that," said Sheila.

"I'm glad," said Peter.

"I'm not a kid," said Sheila.

"It's late," he said. "Let's get something to eat."

For dinner they ate hamburgers at a diner around the corner. Peter wasn't much of an eater, but Sheila was starving. She finished her meal and most of his french fries.

Sheila moved his plate closer to hers on the table, so she could easily sop up the ketchup on her plate with his discarded scraps. She said, "Is this your first time on a trip like this?" She was trying to gauge exactly what kind of trip this was going to be. The truth was she had never really been on a trip, and she wanted to figure out how things were going to work.

Peter looked up. "Oh no," he said. He shook his head. "I've been all over the place. I've been to Lincoln, Nebraska. I've been to Nashville, Tennessee."

"When did you go to all those places?" Sheila asked.

Peter said. "I'm twenty-six years old. I've been a few places."

"But never Chicago."

"My first time," Peter said. He smiled hugely without showing his teeth. He had been fingering a book of matches, as if getting ready to light one. Of course, the diner was nonsmoking, and though his cigarettes were nowhere in sight, each time he came close to snapping one of the matches between his fingers to ignite it, Sheila felt nervous. Finally he set the matches on the table and looked up at her. "You too, I guess?"

"What? Oh yeah." Sheila hadn't really wanted to admit that aside from family camping trips it was her first time away from home, but Peter seemed edgy; she wanted to offer him some-thing, to set him at ease. "It's my first time staying in a hotel," she said.

Peter whistled. "Wow, I guess I should have checked us into somewhere nicer, tried to impress you a little bit."

"Oh, I don't know. It seems real nice," Sheila said.

"There's cable TV," he said. "I guess that's something. There's a continental breakfast."

"There's a pool," Sheila said. She had seen tile arrows pointing around the lobby, smelled the certain stench of chlorine.

"Hey, there is a pool, isn't there?" Peter brightened for a sec-ond. "I say first thing we do when we get back is dive in."

"Deal," said Sheila, and they smiled at one another across the booth, carefully, politely. Sheila noticed then that his foot had brushed up against her leg under the table. She wasn't sure if he noticed or not, but she left her leg where it was. It was only later, when they were walking back to the hotel, that it occurred to her that they hadn't packed swimsuits. That they hadn't packed any-thing. It wasn't going to be that kind of a trip.

She stopped on the sidewalk and turned to him. "What are we doing here?" she asked.

Peter took her hand. He said, "You know, don't you?" He was looking at her so seriously, it seemed to Sheila that no one had ever taken her so seriously in her life. He said, "Isn't that why you asked me to point the gun at you?" He seemed then as scared as she was. It was true that she had asked him to do this, but it was at his suggestion, and anyway, she thought he would direct things from there. Sheila considered the possibility that this was how all such arrangements began when there was the irrational question of desire hanging around in the corners of every half-thought. It came down to this: a series of actions, a series of reactions. He would say something, and then she would say something, then there would be time to interpret, to analyze, before acting again. She thought of hearts beating under floors, hearts inside drawers. It was no wonder there were so many casualties. But the important thing now was to keep reacting. The important thing now was not to stop.

She had never shared a bed with anyone before. Even in her parents' house, she and Andrea always had their own rooms. When they got back to the hotel Peter fell asleep still in his clothes, on top of the covers. Sheila tried not to be disappointed; she had been hoping for more attention. Sheila tried to sleep, but she could feel his weight next to her. She watched him while he slept, as if she might miss something if she dozed off. Peter was on his back, stray strands of hair over his eyes. Sheila cautiously pushed one of the strands behind his ear with the tips of her fingers. He blinked, opened his eyes. He smiled at her and closed them. When his breathing steadied again, Sheila began playing with the buttons of his shirt, and before she'd really considered what she was going to do once his buttons were unfastened, she found she was pressing on them, silently encouraging each one to fit through its little neighboring slot. She had wanted to get a good look at him. Under his shirt, Peter was wearing a ribbed sleeveless undershirt, the same kind Donny wore around the house, but Peter's shoulders were thinner and darker, like a boy's.

"Hey, go to sleep," he said with his eyes closed.

"I can't sleep," Sheila said.

"You should try."

Sheila licked her lips. She traced the lines of his undershirt with her thumb. Peter gave a little grunt after a minute and lifted her up on top of him.

"Hmm?" he asked, although she hadn't said anything.

Immediately she felt panicked and exhilarated. There was

nothing to say, so she kissed his eyebrow quietly, in a spot where there was a little white scar, a small response to his odd question. In reply, he pulled her face down to his and kissed her mouth. The other boys she had kissed didn't kiss so hard. Peter gripped her face between his hands when he pushed his tongue into her mouth. He pulled her face away from his and eyed her with a quiet reprimand. "You don't look a day older than sixteen," he said.

Men took her for an early twenty-something all the time, but Peter didn't seem to care what her answer was to this charge, because suddenly he became very awake, his hands moving quickly under her clothes. She had his attention, and now she was going to have to figure out what do with it. She had heard the men who sat in a line at the bar she went to with her sister say to one another that there were two types of women in the world: flirts and cock-teases. When the girls walked away from the bar with the words ironed into the asses of their sweatpants, the men decided which category each fell into. *Flirt?* they asked one another. *Nope, definitely a cock-tease.* Sheila had wanted to ask someone, but didn't: Which one was better? And: Weren't they kind of the same thing? But she wasn't stupid enough to say this kind of thing aloud. She understood that only a girl would get hung up on such distinctions. She ran her hand along the place where Peter's belt fastened shut, understanding that once she got him out of the jeans, she had no idea what to do with what she was sure to find there. But Peter stood abruptly before she could do anything else. He said, "Are you sure about this?" and Sheila nodded.

"Okay," he said. He kissed her neck and grabbed his wallet from the dresser. "Back in a minute."

The door slammed and she was alone in the room. She flopped back on the bed and studied a crack in the ceiling. Back in a minute? Hadn't that been the contents of the note she left on the locked door of the gas station after she turned off the pumps? Had she done something wrong? Should she take off her shirt or something while she was waiting? Sheila scooted to the end of the bed so she could see herself in the mirror above the dresser. She pulled her hair out of its ponytail and peeled her shirt over her head. "Hi," she said to the girl in the mirror, but then she felt ridiculous for saying anything to that idiot in her underwear. She was still sitting there trying to decide if she should put her shirt back on when the door swung open again. Peter walked to her quickly, placed his hand in the crevice of her side above her jeans and kissed her. In his hand there was a small yellow box. Already Peter was removing the rest of her clothes; he was waiting for her to reciprocate. "Will you put it on me?" he asked, pushing the box into her hand.

Sheila willed herself to finish what she'd started. Don't be a baby, she told herself. Don't be a flirt. She fit her hand under the buckle of his belt and unfastened it. She ripped the packaging away from one of the condoms, and she was holding it up to him when Peter pushed forward so that he was already in her hand. Peter pulled the rest of her clothes off, and he looked a little like he was going to cry. At first it didn't feel like anything, then it sort of felt like something, but she was afraid it was not the right thing, and then she realized she wouldn't even know if it was the right thing. She thought of asking him what it was supposed to feel like, but when she looked up at him, it was clear he was feeling something, the way he was pulling her thighs closer to him and gasping for breath like someone coming up for air from underwater. The smell of latex stung in her nostrils. Andrea had advised her that even if she didn't like it the first time — and eventually, she would like it — she should make a lot of noise, or the guy would think there was something wrong with her. But every time Sheila opened her mouth, Peter cupped his hand over it and smiled, asked her if she wanted to wake everyone up. Each time she opened her mouth to sound pleased — pleased in the way one was supposed to sound while having sex for the first time with another person — Sheila had to focus to be sure her mouth produced a moan instead of a question. The question her mouth was trying to form still wasn't entirely clear to her, but it had something to do with the women who had been in the car on the shoulder of Interstate 80. She looked down at her skin, her body beside his, below his, but alternately, in place of her own, she saw the girls' narrow bodies, as they had been wrapped around the steering wheel, the glove compartment. Then Peter started gasping again and he pulled away from her fast, closing his eyes, helpless to whatever it was that was passing over him. Sheila breathed in and the air tasted sweet and she felt an odd calm settling in her own body like a kind of quiet accomplishment.

She woke to the sound of him stumbling around the room looking for his clothes. He had already pulled his jeans on but his shirt was lost, somewhere under the sheets, under the other things in the room. Peter was on his hands and knees near the foot of every piece of furniture, trying to keep quiet, and he looked so earnest in his search, she watched him for several more seconds, admiring his arms, his back, the backs of his hands pressed out on the floor, before it occurred to Sheila that the reason that he was looking for his shirt was because he was going to leave. She bit her bottom lip to stifle something rising. Of course this is why you were never supposed to have sex with someone on the first night; this is what the poets, with their falling-out hearts, always failed to consider. All the poets were men — those idiots! — and there was something else that complicated it all to feel these same things as a woman, she was remembering now, something mothers said about cows and the price of milk, but she couldn't recall if the girl was the cow or the milk or what, and anyway, what was the difference! Peter had found his shirt now and already he had his hand on the chain of the door.

"Wait!" She was sitting up in the bed now, the sheets tucked around her chest. Peter turned.

"What time is it?" Sheila asked. It was difficult to say with the shades drawn, but it didn't matter. She needed to say something. She tried to stay confident, to stay calm, to ignore the red digits on the bedside clock and on the clock above the television across the room that had already answered her question: 9:45 A.M.

Peter retreated from the doorway and sat on the end of the bed. He looked at her cautiously as if she were a rabbit or a finch or something that had just appeared in the bed and addressed him in his own language.

"Hi," he said. He inched closer slowly.

"Where are you going?" Sheila said.

"They take away the breakfast stuff in fifteen minutes," he said. "I thought I'd try to find us something to eat."

She studied him to see if this was true.

He said, "I left you a note."

She turned to the bedside table and held the piece of paper up to her face. It said:

Free breakfast ends at 10. I'm not sure what you usually eat in the morning so I will just try to bring up a few of everything and you can pick what you like from it. You look pretty tired, I don't think I should wake you up, but if you wake up in the next 15 come meet me in the lobby kid.
Peter

She looked up from the hotel stationery and met his gaze. He was smiling at her, but only with his eyes. Sheila leaned closer to the end of the bed, where he was waiting. She said, "Quit calling me kid."

He leaned over her now, balancing on his forearms so that only the sheet was between them. "What do you want me to call you?" he asked.

She looked at him. She wanted to say, *What about that name that you called me last night when we left?* But she was afraid to say it aloud, as if there were some spell, some understanding, some balance between them that she didn't want to upset by talking away the mystery of the thing.

Peter didn't wait for her to say anything. He let his forearms drop and his weight rested on her. When she went to kiss him, she could feel him tense and relax against her as if every muscle were concentrated on a reply, and when she asked him if it would be okay if they just got breakfast somewhere else later, he didn't bother responding anyway and already he was working at her neck and her shoulders with his mouth.

That afternoon Peter went to see about a place for them to stay that wouldn't cut as deeply into their funds. He knew of a guy in Humboldt Park who owned a building. Sheila was alone in the hotel for most of the afternoon. At three, she picked up a pay phone and dialed her sister's number. It rang five or six times and then Donny answered. Sheila hung up. She called back in an hour. This time Andrea answered right away.

"Andy, it's me."

"Jesus Christ, where are you?"

At the sound of her sister's voice, Sheila faltered. She hadn't counted on that. She had to catch her breath and speak slowly.

"I just wanted to let you know I'm okay."

"Okay? Well, where are you?"

"I'm not close by," said Sheila.

"Sheila, don't fuck around. There'll be a missing person report filed on you with the cops by the end of the night. The Sinclair station's all over the news. Dad's about had an ulcer."

"I don't want you to worry."

"Tell me where you are."

The thought occurred to her then to tell her sister that boys *don't* always like it when you make a lot of noise. Some boys cover your mouth in their hands, she wanted to say to Andrea. Here, on the telephone, Sheila felt the strange impulse to confess to what she had done with Peter. Andrea's voice on the other end of the line sounded more like home than she'd anticipated. She could hear the worry, the phone calls, the prayers, the neighbors' casseroles, the police visits, the aimless car rides up and down the Coralville strip.

"It's okay," Andrea said. "You can tell me."

Sheila swallowed. "I'm," she said. Like that, the entire thing could be over. Peter had given her an out. *You could say you were kidnapped if you wanted to bail on me.* She was terrified for an instant then, and she wanted her sister to tell her it was okay. And here Andrea was making it easy for her. But she hadn't been kidnapped. She had asked Peter to take her with him. Don't be a baby, she thought. Don't be a flirt.

"Honey, where are you?" Andrea said again.

Maybe that was the difference between a flirt and cock-tease, Sheila thought then. A flirt was a woman who moved between this and that without any real sense of direction, of decision. A cock-tease pretended she knew what she wanted. She put her hand firmly around the thing and said, this is it, but then she got scared and faltered; she got scared and ran away from what she had started.

"I'm not in Iowa," Sheila said into the telephone. She fit the phone neatly back into its cradle, and promised herself she would call back soon, as soon as she figured out what she was going to do.

Sheila went for a walk. She found a diner at the other end of the street where she bought herself a slice of pizza for an early dinner. An Italian man with a receding hairline worked the register. She ordered a slice with sausage and green peppers.

"American girls, *allora*!" he said. "Chicago girls! They are never afraid of a little sausage, no?"

"No," said Sheila.

"And I can see that you practice sports," he said. "Tell me, which sport do you practice?"

"I don't practice sports," said Sheila, fitting her tongue around his awkward English in reply.

"But you are so thin!" exclaimed the cashier.

In Iowa, it was easy to cut male advances short. Sheila had learned a couple of handy phrases: "Please go piss up a rope," and "I don't trust you any farther than I could spit you." She could immediately see that such phrases were not useful here. She had started learning idioms in her French workbook, and that's exactly what her little phrases were. The further you moved from home the less sense they made. It was good that she was not going to France. Just how had she expected to communicate! Sheila fumbled nervously with her wallet to pay the Italian, counting out her spare change as quickly as possible. She thought of Ned with his piles of pennies, and she felt, suddenly, that she had somehow betrayed him.

She found a small convenience store in a strip mall on the same block as their hotel. The little plaza was tucked beyond the sidewalk on Clybourn Avenue. The Sinclair station had been surrounded by similar architecture. There were few stores that survived as self-contained structures even in Iowa. But here, there wasn't the land between them. The space felt cramped, threatening to spill over, barricaded as it was by rows of metered parking on either side of the moving lanes of traffic.

Sheila walked in and asked the boy behind the counter for a pack of Peter's cigarettes. "I said straights," said Sheila, when the boy pulled down filtered, and Sheila saw how it would be to be Peter, having to repeat that same thing all the time. It was only when the boy — who was clearly younger than Sheila by a few years at least — asked for her ID, that Sheila noticed that the name on her driver's license was different. Her smiling picture was the same. Under the picture it said her name was Gwendolyn Stacy.

When Sheila returned home that evening, Peter was asleep on the bed. It was just starting to get dark in the room. She threw her purse down and sat on the foot of the bed. She had come home with the ID clutched in her hand, ready to confront him. Now she only watched him. Peter slept like a child, deeply, oblivious to her presence, as if he expended so much energy during the day that once a certain hour hit he had no choice but to give himself over to sleep. Sometimes his breathing went syncopated, worrying over some uneven thread of a dream she imagined. Sheila looked from Peter to the driver's license in her hand. Whoever had done it had done an expert job. It was nothing like the fake IDs she had seen at her high school. The name Gwendolyn Stacy was so seamlessly merged with her personal data: eye color, hair color, height, weight, etc., it looked like it would be difficult for an authority figure to question. She felt a twitching in the muscles of her stomach as the thought took root that maybe Peter had nothing to do with the ID. It was too good to be a fake. "Baby," Peter asked from the other side of the bed. "Is that you?"

"I'm here," Sheila said, shifting her weight closer to him. Then she pulled off her clothes, fit her body in the crook of his arm, and went to sleep beside him.

In the morning, Sheila woke to the sound of pages rustling by her head. Peter was flipping through the brochures that were kept in the drawer of the nightstand. *Chicago's Most Popular River Cruise*, said one. Another said, *Experience the Adventure of Navy Pier!*

"A river cruise?" said Sheila. She wrinkled her nose. "What's this?"

"Just an idea," said Peter. "I thought we might do something like this today."

"Isn't that kind of a tourist thing?" asked Sheila.

Peter shrugged. "We're not from here. We're like tourists."

"I guess," said Sheila, but she didn't like considering herself as such. In Iowa, there was a distinct delineation between those who lived in the town year-round and those who filtered in and out by semester schedules to attend the college. These boarders, renters and deserters, were treated not exactly with disdain, but there was a general sense that they were temporary fixtures — bathmats, hairpins — evaporated from town before you bothered to learn their names.

The river cruise was an architecture tour, winding by some of the city's most significant buildings, and the boat held fifty people in plastic folding chairs on its deck. Their guide was a lifelong Chicago resident with a hot pink visor and a megaphone. She looked to be about seventy-five, and though very knowledgeable about the city's architectural history, she seemed most eager to dispense information about ordinances ruling land on both sides of the river public property, owned by the city. When coasting by luxury condos, the guide would assert, "Bring a picnic back to the yard here if you like — this is public property!" or "The employees that work in this building never use their riverfront property. But you can — this is city-owned, anyone's free to use it!"

It seemed strange to be so emphatic, the small swaths of riverfront grass being least exciting beside all the stainless steel edifices rising up from either side of the riverbank like giant dominoes. But Peter was similarly taken with the idea.

"Did you hear that?" he whispered excitedly to her. "Public land."

Sheila smiled, but she said nothing.

Peter slipped his hand into hers. "We could come back at night with a blanket. Look at the stars."

They had just driven three hundred miles away from a place where open land was everywhere and the night sky was so pockmarked by light, you could read by its glow. "We're in the middle of the city," Sheila said. "There are no stars."

"Shhh," Peter said, and he covered her mouth in his hand again, as if he didn't want the others to hear her pronouncement. "Come on," he said. He removed his hand from her mouth and brushed her bangs off to the side of her face. It was difficult to say whether he was joking or he was suggesting that the stars were the same here as anywhere, and it was she who needed to make an effort.

The tour guide carried on with her megaphone as the boat snaked along the river. *Public land this! Mies van der Rohe that!* Sheila had stopped listening, but Peter nodded along to the tour guide's recommendations as if they were essential, necessary for their shared survival. Sheila decided then she would do what he asked of her. She would feign sight of entire constellations if that much were necessary.

But in the middle of the night, her mind began to race again. She could choose what to believe, but she wanted more information on which to base her choices. While Peter slept, Sheila tiptoed from the bed beside him and silently pulled his duffle bag into the bathroom. The gun was on top, and she pulled it out and placed it in her own purse. It felt lighter in her hand than she thought a gun would feel. It made little difference in the weight of her purse. Sheila stuck her hand back into the duffle bag. In his wallet, she found the ID that said his name was Peter Parker. Behind it, she thought she would find her own ID, but in its place were two old laminated cards belonging to two men who looked vaguely like the man she was sharing a bed with. In both of the laminated cards, the names had been gouged out through the plastic, rendered illegible.

There was a knock on the bathroom door.

Sheila flung the door open and held up the handful of IDs. "What the hell is going on?" she asked.

"Oh, I wanted it to be a surprise," he said. He sounded disappointed. "Look in your own wallet."

"I already did."

"Did you notice anything?" he smiled.

"You changed my name."

Peter shook his head, as if this part had nothing to do with him. "I changed your age so we won't always have to stay in at night. You can't get away with flirting with the bartender here like you did in Iowa." He smiled. "They don't even let you through the door if you're underage."

Sheila paused.

"Thanks," she said slowly.

Peter kissed her on the cheek. He smoothed her hair behind her ear.

"I really like you," he said.

Sheila took a few steps back into the bathroom, her stance softening. "You do?"

"Of course," Peter said. "Why do you think I asked you to come with me?"

"Actually, that hasn't been made entirely clear to me," Sheila said.

Peter advanced into the bathroom, and Sheila could feel his reflection in the bathroom mirror moving closer as Peter moved closer. She felt surrounded. He said, "When I saw you in the station, I felt like I already knew you. I felt close to you instantly, like we had already met somewhere else, somewhere in the past that I couldn't quite place. Like you reminded me of someone I had already known, but had lost."

"Gwen Stacy," said Sheila.

Peter looked at the floor. "Is that okay? Does that bother you?"

Sheila said, "I haven't decided yet. I mean, she's a character from a comic book, not a real person. You get that, right?"

"Of course," Peter said, "but understand, I've been waiting my entire life for someone like her to show up. And you remind me of her. Or, in some way you are her and I know you're meant to be here with me. Now if that scares you, I'm sorry, and I don't want you to stay if you don't feel the same. But maybe we could spend a little more time together and, I don't know, see how it goes."

Oh my God, Sheila thought, he's fucking crazy. I'm sleeping with a crazy person. But she wasn't scared. She was scared when she wasn't with him, when she felt like she had to investigate and assemble clues on her own. When he spoke to her like this, she felt exhilarated, like maybe she actually *was* Gwen Stacy, maybe this was why nothing else in her life had ever felt like the right thing, because the right thing was to be here with Peter.

Sheila looked him in the eye. "I'm not scared," she said.

Peter kissed her other cheek, the one he hadn't kissed before.

The gesture felt calculated for a moment, like he was trying to balance something obscure though this small sign of affection, but Sheila let it go and decided to be thankful for the symmetry. It was all a matter of deciding how to interpret information, she told herself. "I'm real glad to hear you say that," she heard him say then. He said this quietly, and again Sheila nodded. "It means a lot to me," Peter said.

"I'm not scared," Sheila repeated. "We're doing the right thing."

Peter smiled. "I knew it," he said. "I knew I was right about you."

Then he started to pull at the buttons on his pants, as if to use the bathroom.

The following night they used Sheila's new ID in the hotel bar. The bartender didn't look at her name oddly, as she expected he would. He glanced at it through the plastic sleeve of her wallet and said, "What are you having?"

"Vodka tonic," said Sheila cautiously.

Peter ordered a beer and they found a table in the corner. He announced that they were going to run out of money, which Sheila had already figured. They had only been there for three days, but living exclusively on the stolen money wasn't a sustainable plan. Sheila understood if it ever came down to an emergency, she had money saved in her bank, the money she had been saving for France. But she didn't want to touch that. She didn't want her bank tracing her location after a transaction; besides, that money had nothing to do with this.

"If you want to stay here, we'll have to start looking for new jobs," he said. "Do you want to stay in Chicago?"

She thought she did. She knew she wanted to be where he was. But what she had been craving was a plan, a ready-made

101

plan that she could latch onto and live inside of, and the more time she spent with Peter, the clearer it became that there didn't seem to be any semblance of a plan at all. Aside from the river cruise, she hadn't seen more than two blocks in either direction of their hotel. She was giving her father an ulcer.

"Who are the men whose IDs you have in your wallet?" she asked.

Peter nodded, as if confirming the question was a fair one. He said, "They're brothers."

"Are they real, or made up?"

"No, they're real."

"Who are they?"

"Me and my dead brother," he said. "Jake."

"I didn't mean . . . um," she trailed off. "Sorry."

"Well, what for? He died years ago."

"You miss him?"

"He was much older than me. He died when I was a kid and left me all his comic books."

"Well, then which one are you?" asked Sheila.

"If I had to pick one, I guess I'd be the original," Peter said. He was smiling that goofy, half-crazed smile he sometimes had. "Lee and Ditko's, back when the mechanical web-shooters were designed by hand. None of this bullshit inflation with organic spinnerets — I'm just not interested in that."

Sheila stared. Two thoughts came to her at once, quickly, and settled uncomfortably in her chest. The first was that the supposedly hard and fast rules by which the regular world functioned were actually blurry, irregular, like the borders between state lines, how it was difficult to pinpoint the exact moment when one territory became another if you weren't on the strip of the Interstate that marked the transition with a welcome sign. That the logic she had thought governed the world of adults was a hazy thing, no more certain than the lies they told to children. But the second thought came just as quickly: anyone could play this game. Sheila narrowed her eyes. "I mean, which brother are you?"

"The younger one," he said. "The baby."

"What's your real name?"

"What's the difference?"

"But Peter isn't your real name."

He looked at her hard. "Nobody reads comic books anymore," he said. "So it might as well be."

Sheila looked Peter in the eye and reached out across the table. She gripped his chin between her two fingers, and held him there. She dropped her voice and spoke low. "Lots of people read comic books still," said Sheila. She knew this to be true, and she would stand by it. There were readers everywhere; there were movies being made all the time. What right did Peter have to single-handedly commandeer the story? He wasn't doing it without her input. She tightened her grip on his face, held it still, and his mouth — half-opened as if in reply — sat mute by her hand, waiting.

Sheila let go of his face and put her hand back around the glass of ice that held her drink. She tipped back the glass and felt the last of the vodka coat the inside of her mouth. She placed the glass down on the table, and allowed her eyes to meet Peter's. At first he just stared. He ran his own hand over his chin, as if tracing the impression she had left. "Okay, sweetheart," he said softly, "you're right. Lots of people read them." But still he didn't look away, and she didn't look away, and in that lapse something shifted, as if the empty space between them were growing angles, edges, something sharp enough to reach out and grab and form into what you wanted.

"New rule, starting now," said Sheila, and Peter nodded. "No more calling me *kid*, no more *sweetheart*, no more *Sheila*. You call me my name as it's printed on my ID, and I'll do the same for you. Deal?"

He looked at her uneasily for a second. "Okay," he said.

"Say it," she said.

"I said we have a deal," he said.

She shook her head. "I want to hear you say my name."

"Gwen," he said. "We have a deal."

Sheila smiled. Under the table, she slipped her hand onto his knee.

His friend in Humboldt Park had said that they could crash in the loft for a few weeks, no more than that, or they'd need them to help make rent. Technically, she and Peter were fugitives. Sheila knew this, of course. But they had started to depend on each other. It was thrilling, and in a way, everything changed when they were in the apartment together. She felt less like a runaway and more like his girlfriend. She had never been anyone's girlfriend. Peter draped his arm over her shoulders as they walked down the street together, like he wanted to protect her, to be on both sides of her at once. But he was helpless too. Sleeping beside her, he would call her name and ask her for things, and it made her feel powerful, so she understood that he wanted her to protect him as well. This was part of the deal.

Sheila met a pretty Czech girl named Iva who lived downstairs and had also recently left her home. She cleaned houses with a group of women, all from different places. Iva came upstairs to introduce herself one of the first nights, and Sheila took to her right away. Iva was a somewhat recent immigrant to Chicago, with a passable — but far from perfect — command of the English language, and Sheila instantly saw an ally in her. She went and knocked on Iva's door the following night, when Peter wasn't around, and asked her for a job.

Iva looked at her carefully. "You want to clean houses?" She seemed incredulous at first. "The work is hard. Floors we clean on our knees, you understand this."

"I get it," Sheila said. "I know how to clean."

"The bathroom in your apartment," Iva said. "I saw it yesterday. It is not so clean."

"We just moved in," Sheila assured her. "I haven't had the chance."

Iva stared at her for another second, then disappeared into her own bathroom. She came back with a bottle of bleach and a sponge. "We try it?" she asked. "A test."

Sheila took the bottle of bleach and the sponge from Iva, and before both women walked up the narrow stairs to Sheila's apartment, Iva opened her fridge and grabbed two bottles of beer to take upstairs with them.

Iva opened one beer and looked in Sheila's cabinets for a glass, but there weren't any there. She looked confused for a second but let it go without saying anything. Then Iva took a sip from the long neck of her beer bottle, licked her lips, and sat on the closed lid of the toilet while Sheila got on her hands and knees and did her best with the bleach and the sponge in one of the blackened corners. Iva opened the second beer and smiled as she set it on the edge of the bathtub for Sheila.

"You are too young for him," Iva said.

Sheila, scrubbing at the tiles, felt her face get hot. She looked up at Iva. "I'm not as young as I look," she said. But she could feel the color in her face and was sure that just then she looked even younger.

Iva smiled. "He knows how many years you have?"

Sheila nodded. She pushed a loose strand of hair behind her ear. She continued scrubbing.

"How many?"

She had been ready to say twenty-one, but as she turned and sat on the tub to take a sip from the beer that Iva had offered her, she felt here was an opportunity to speak the truth and see how it sounded. The possibility was liberating. It was the same with her name. After demanding that Peter call her Gwen, she had introduced herself as Sheila to Iva without thinking twice. It felt good to be able to control this, to exercise authority over when she was one thing, and when she was another. "Seventeen," Sheila said. "I'll be eighteen next week."

Sheila was afraid that Iva would reprimand her, the way her sister might have, but she could see right away that she would be rewarded for her honesty. Iva nodded. "He has a nice face, your boyfriend," she said. "But he looks very sad, I think."

It was the first time anyone had referred to Peter this way, and Sheila felt her heart knock things around in her chest. "He is too sad," Sheila agreed. "I'm going to work on that."

"Yes," Iva said. "I imagine you will have success." She reached out and touched the ends of Sheila's hair that hovered near the tile floor while she scrubbed. "Very pretty," Iva said, "but you will need to tie it back to work." Iva took a black rubber band from her own wrist and offered it to Sheila.

Sheila nodded; obediently she fastened the band into her hair.

"I pay in cash," Iva said finally. "The women whose houses we clean will leave the payment in cash, and we share it."

"That works for me," Sheila said.

Iva smiled a little then in the corner of her mouth like of course she knew it worked, or she wouldn't have mentioned it. Her smile remained couched in the corner of her mouth as if to say, I know you have something to hide, but you're not alone in this.

Sheila started cleaning houses. No one talked to each other much except when articulating the full name of a cleaning product. "Clorox Bleach?" someone would shout from the bathroom down the stairs. "Murphy's Oil Soap!" the girl in the kitchen would respond, and the two would meet halfway up the stairs and make the exchange. The houses they cleaned had many bathrooms on each floor. "A waste!" Sheila heard one woman say, as she moved between bathrooms with a sponge. Sheila had never thought of the two bathrooms in her parents' house as excessive; there was one on each floor. Now she could see how little one needed to survive.

It didn't take long to discover that Iva spoke French as well as English, and so sometimes Sheila would speak with her in her own stunted French. "What age do you have?" they asked each other over and over again, and each time Sheila answered honestly, it felt just as good as it had the first time. "How does Chicago please you?" The way that Iva said the name of their city, Chicago sounded like the most exotic place in the world. But of course, that was a trick of the tongue; that was the French, making every word in Sheila's life sound like a huge soiree with lace tablecloths and pointy shoes, while her hands were wringing out a dirty sponge in some rich woman's bathtub.

Peter had taken a job in a family restaurant, washing dishes. He was getting paid under the table, and often returned with a small roll of bills to sort. His arms were always pink when he came home, from all that hot water. The hairs on his arm were matted in every direction.

"You look like a haystack," Sheila said to him, petting his arm.

"So do you," said Peter. He didn't take his eyes off hers, as if there were a whole mess of hay in her eyes, a maze or something.

There was a balding preacher on a post at the street corner near her home in Iowa who would yell at passersby on Saturday mornings about hay and eyes. "It's easier to pass through the eye of a needle, than to find a needle in a haystack." Or, "Look how you see a fleck of dust in your neighbor's eye but not a haystack in your own." Or something like that.

Sheila looked from Peter's eyes to his arm and back again.

"Parker, you're insane," she said. She smiled and drew her hands around his neck, pulled him into her. "I'm sorry to say, you don't make a bit of sense."

"Of course it makes sense. It means we're the same," Peter said. He walked her toward the window that looked over the park. "We're good together."

She leaned into him, offered him all her weight. Peter kissed her on the mouth. He started to pull off her clothes. Sometimes they would go to the bed right away, but sometimes he wouldn't let her touch him. He would remove her clothes slowly and stare and say things under his breath like, "Oh," and "Oh, God."

Other times, she would enter the apartment and find Peter staring off into space with this blank look on his face, and when she approached him, he would brighten; he wouldn't take his eyes off her. He wound his arms around her tightly as they slept. She tried to ask him questions. But Peter didn't like to talk about himself. She'd asked him how his brother died:

"An overdose of something," he'd said. "A little of this and a little of that."

"On purpose, you mean?"

"Well that's not the way it was explained to me at six, but yeah, on purpose. That's one way of saying it."

She'd asked him how long he'd lived in Iowa.

"Oh, a while," he'd said. "Too long."

Sheila walked to the other side of the apartment and poured herself a glass of water. The front room was large, but there were several small holes in the front window, the size of bullets.

"The neighborhood did not used to be so good as it is now," Iva had cautioned.

There were rats in the alleys, with long pink tails. Of course, they only wanted to eat. Everyone's garbage was heaped together in piles behind the apartment; who knew what one could find. The city of Chicago had put up signs in the alleys that said: TARGET, RATS! with a crude illustration of a rat electrocuted by a bolt of lightning. Did it mean that traps were set? Or that tenants should consider setting such traps? The eyes of the rat in the illustration were exaggeratedly frozen, as if in shock, and it made Sheila wonder where all these rodents had come from, how all these animals had found their way to the city in the first place.

Her coyote in Macbride Hall had likely never lived in Iowa like most of the animals there; it was either shot upon arrival in the Midwest, or it was a gift from scientists in Nevada or California. It stared straight forward. Maybe they didn't know how to arrange it, the limbs and everything. In the case at Macbride Hall, the coyote kept so still. None of its natural prey and predators were around; there was nothing to chase, nothing to run from. It was difficult to know one's own body, surviving in a place outside of the natural, predetermined one. There was nothing obvious about what to fear; there was no expectation about what to desire.

In the bathroom that she shared with Peter, his razor sat on the shelf beside her soap and what her mother would call her *feminine hygiene products*. She remembered her mother encouraging her to wrap up the used applicators in toilet paper before throwing them in the bathroom trashcan. "Men don't want to see that kind of thing," she'd advised. As if there were a constant stream of strange men visiting the house rifling through the garbage for evidence of Sheila's period! Now that she was actually living with a strange man — or anyway, the only man she'd ever lived with save her father — she took comfort in the sight of their bodies' overlap: stray strands of her hair stuck to his bar of soap in the shower, his used condoms mingling with her tampon packaging in the trash. The box of tampons boasted in three languages about the everyday importance of enjoying being woman, *Être une femme, c'est formidable . . . tous les jours!*

Sitting on the toilet, she smiled into her thighs.

One night as they were lying in bed, a woman on the street was yelling up to one of the apartments nearby, "An accident, you Don Juan asshole? Is that right? I'll show you accident!" Sheila heard glass, presumably a windshield, shattering. She heard a man shouting in a language she didn't understand. She heard sirens.

Peter wound his arms tightly around her in the bed like he wanted her to know she was safe.

"You and your boyfriend maybe should be more quiet," Iva advised one day as they knelt on the floor of a kitchen, scrubbing side by side.

"Quiet how?" Sheila asked.

"Mmm," Iva mimicked, "Oh, oh, oh."

Sheila smiled and stuck up her middle finger, and then she went to squeeze her rag out in the laundry room sink. Iva followed. She put her head on Sheila's shoulder as if to rest for a moment. "A joke," she said quietly, in truce, in apology. "I know you have not many of them in this country, but it is only this."

"At least I'm getting some," Sheila said.

"Some what?" said Iva.

"It's an expression," said Sheila.

"What are you getting? Some sex? Yes, it is obvious because you are very loud."

Sheila laughed. "Yeah," she said. "You mentioned."

Iva said, "I can say, 'I am getting some,' and it means I am getting some sex."

"Also," Sheila said, "you could ask, 'Are you getting any?'"

"And it means the same?" Iva looked at her as if incredulous that such innocuous words could become so loaded in context. Sheila recognized this feeling from French. Put an accent mark in a different place or switch two letters around and you could think you were talking about vegetables when in fact you were talking about genitalia.

"Have you been with a lot of guys?" Sheila asked.

Iva began to count off on her fingers. She didn't get very far before she held her hands up, but it was still enough that she had to pause to count them.

"I've only ever been with Peter," Sheila admitted.

Iva smiled, "Yes, I know."

Both women squeezed their rags and went back to their knees in the kitchen.

"I am pleased for you," Iva said from the other side of the dishwasher. "And the next time I get some, I will be sure you hear me get some."

Sheila smiled into her sponge, "C'est formidable, mon ami." At first, she couldn't put her finger on what set her so much at ease being around Iva, until she remembered that it had been a long time since she had someone she might refer to as her friend. She thought of Anthony then, of the friend he had been to her in those first weeks of sharing their lunches in the Large Caf. She pictured him sitting alone now at their lunch table. His eyes looked the same way they had when he walked away from her after she'd kissed him. She wished there had been some way to apologize to him. She wondered if he had asked another girl to the dance. She wondered if the girl had said yes.

Would it be accurate to say that they willfully ignored the fact of their criminal status? They had been living in the apartment for nearly two weeks now. Their actions were not something they acknowledged aloud. It was the way it had been with the name, the way he had used it the first night in the station, and it seemed to initiate this understanding that she didn't want to disrupt by talking the thing away. So too with their crime. Andrea had said the gas station was all over the news. And why wouldn't it be? It was no small thing to rob a business and cross state lines in a stolen vehicle. But Peter and Sheila didn't have a television or a radio and they made no effort to seek one out, at least for a time, as if to deny the possibility of danger, like children who close their own eyes with the hope of not being seen.

But Sheila didn't need to see the local news at night to sense the danger. She was starting to feel lingering glances cast in her direction, even the women with whom she cleaned houses, save Iva, seemed to regard her with a slight sense of distance. It was difficult to say whether it was because she didn't speak their language, or because she was a wanted criminal. After work that day Sheila stopped at the drug store at the corner and bought, for herself, a box of hair bleach, lipstick, eye makeup, red nail polish and, for Peter, a pair of black plastic-framed eyeglasses and a pair of desk scissors — all for under forty dollars. She reasoned it was time to make an effort to look less like themselves. When she knocked on Iva's door with the box of hair bleach, her friend immediately smiled. Sheila sat on the lip of the bathtub in Iva's bathroom, while Iva stood behind her in the mirror with plastic gloves on her hands, massaging the platinum dye into Sheila's scalp.

"I always thought it would be fun to be a real blond," Sheila explained innocently.

"Very beautiful," Iva said. "Like American movie star."

"Think Peter will be surprised?"

Iva stifled a smile. "I think you will get some."

Sheila felt the impulse to reach for Iva's hand, but because it was covered in the plastic glove, she reached for her wrist. Iva was funny in English; she was funny in French. She didn't take herself so seriously that she wouldn't mind laughing at her own expense. But the times Sheila heard her friend speak in Czech, it filled her with an incredible sadness that she couldn't explain. To hear the speed and seeming force with which Iva spoke to the other women, Sheila felt the Iva she knew was only a shred of the real woman, what this woman must be like in her own language.

"Iva?" Sheila asked. "What are you doing here?"

A thought crossed Iva's face quickly, as that other Iva, the version of her friend that was more solemn, that had survived something. "A chance to begin again. The same as you, no?" she said.

Sheila looked at the floor.

"Not important," Iva said. She raised Sheila's chin with her gloved hand, so that both women faced the mirror.

Sheila nodded. "Thank you, Iva," she said.

"It is nothing," Iva said.

When Peter arrived home from work that night, Sheila had already prepared dinner. She had applied a coat of nail polish and spent a good half an hour in the bathroom mirror with the eye shadow and mascara and all the various accompanying brushes. Soaked in black paint, her eyelashes were longer than she could have imagined. Everything about her was exaggerated. She felt like the animated or Technicolor version of herself. Then she sat and waited for him at the table, waited for him to notice her.

It didn't take long. The second he opened the door he took a step back.

"Jesus Christ," he said.

Sheila turned. "You like it?"

He walked quickly to her. He reached out for her waist and pulled her to him. Sheila smiled. She thought he was going to kiss her, but then he pulled her away just as quickly, his hands still on her waist.

"What the hell are you doing?" he said quietly. "Why are you doing this?"

"Doing what?" Sheila asked.

Peter eyed her with a look of reprimand.

"You look like her," he said.

"Who?" Sheila said.

"Who," Peter repeated, half a laugh. He gave her hair a little tug. He kissed her then, but the kiss was rough and difficult. He wasn't kissing Sheila; he was kissing the other woman. "You're going to drive me crazy," he said simply.

"You started it," said Sheila.

Peter nodded. "Yes," he said.

"That's not why I did it anyway," Sheila said. "You know we need to disguise ourselves, our identities. Don't pretend you don't think about it."

"About what?" he asked.

Sheila stared. "We broke the law, Peter," she said. "We're wanted criminals. People are looking for us." She went into her handbag and produced the black plastic glasses she had purchased for him. She held them out. "I tried them on in the store. There's no prescription. The lenses are a little scratched, but if you squint you can still read and see enough of everything."

"I don't wear glasses," he said.

"Well now you do," she said. "Try them on."

Obediently, Peter placed the eyeglasses on bridge of his nose.

Sheila nodded. "Good," she said, reaching into the plastic bag to reveal the scissors as well. "And after dinner we'll see about your hair."

Several nights later, Sheila woke up cold. First she noticed only that the sheet was missing, crumpled in a heap at the foot of the mattress, half on the floor. It was as she sat up to retrieve the blanket that she noticed that Peter was not in their bed. She heard a mumbling sound and saw the bathroom light was on; she stood up from the mattress to investigate only after fifteen minutes had passed and Peter had not returned.

The first thing she identified was that the kitchen tap was left running. Sheila turned off the faucet and advanced toward the light in the bathroom. In the bathroom, the tap was also running. Beneath the sink, Peter was sitting on the bathroom floor with a glass of water in his hand. Between gulps from his glass he mumbled something under his breath, something Sheila couldn't make out. Once his glass was empty, he reached to the running faucet and refilled it, then repeated the action. Sheila watched this continue for several minutes before she crouched on the floor beside him and placed her hands on his shoulders.

"Peter," she said.

At the sound of his name, he looked up at her, but his eyes were glossy and difficult to make contact with, like the eyes of an animal in pain or fear. She shook him again by the shoulders. "Peter," she said again.

"Gwen," he said now, as if relieved. He repeated her name several times, greedily, comforted at the sound.

"You were sleepwalking," she said. "You were drinking water in your sleep." She put her hand on his forehead like her mother used to do, feeling for fever.

Peter shook his head, embarrassed; he began to stand up from the bathroom tiles. "I was having a bad dream," he said. "You were underwater and I couldn't find you."

Sheila smiled. She guided him back to their bed and pulled her arm tighter around his torso, rubbed his back until she could hear his breathing steady and wander off, like she was the one who would take care of him now. That was the first night she had found him up wandering the apartment.

But after three nights of turning off the kitchen tap, after three nights of finding Peter drinking from the bathroom tap and explaining how he was looking for her in the water, she was frightened. She would wake up, first cold, then angry at him for walking away from their bed, for doing strange things at night that he made no attempt to explain to her in the morning.

"What are you seeing?" she asked him.

"A lot of water," he would say.

"And I'm in the water. Am I swimming?"

He'd say. "Come on. Let's talk about something else."

"Tell me," she would beg on the third night.

"It's a dream," he'd say, "It doesn't matter."

"Stop it," she would yell as she shook his shoulders on the fourth night. Peter looked back at her with wet eyes. "I can't," he said, and the helplessness in his voice would be what scared her more than anything.

The morning of her eighteenth birthday marked three weeks of their shared survival as fugitives, but Sheila woke up thinking it couldn't last much longer. She woke up early enough to watch the first sunlight touch the floorboards through their curtain-less windows. Peter had been up again last night and now he slept beside her, deeply as always. Sheila dressed slowly and let herself out the front door. She purchased a coffee from the café at the corner and crossed the street to Humboldt Park. The park was deceiving, more expansive than it seemed from the window of their apartment, and it was empty at this early hour and looked slightly more sinister than during full daylight. She walked by a boathouse and along a lagoon. She walked through a grove of crabapple trees, and out of the corner of her eye, she caught sight of an animal watching her, as if charting her movements, something fierce in gaze and sharp in bone structure, but when she turned again, she only saw a collie sniffing around plots of perennial flowers. It happened several more times, this feeling of being watched, her progress through the park guarded by something wild, but always by the time she turned on her heels to catch her pursuer, the park returned to a benign landscape. The truth was she was glad for the distraction. She walked for forty minutes, aimlessly at first, then more purposefully, and tried with everything she took in not to think of her father this morning, not to think of him waking up for work on the date she was born and brushing his teeth or tying his shoes or reading the newspaper.

Walking from the perimeter of the park, Sheila passed a payphone. She stopped and clutched the receiver in her hand. She thought that it would be enough only to hold it, but before long she was fishing around in her bag for spare change and dialing. She could picture the telephone on the nightstand beside her parents' bed. Her father picked up after a single ring.

"Hello?" he asked. His voice had the slow panic of interrupted sleep.

"Dad," she said. And already she could hear every noise in the room, her mother shrieking in the background, her father covering the mouthpiece of the telephone and saying, "It's her."

It was her father who spoke first. "Sheila," he said. "Your mother's worried sick."

"Dad," she said again. "I'm sorry."

"Nothing to be sorry for," he said. His voice was strangely calm and steady. "Are you safe? Did they hurt you?"

"I'm okay," Sheila said. She could feel a sob building in her throat. "Dad, I have to go."

"Now wait a minute," she heard him start, but she made herself put down the phone before she could hear the rest.

She told herself it was better to let them know she was okay, that she was safe, than not to have called at all.

When she arrived back at the apartment, Peter was up and dressed. He looked at her slowly. She could see that her absence from the bed this early had worried him, but this he was trying to disguise. "Have you eaten?" he asked.

"Only coffee."

"I thought I would take you to breakfast," he said.

It was difficult to discern whether he understood the significance of the day, or if he just had a craving for an omelet. He was more delicate since the sleepwalking had started. It seemed like the smallest things she said, even in jest, could hurt him.

"I bet my parents are really worried about me," Sheila said.

Peter nodded. "Maybe you should think about going home."

Sheila felt her eyes fill. "I don't want to," she said.

"Okay," Peter said. "You don't have to." He put his arms around her, dried her face with his fingers. "You know I want you with me, but you do whatever you feel is right. You make the rules, okay?" Sheila nodded. He kissed her forehead. Then he said, "Wait here." He retreated to the bedroom and returned with something stashed behind his back.

"What's this?" Sheila said.

Peter exaggerated the gesture of concealment and took a step forward.

Sheila tried pulling at each of his arms, but Peter wouldn't reveal the object until she promised to sit down and close her eyes.

Sheila complied, sitting on their bed, with her legs folded beneath her.

"Okay," she said. "I'm ready."

Peter said nothing, but she could hear him kneel on the ground, beside the electrical outlet. Then she heard the sound of static and from it the Frenchwoman's voice began to speak.

"Je ne sais pas," the Frenchwoman said.

"Je ne sais pas," said Peter.

"Je ne sais quoi," the Frenchwoman said.

"Je ne sais quoi," said Peter.

Sheila kept her eyes closed for a moment and listened. She had left her CD player in the gas station and hadn't heard her lessons since. It was a level-one lesson and all he was doing was repeating, so the dialogue was nonsensical, but it didn't really matter. Peter's voice was soft and unsure of itself as he repeated after the Frenchwoman. When Sheila opened her eyes, Peter stopped the tape abruptly, as if suddenly shy.

"Do you like it?" he said.

Sheila felt something, like desire, rise in her gut. "Your accent needs a little work, to be honest," she said.

Peter looked at the floor, but he smiled.

"Where did you get it?"

Peter leaned nervously over the tiny, black buttons, as if they were the teeth of an animal. "A little pawn shop on Chicago Avenue," he said. "They barely sell these things new anymore, so — " he trailed off. "Happy birthday, Gwen," he said quietly, and he touched her face where her cheek met her chin.

Sheila stood beside him. With one hand she pressed the play button on the CD player, and with the other she took Peter's hand and walked him back to the bed. They lay still, side by side. The Frenchwoman spoke; Sheila and Peter listened. The familiar rhythm of her voice filled the room like a mother's, and Sheila felt content just to let the sound soak up around them without reacting to the words.

In the pauses between each French phrase, Sheila heard not Paris, but Iowa. She heard the stillness of empty fields of quiet crops, of parking lots at night with only insects moving, the stillness of her parents' kitchen in the long afternoon hours. Iowa was the last place she'd heard French like this. She understood then that she was not going to Paris. She had saved all her money to get as far as Chicago, and now she was here, with Peter, working hard not to let the French make her miss the home it called to mind.

On the bed, Peter took her hand into his and squeezed it.

Sheila bit her lip to discourage a tremble.

"We're going to make it. It's working," Peter said. He pressed his mouth to her temple. "Everything is going according to plan."

And a part of her thought, *What plan?* But so what if the plan was hazy and unknowable in its entirety? An arrangement was beginning to form, rules they agreed on. She saw how he would take care of her, except for when she took care of him, and how they would pool their money and work to eat, and this was one way to leave the place you'd known too long and make a go of it. This was what a plan looked like once you stopped obsessing over the culminations and actually started to live inside it.

Yes, she wanted to say. She wanted to agree with this logic, to adopt it as her own. Instead she said, "I want to know where you go at night."

"But I'm always right here," said Peter, "beside you."

"Take me with you," she said. "In one of the dreams."

Peter shook his head. "Don't," he said.

The Frenchwoman was still speaking, but she was background noise now. The names of the things she said had become irrelevant.

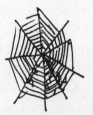

CHICAGO. IT SEEMED unlikely that you could get to a place like it, another world entirely, after only four hours in the car. There were parks and avenues stuffed with skyscrapers, there was a lake that you'd have sworn was an ocean for its size and for the way the waves pulled themselves out onto the sidewalk. The city Peter had dreamed every night for a week retreated to the back office of his brain, to be replaced by the thing itself. It at first seemed purely speculative that people actually lived here, but he saw them, all right: filling their cars with gas, walking their dogs. Those were the surefire signs of residence — cars, dogs.

In the hotel, there were rules posted everywhere. By the pool: NO RUNNING. NO DIVING. NO HORSEPLAY. By the bar: NO ID, NO SERVICE. WE RESERVE THE RIGHT TO ASK FOR IDENTIFICATION OF ANYONE WHO LOOKS TO BE UNDER 35. Out front of the lobby: NO SMOKING WITHIN 15 FEET OF THE ENTRANCE. With every cigarette, Peter walked the requisite fifteen feet before rummaging in his pocket for a match and even in this ridiculousness, he felt content to be abiding by the rules of this other place.

Later — near the apartment he'd secured for Gwen and himself — squirrels darted between trees with hedge apples, giant and unwieldy, stashed between their front teeth. There had been talk, all over the middle of the country, of wilder animals — coyotes, cougars — crossing into the borders of cities and roaming the streets by night. Peter felt as if he had reached a place where so many living things converged, he sometimes had to close his eyes so as not to get overstimulated. He found an ad in the paper for a partially furnished apartment in Humboldt Park, a weekly rental, and he'd told Gwen that a friend of his had hooked them up. He didn't want her to know how much of their money was going to the place. He had put down two weeks' rent, because the landlord had been a bulky man who asked no questions and did not ask him to sign anything. It was an investment really, cheaper than the hotel room in the long run. Safer too.

When he walked Gwen into the apartment, she ran excitedly from the sink to the table, from the window's view of the park to the mattress on the floor — you'd have thought he'd secured a penthouse suite. The apartment was borderline decrepit, sure to be full of cockroaches, but Gwen clearly was impressed, and in a way it endeared her further to him. At the time, watching her run through the near-empty room — touching everything, securing her arms around his neck — the stolen car and money, the gun and the police seemed to exist in some other reality that had nothing to do with Peter Parker, nothing to do with the woman he loved.

They had been living there two days when the Czech girl who lived below came up the stairs to introduce herself.

"You are from here?" she asked. Her name was Ivana — "Iva is for short." She was likely Gwen's age, but spoke with the low, throaty tenor of Slavic translation, which made her seem older, more sage than both Gwen and himself.

"No," Peter said. "We're new to the area."

Iva nodded. "Two years I have been here," she said. "I can explain."

Which made it sound to Peter as if she would explain her journey from Eastern Europe, how she came to live in the Midwest from the Old World sophistication of opera houses and finely fermented beers. But what she had come to explain was purely practical advice. She explained how the man who lived on the corner sold drugs, how they would hear the people waiting for him in the alley. She explained how at night they were never to walk on the park side of the street, but to stay to the house side, where there were streetlamps, to avoid getting mugged.

"Sounds like a nice neighborhood," Gwen said.

Iva said, "It did not used to be so good as it is now."

Which Peter took to mean that the place could grow on you. He could see that.

"We heard animals last night," Gwen said. "In the alley."

"Rats," Iva said. "Also" — here she paused, mimed the act of howling — "how do you say this?"

"Wolves," Peter said "Dogs."

"Coyotes, she means," said Gwen.

"Yes, this," said Iva. "In the alleys, also sometimes in the park, you hear them."

"But have you seen them?" Gwen asked.

Iva waved her hand dismissively at this, as if her expertise in such areas was being challenged, though Peter could see that it was only that Gwen *wanted* to see one. She was funny about things like that. Whenever they saw a dog being walked on the opposite side of the street, Gwen would practically knock Peter down to coddle the thing, to work her fingers into its coat.

"You are very patient," he'd heard her confide plainly to a dog that was tethered to a bike rack outside a bar once, while checking the dog's tags for the proper name with which to address it.

"Toast," she'd added before Peter pulled her from the ground where she knelt.

Iva continued, "They have to be removed."

"Removed?" Gwen repeated.

"Sure," said Peter. "Creatures like that could cause a lot of harm in the city. They *eat* dogs."

"But they return," said Iva. "If you want to see them" — she was talking to Gwen exclusively now — "you must go to the lake. There they travel in packs."

He could see Gwen had not yet exhausted the topic, so Peter took the opportunity to step outside for a cigarette. There was a rickety bit of porch on the side of the house, where if he strained his head, Peter could make out the dark expanse of the park. He liked being close to so much land. He knew he had become distracted, that he'd lost sight of his mission, but looking into the bulk of darkened shapes — barely visible suggestions of what was really out there — he had the distinct feeling that things were starting to come together.

How exactly to go about making things come together was unclear. It was his first calling — if it could be called that — or anyway, it was the first time he had chosen to try to follow the sketchy details from a dream to try to effect a change, and so far, so good, but now what? He had a weapon, which seemed important. But what exactly was he meant to do with it? Toward whom was he to point it? Peter imagined breaking and entering into the bathrooms of the city's loneliest men and making demands. *Come out with your hands up or I'll shoot!* The entire proposition was absurd. In stories, those who hope to do harm call attention to themselves. They kidnap public figures; they steal potent potions from scientific labs and unleash monsters of their own creation on the general populace. But what about the small and quiet criminals who hope to make no noise in their work? How to save someone from himself?

The first week in Chicago he had snuck away for an hour or two with the pretense of looking for work, but instead, he wandered the city, looking for clues. He rode city buses. He walked the perimeter of parks. He found several small scrap yards, and he spent the better part of a few afternoons wandering through the smashed up cars and piles of trash. He saw nothing that resembled the isolated fragments from his dreams. The thought occurred to him that it was Gwen who would have to lead him. He had the foresight, yes, but she was there with him for a reason. He remembered the way she had slapped him, straight out of the comics. He could do nothing but continue to look for overlaps, make meaning of coincidence, and encourage her to keep improvising until things started to resemble the stories he knew.

In the meantime, he washed dishes. He washed dishes in water so hot his arms stung long after he'd removed them from the scalding basins. There were three sinks, a process: wash, rinse, sanitize. After sanitization, it was contrary to health codes to rinse a second time. He'd lift the dishes from their third bath still covered in suds — the fluids of sanitation — but under no circumstances was he to ever rinse this dish again, whatever he might think. This was explained to him by his supervisor at the Greek restaurant, and explained again routinely by the prep cooks who chopped garlic and destemmed spinach beside him.

"Peter, no good! No good!" they yelled.

Victor and Diego had worked their way up from dishwashing to kitchen prep, and as such, they were willing to help Peter do the same, if he stuck around long enough. Of course, he would not stick around long enough. He was being paid cash under the table; this way there was no need to hand over his social security number or personal information that might link him to the robbery of a gas station and a taxi three hundred miles away. But already he was beginning to understand the constraints of the clandestine existence he'd forged for Gwen and for himself.

Gwen had taken up Iva's offer to clean houses with her, and she too would come home with her hands cracked and brittle from so many cleaning products. Sometimes, he felt bad he had brought her here. She clearly could have done better for herself than squeezing the water out of sponges all day. But Gwen insisted that this is where she wanted to be.

They had only lived together a few weeks, but already patterns were beginning to form, routines he began to expect and look forward to. Every night they made dinner. Peter did the shopping. Gwen pulled the pan out from beneath the sink and threw whatever he bought inside of it, closed the lid. After dinner they went for walks, long walks, in which Gwen wound her arm through Peter's and they pointed out houses to one another where they might have lived in another life, if Chicago were their city, and not just this place where they were. They walked along the thrift shops on Milwaukee Avenue and tried on clothes they sometimes bought. Peter had packed a change of clothes in his duffle bag, but Gwen had come to Chicago with only the clothes on her back, so it was far from frivolous to use some of their shared funds to buy a new pair of jeans or T-shirt.

The last time they'd gone to the Salvation Army, Peter had run his hand along the material of a navy blue dress with buttons and a cloth belt. While Gwen sifted quickly through hangers in rows, Peter pushed the dress into her hands.

"What's this?" she said.

"Try it on," he said.

"I have nowhere to go in this." Gwen held the dress up to her shoulders.

Peter shrugged.

"You're blushing," Gwen said. "Give it to me."

When Gwen pulled back the curtain of the fitting room, Peter paused for a moment before he stepped behind the curtain with her.

"Only one person allowed in the fitting rooms at a time," a clerk called from the counter.

"I'll just be a second," Peter said, but quietly for only Gwen to hear.

The dress was old-fashioned and it was cut for a woman with a bit more bust and hip to her, but it hardly mattered. Peter stepped closer to the dress and fixed the collar where it rose awkwardly in the back of Gwen's neck.

"What's the big idea?" she asked.

Peter reached for the rubber band that held back her ponytail and tugged twice to free Gwen's hair from it. He placed his hand at the small of her back and turned Gwen toward the mirror, so she could see herself, so she could see how in this dress she was a spitting image of the Empire State University science major who would become Spider-Man's first love.

"Put on the dress," Peter would sometimes say at night, and Gwen would obligingly walk out of her jeans in the bedroom and slip her arms through the fabric. Peter breathed deeply into the material that covered her shoulder as he held her and felt that he was breathing in so much that he had lost.

The way Spider-Man had clutched at Gwen Stacy's body after she died, like there was nothing he could do to make things right, Peter remembered. He remembered Jake curled in a heap in his childhood closet, his fingers twitching. He remembered his mother staring off into the buttons of the microwave without touching a number to heat her dinner. Peter held Gwen in their bedroom in Chicago and breathed in the smell of her hair.

"Okay, that's enough," Gwen would say then, and she'd put the dress on a hanger and return it to their closet. And it was. Even seeing her in it for five minutes like that was enough to conjure a world of loneliness and so affirm their reason for coming.

The truth was it had been easier than he would have ever imagined to coerce Gwen into the car with him. It was as if she had been sitting there in the station, waiting for him to show up. Peter had anticipated that the entire prospect would require some convincing, and so he had planned to tell her everything — the nightmares, the comic books, the way his brother had died — but Gwen had asked him to point the gun at her. Gwen did most of the talking in the car. Gwen had removed his clothes, unprovoked, on the very first night they shared a room.

Peter had been with a few local girls in early adolescence, he had visited a prostitute more recently; once, regrettably, he had slept with a fare in the back of his cab, but these had been quiet, efficient exchanges, the scripted trajectory from grope to release that he had learned from movies along with everyone else. None of this had prepared him in the least for the patient concentration of Gwen Stacy slowly unbuttoning his shirt — as if not to wake him — while he pretended to sleep. Peter had understood that if he opened his eyes, Gwen would be there, inches from his face, the blond ponytail that she favored hovering between them like an intermediary, ready to bargain. He had told himself that he wouldn't touch the girl, though every hour of the drive he'd felt increasingly prone to question this rationale; she was young, and, at the time, he wasn't even sure how young — she was almost certainly lying to him about her age. But young, possibly a full ten years younger; seventeen, he feared, was not a bad guess. When she had finished with the buttons, she started to trace lines in his skin with her fingers. Peter cleared his throat. He fought the impulse to open his eyes. He'd said, "Gwen, go to sleep."

"I can't sleep," she had said. "Obviously."

"You should try," Peter said.

Several minutes went by and Peter thought he had successfully evaded confrontation, when he felt something flicker twice between his ribs. Peter exhaled, lifted her on top of him and looked her in the eye. "Hmmm?" he asked.

"I didn't say anything," she said.

"You didn't say anything," Peter repeated. "Did you just lick me?"

Gwen shrugged. "Uh, I guess, yeah I did."

Peter closed his eyes. But their speaking somehow seemed to grant her further access, permission to continue. She kissed his face — eyebrow, chin, ear — quietly, and it was only when he began to push off her clothes that her demeanor shifted. She became loud, sharp in her movements, which gave Peter the distinct feeling she was performing for him — or worse, that he was her first — a thought that Peter quickly pushed from his mind, even while he was covering her mouth with his hand.

"Shhh," he whispered. "Do you want to get caught?"

Gwen had giggled into his hand at his little joke, which really was no joke at all. The old thrill of getting caught having sex, in this case, did not apply. He had paid for the room; it was theirs to use as they wanted. Getting caught, in this case, applied to each of their joint actions leading up to the acquisition of the hotel room, a laundry list of morally questionable decisions.

And so while he might have preferred to wait to consummate whatever they were going to be to each other, it was Gwen who had pursued him. It was Gwen who had unfastened the buttons of his shirt and pushed her hand along the flat plane of his stomach, and it was Gwen who had made so many strange noises, so much like something in pain, that when Peter thought back to this first night, he had to work hard to remind himself that he hadn't forced himself onto her. She seemed to oscillate between wanting to run things and wanting to follow his lead. She had asked him that night in the bar to call her Gwen, to retire all other names for the purpose of addressing her, and he had agreed, complied; besides, it was the name he had always used in his mind to address her even if he didn't do so with his voice. So he was glad that she wanted to take the name he had offered her, but also it made him feel a little uneasy, like there were parts about the rules they were making that only she understood.

For the first week, he'd allowed himself to be distracted.

"What would you rather be?" Gwen would ask. "A collie or a greyhound?"

"A collie," he said. He kissed the underside of her wrist, where her veins crossed paths.

"Montana or Wyoming?"

"Wyoming," Peter said.

Gwen wrinkled her nose at him. "Invisibility or x-ray vision?"

Peter sat up. "What kind of question is that?"

"The one I'm asking," Gwen said.

"Invisibility." He said it quickly, but he could feel pressure building in his face, the shame of thinking himself special.

"Why?" Gwen said.

"How should I know," he said.

It got quiet for a minute.

"It's okay," Gwen said after awhile. "I would want to be invisible too."

More recently — perhaps as he grew to care for her more, perhaps as she grew to share more in common with the Gwen Stacy whose stories he read as a child — Peter had become lazy with letting the messy contradictions in his brain hang loose for her to see. The other day Gwen had asked him, apropos of nothing, "So what do you think will happen to us if we get caught?"

"Nothing will happen to you," he assured her. "It's a good thing we put on that little show with the gun for the security camera. We can say I kidnapped you, and no one would question it."

Gwen laughed. "How many years do you think you would get?" She was tracing her fingers in patterns along the small of his back, teasing him, testing him.

"Oh, ten? Twenty?" Peter said. "It doesn't matter." He leaned in for her mouth, bit her lip softly. "We're not going to get caught."

"And if I say that I chose to leave with you, what would happen to me?" Her fingers ceased their tracing pattern along the waist of his jeans. She was waiting for him to answer.

"You wouldn't say that," Peter said.

"And if I did?" She persisted.

"You wouldn't go to jail," he said. "Your father would pull some strings."

"What strings?"

"You know, with the law. It helps to have a father who's the chief of police."

Gwen wrinkled her nose. "My father's an accountant," she said.

"Admiral Stacy?" Peter said. He shook his head. "Only if by accountant you mean he's accountable for the safety of the entire New York police force."

Gwen continued to talk over him. "He's an accountant. He's never even been to New York! He's fifty-two years old, and he has high blood pressure. He taught me to read. He took me camping in the Ozarks every summer until I turned thirteen."

"I have a hard time believing he'd have time for so many vacations!" Peter said.

"Stop it," Gwen said.

"What?"

"Forget it."

"We're just playing."

"I don't want to play like this," she said, and she turned from him suddenly, brusquely, and pretended to sleep.

"Gwen?" he said.

She faked a snore.

"I guess I'll sleep on the couch," he offered.

"Good idea," said Gwen's back.

They didn't have a couch in the apartment. She knew that, obviously. Peter dragged a blanket and pillow to the cushioned chair near the window and began making a bed for himself there. He looked out the window to the park where there was a man sorting methodically through the trash can, seeming to catalog the contents of each object he extracted. An order existed in the most unlikely things if you just waited to detect it. Peter dozed off after a while, and when he woke up, it was because he could feel her standing over him. For a moment he thought he was dreaming, the old dream as it had come to him in Iowa, kneeling over his bed — he held his breath, he waited for it — but this was different.

"Hey," she said.

"Hey," he said.

"You were sleeping?" she asked.

"I guess so," he said.

"I love you," she said quietly, simply. "That's why I can become her when I'm with you."

Peter nodded.

"But if you confuse my father with some stupid cartoon character again, I'll leave."

"Admiral Stacy is hardly a cart — "

She put her hand up to silence him. "Cartoon, comic book, whatever. Listen, I like who I am when I'm with you — enough to want to alter certain parts of myself, even. But don't let it make you arrogant enough to think you can go around changing everything. You can't play God in other people's memories, mess around with other people's families."

"I'm sorry," Peter said. "It has nothing to do with your father. It has nothing to do with us."

"I know that," she said. "I wanted to make sure you knew it."

"Of course," he said.

"Also," she paused, "I know what happens to Gwen Stacy."

"What do you mean?" asked Peter.

"She gets killed."

"Yes," said Peter.

Gwen stared. "Maybe you better tell me what happened to her?"

Peter looked at the ceiling, then back at her. "The Green Goblin kidnapped her. He brought her to the top of the Brooklyn Bridge to get Spider-Man's attention. But just when Spider-Man arrived, the Green Goblin pushed Gwen over the edge."

"And Spider-Man doesn't save her?"

"He tries to. He flings out his webbing. And it reaches her; his web wraps around her thigh as she's falling. So for a second it seems like he's rescued Gwen, but when he pulls her up to the bridge, she isn't moving."

"Because she's dead," Gwen offered.

"Pretty much," Peter said. Of course it was more complex than that. There was the issue of responsibility that would plague him for a long time, because the fact that she was dead was one thing, but the cause of her death was another, a question that would remain obscured and unanswered to him.

Gwen swallowed. "This part of the story doesn't have anything to do with us either."

"Of course not," said Peter.

She studied him around the eyes until she decided this answer would satisfy her. "Come back to bed with me?" Gwen asked.

Peter smiled. "Yes," he said. "The couch was kind of starting to hurt my back."

She kissed him and pulled him back into bed with her. She rubbed his back until she fell asleep, leaving him alone in the room.

All this time the dreams did not return. Peter had been trying to channel them. He had been trying to encourage a sign that he'd done the right thing to "kidnap" Gwen, or whatever you wanted to call it, to rob the gas station, to cross state lines in a car that was not his own. But the dreams did not return, and Peter began to worry that he had taken Gwen for a reason that was slowly receding, that he'd convinced her to accompany him on a quest whose rules she didn't understand, because, of course, he hadn't explained them. It had seemed for a time that Gwen had intuited their mission, for she had been a very take-charge kind of girl initially, but that too was waning, and now Peter wasn't sure he trusted these motives himself. Peter resolved in this moment to stop overlapping this childhood story over the very real woman whose bed he shared. So he kept quiet about their responsibility, he stopped searching for overlaps, stopped waiting for the dreams to direct him, forgot about all of it for a time and allowed himself to focus on nothing but his love for her, and his desire to preserve it.

Gwen was developing her own ideas of how things should be directed with respect to their identities, and they weren't always in agreement with Peter's. The day of their joint makeovers, Peter sensed it was the beginning of the end. But to clutch a fistful of that hair! Peter barely had time to process the difference in her before Gwen began introducing the change she had in mind for him as well: glasses, a haircut. She had her reasons. They were wanted criminals; their faces were on the news. Surely this was true, but this truth wasn't a reality that Peter spent much time considering. He knew that they would not get caught until they had accomplished what they had come here to do. Of this he was so certain, that in the first two weeks, he didn't bother thinking of their mutual safety all that much, in terms of the law. But now safety was on the forefront of his mind. She was flirting with disaster designing disguises straight out of the comic books. She had held up the glasses and told him to put them on, and he had complied. He pushed them up the bridge of his nose and blinked his eyes. Watching her movements around the kitchen through the smudged plastic lenses, her body blurred, the general outline intact, she was Gwendolyn Stacy in the flesh.

"You're next," Gwen said. She produced a pair of scissors from the plastic bag on the table and gave a few preemptive snips in the air, like a gunshot signaling a race has begun.

He had let his hair grow for the past few months, and the longest strands now touched the collar of his shirt, but it was due to laziness more than choice. Sitting in a kitchen chair, watching snips of his black hair coast to the floor all around him, around the blond blur that was Gwen Stacy, he felt completely devoted to her, he felt his love for her deepen and expand even as his fear grew.

It was a few days later when Gwen came home from work talking about a place Peter had seen in a dream. She and Iva had started cleaning some new houses in Lincoln Park, blocks away from one branch of the Chicago River.

"There was this river filled with scrap metal," Gwen explained over dinner. "It was floating on huge barges — piles of smashed up cars, stuff like that. Really strange looking."

Peter felt the muscles in his stomach tense. It was starting to happen. She was going to lead him. "Where was it?" he asked. He swallowed the bite in his mouth. "Could you find your way back?"

Gwen looked impressed with herself to be carrying information that was somehow valuable to him. "Yeah, I think so," she said.

"Tonight," Peter said. "After dinner."

Gwen shrugged. "Sure."

After dinner, Gwen disappeared for fifteen minutes into the bathroom while Peter did the dishes. It seemed to be his lot lately, dishes at work, dishes at home, but he didn't mind; he felt useful. He was just finishing up on the last of the pans when he heard Gwen behind him. "About ready?" she asked.

The dress. She had changed into it without him asking her to, and the sight of her standing on the other side of the kitchen table in it without proper preparation made him feel the need to steady himself against the counter.

"What are you doing?" he asked.

"What do you mean?" asked Gwen.

"Why are you wearing that?"

"Oh, this?" Gwen said, as if it were any random article of clothing. "I thought you liked it."

"I love you in that dress," he said. "But I didn't think you liked to wear it out of the apartment."

"Well why shouldn't I?" she asked. "It's comfortable, and I have a pretty limited wardrobe here."

Of course it was reasonable for her to want to wear the dress for reasons that had nothing to do with him, but surely Gwen understood that there was more to the dress than that. She was smart enough to understand that in wearing it, she exercised a kind of power over him.

"Do you want me to change?" she asked.

"No," he said. "You look great. Let's go."

They left around nine. As the bus turned onto Cortland Street, Gwen pulled the cord above their seat to request a stop. They walked under an expressway viaduct and crossed a busy street. At first, it didn't look familiar at all. There was a slight incline up Cortland past a gas station, past a steel banner that announced the workplace of A. FINKL AND SONS FOUNDRY. Then the bridge appeared, and beneath it the floating metal just as he'd seen it. Gwen joined him on the bridge and together they looked out onto the barges and watched how slowly they moved down the river. "Just like I said, right?"

He felt a shiver pass through him. "Let's keep going," he said. "See what else is here."

They wandered closer to the scrap pile itself, inside an open gate, past several NO TRESPASSING signs, and watched the metal as it was collected and distributed by a giant metal arm. Even in this there was an order. Peter followed the route of several rounds of scrap, as it made its journey from the haphazard pile to the teeth of the crushing mechanism. He had been standing, watching for several minutes, when he felt the first explosion.

Giant billows of smoke rose from the scrap yard, and then the bursting sound rose with it. Two smaller bursts followed. Peter grabbed Gwen by the arm and started running, past the gate and the posted signs. He ran to the edge of the metal fence and ducked behind a gutted car parked there. He pulled Gwen to his chest, trying to keep the smoke from her face. He was thinking, *Forgive us our trespasses.* It was a phrase he remembered from his mother, part of the prayer she would say before they ate supper at night, and now it played on a loop in his brain — as if testament to the fact that he didn't belong here, that this shaking ground and smoke had nothing to do with him. He covered his head in his hands and waited for the ground to stop shaking, waited for the smoke to clear. *Forgive us . . . Forgive us . . .* He remembered hearing you weren't supposed to breathe in smoke, so he batted at the thick air with his hands, looking around, trying to get his bearings. The first moving thing he saw was a black man on a bicycle. Peter called to the man from behind the car.

"Get down," Peter yelled. "Over here."

The man was walking his bike from the scrap yard, as if completely oblivious to all the rising smoke and dust.

"What you mean 'get down'?" the man yelled back. "The fuck you think you are, Gaza?" The man started to walk toward Peter and seemed surprised to see Gwen there as well. He shook his head for a moment as if reluctant to confirm that there was a girl there in the scrap pile. "Evening, miss," he said finally, laughing, removing his cap. He offered Gwen his hand, and she accepted it.

"Thanks," Gwen said. Now she was snickering too.

Peter lifted one knee from the pavement. He felt suddenly ashamed, but still more confused than anything. Of course Chicago was not known for its roadside explosions. "The smoke," Peter said, as if in defense. "Something went off."

The man laughed. "Happens all the time. Some asshole puts an engine in the scrap pile . . . Kaboom." He mimed the force of the explosion with his two hands, then offered one to Peter.

Peter accepted the lift. He dusted off his knees. "Fuck," he said. He shook his head.

"*Fuck*, that's right," the man repeated, still laughing. "Where you from? Not here."

Peter noticed the man's bicycle again, now leaning against the car where they had taken cover. It was so small, it looked like a child's bicycle, and behind it there was a slack bit of rope that kept it tethered to a shopping cart. The shopping cart was filled with scrap metal.

"We're from New York," Gwen said.

Peter gave her a look. "You work for the foundry?" he asked the man.

"I work for myself," the man said. "Finkel pays by weight. I gather what I can." The man looked them up and down again, then between them — from Gwen to Peter and back again — as if he was contemplating something. His gaze rested heavily on Peter finally, and Peter could feel the man sizing him up as if comparing his features to something else he'd seen. Peter thought of the grimy, heavy-lined police sketches that depicted kidnappers. He wondered if such a sketch existed in a rough approximation of his own face.

"You lost? You in the wrong neighborhood."

Peter pushed his glasses up the bridge of his nose with his finger. He put his arm around Gwen's shoulders. "We're on vacation. We're out for a late night walk," he said. He tried to smile. "Is that a crime?"

It occurred to him that if there was a reward being offered in exchange for information, this man could use the money. His brain raced, and he tried to think of something to say.

But before he could say anything, Gwen's face was next to his, her mouth beside his mouth. The kiss was quick, but he could feel Gwen directing it; he could feel the small bones that were her teeth tense behind her thin smile. It was more certain and steady than anything he could have managed. When she pulled away, she said, "Honey, it's late. Let's go home."

Peter nodded, took his cue. He said to the man, "We better be getting back."

The man shook his head and smiled at something over their heads where the scrap pile rose behind them. "I see that," he said, nodding at Gwen. "But don't be walking no more round here at night. Ain't no place for walking," he said. He picked up his bicycle and the scrap metal in the shopping cart rattled beside it. "You're not supposed to be here."

Gwen laughed all the way home, on the walk back down Cortland, and when the 73 bus let them off at their stop, Gwen launched into it again. "Parker, you saved my life," she said for the hundredth time. "The next time I'm in imminent danger, I'll know who to call." She laughed, trailing off.

"Could you maybe stop saying that?" Peter said. "I mean you don't even know what you're talking about, do you?" He said it more sternly than he meant to, but it was irking him somehow, this cute way she just happened to want to slip into the dress, the way she was playing at being a damsel in distress. "Have you ever read a single one of the comic books, Sheila?"

"Don't call me that," she snapped.

"It's your name, isn't it?"

"As much as yours is whatever you scratched out of your driver's license."

He felt as if he had been punched in the stomach, and he wanted to return the blow. He couldn't explain it. He wanted some power over her, as a kind of counterforce for that which she held over him. It was as if she hadn't noticed how close they had come to being identified. But if not, why did she kiss him in that moment? With the kiss, she had absolved him.

Once they were in their room again and began undressing for bed, Peter tried to smooth things out.

"Listen," he said. "I'm sorry I tried to save you from that fake explosion. Okay?"

"Forget it," Gwen smiled. She kicked off her shoes in the corner. "Never happened, right?"

She was still angry with him, but she pretended to laugh. She really did love him; he could see that. She was such a sweet and sensible girl, his Gwen; she was perfect, really. Peter took a few steps toward the bed and held out his hands.

Gwen shook her head. "Lose the street clothes, Parker," she said suddenly, fitting her fingers into the waistline of his jeans, pulling him in. "And then maybe I'll think about letting you near me."

He started to remove his clothes, his shirt, his socks. He had started to reach for her again, but Gwen stopped and he saw something shift then in her face, her mouth soured at the corner. She sat up in the bed. She stood. "Oh God," she said. "Oh my God." She placed her chin in her hands and started to sway back and forth.

"I'm just like those other girls," she said.

Peter swallowed. He said, "What other girls?"

"The dead ones on the side of the road," she said. "The ones you were trying to save."

He spoke to her cheekbone, to her jaw, to the place where her hair was stacked behind her perfect ear. He said, "You're nothing like those other girls."

"Why not?" she said. "It kind of seems like you're trying to save me."

Peter shook his head. "No," he said.

"Yes you are!" she was shouting now, pacing around the room. "You tried to save me from that explosion that wasn't a real explosion. You're going to start thinking up ways to save me, so you can feel powerful? Is that what you're doing?"

"No, Gwen," he said. "No." He couldn't explain the explosion. It was nothing he had anticipated. He reacted in the moment, nothing more.

Gwen turned fast and squeezed his arm at his wrist so hard he felt the blood working to push through. She leaned into him close, so that her breath was the only air in the room. She said, "This is not a comic book."

"No, of course not," he agreed.

"You are not a superhero. This thing we are together — you don't own it."

"You think I don't already fucking know that?" he said quietly, but then he got louder. "I've never been able to help anyone in my entire life. Not one. You're the one who saved us in the scrap yard. That man might have recognized us, he thought I was a kidnapper, and you know he did, that's why you kissed me. Don't act like you don't know that, because you do."

Gwen loosened her grip on his arm, and he felt the blood pump greedily, hungrily into his hand and each of his fingers. She held his wrist tenderly now, stroking where his veins showed through the skin.

"How did they die?" Gwen said, quietly now.

Peter exhaled heavily. He pushed his face into his hands. "The one who was driving fell asleep. The car hit the median."

Gwen swallowed. "How do you know that?"

"I saw it happen like that in a dream. I didn't know it was going to happen that night, on that road, with you. I only knew it was going to happen."

Gwen pulled him away from her, eyed him carefully.

She said, "It's always been like this?"

Yes, he was going to say, *always,* but before the words rose in his throat, it occurred to him that it had not always been like this. "No," he said, and his voice began to quiver, to wander off scale, and he pressed his face into Gwen's shoulder. "It started when my brother died."

Gwen stroked his hair, and she rubbed his back, and she said, "Shhh," and she said, "Peter," and then she led him back to the bed and he rested his head on her chest, where he listened to the steady rise and fall of her breath for balance.

When he woke up, it was with a start. Gwen slept beside him, the sheets tucked beneath her chin. The explosion, he was thinking. But what else was there to really say about it? The explosion had not been a real explosion; it had been a dummy, a stand-in, a stunt, a lot of noise and no substance. Ultimately, all he could say was that the explosion had been a distraction from the fact that Gwen had taken him to a place he'd seen in his dream. The implications of what this might mean he could only begin to surmise. But the bottom line was what the man at the foundry kept saying. They were trespassers. They had crossed a line that was meant to remain uncrossed.

With that, the floodgates opened. Later that night, the dream came exactly as it had before. There were the skyscrapers, the scrap yard; there was the narrow river, the strange apartment, and the eyes of the man who lived there. The eyes were quiet and pleading. There was the half a vial of white pills in the medicine cabinet. The man was sitting on the bathroom floor with a glass of water. He sat with his legs propped beneath him. Then Peter was at the sink with the water glass in his hands, and when he turned around the man was no longer there. Peter stood alone in the bathroom. It was while he was looking for the man that it occurred to him that Gwen was not there either. It wasn't clear if she had been there at all this time. "Gwen," Peter began to call through the rooms. "Gwen." He was alone in the apartment for only another moment. Then he was at the lake. He was walking along the lakeshore near the space where a small crowd had gathered. There were cameramen and there were microphones. There was a crowd surrounding a stretcher that was being thrust toward the water. Under the water, something was caught. Something was being prodded at and recovered. He heard someone say, Shallow by the rocks. He saw her blond hair, drenched and floating. When he woke up, it was not in their bed. He was alone in the bathroom with an empty glass and every tap in the house was running, the sinks and tub pooling with Lake Michigan water that Peter drank by the glassful.

The dream would come for three more nights before Peter said something. He woke up in her arms, on the floor of the bathroom. Gwen was smoothing her hands over his hair again. She was leaning into him, saying his name, and he was relieved to hear her say it. But later that night, or the next, or the next, it would happen again, and he was terrified not to say something to her now. The following morning she was listening to her French lesson in the other room with the CD player he had given her for her birthday, brushing her hair in the mirror, when he said her name like it was a question.

"Gwen?"

"Je voudrais un café," the French woman was saying.

"Lady wants a cup of coffee," Gwen said loudly, as if translating for the benefit of a phantom waiter in the bathroom with them. The way she interacted with the CDs lately, when she played them at all, it sounded as if it were Gwen who was trying to help the French woman communicate, rather than the other way around.

"Un café crème," the French woman clarified.

"Cream, hold the sugar!"

"Gwen?" Peter said again.

For a moment, Gwen said nothing, and Peter thought she was too entrenched in breakfast translation to be bothered. But when he pulled her against his chest, she stayed rooted to the spot he held her. She let the French woman struggle through the rest of her order alone. He smoothed her hair in his hand. He said, "Gwen, there's something I need to tell you."

She nodded. He felt her body tense again in response to his weight.

He said, "It has to do with why we're here."

ANOTHER ABDUCTION, ANOTHER RUNAWAY, another kidnapping, another set of dough-faced middle-aged parents appealing to their God to bring back another child unharmed. Every night, it seemed, there was one of these stories on television. But the lines blurred. Sometimes the kidnappers were victims, the runaways were perpetrators, the abductees complicit in their own demise. This was what made a captive audience of the nation — one never could anticipate the twists and turns of a story like that. You started with an innocent victim who captured the hearts of viewers everywhere, and you hoped for the best. But sometimes she was secretly a prostitute, or maybe she had tried to kill the wife of her illicit lover five years ago, stuff like that. Tonight there were the parents saying what a good girl she was, good grades, driven, kind to her neighbors, a real gem of a kid, this girl. Sure, sure, Novak thought. The mother was a little overweight, tearing up with a photograph clutched between her two hands. The father was solemn, quiet, brooding, holding the hand of his wife, and you could tell he was broken up about the whole thing, but he wasn't going to cry on national television.

A runaway himself, these stories interested Novak. His own

family had never searched for him, never notified the cops, never wept on television. And while initially, that had been exactly what Novak had wanted, while it seemed for a time that he was going to get away scot-free, it didn't take long to resent the fact that no one had ever bothered to pursue him. It felt after a while like they had been the ones who had chosen to abandon him instead of the other way around. Novak had failed at enough things to not try much anymore. He had failed at pleasing his family. He had failed in love. The only way he succeeded in maintaining any kind of income at all was through his work at the foundry, but even that was precarious. He'd messed up his lower back years ago working construction, an injury that he'd never had properly looked at, and it had grown into a kind of chronic pain that he was only able to keep at bay through a careful balance of pain medication, sedatives, and antidepressants. The first few times he stumbled into the television crew at the lake throwing coyote props into the water, he thought he was seeing things. If he missed a dose and doubled up later, there were sometimes side effects. But he wasn't seeing things. Things were just legitimately that messed up.

The coyotes were rumored to be hailing primarily from wildlife preserves in the suburbs. They had lost their packs, for reasons said to be obscure, and were heading east, toward the lake, as if by instinct. They were isolated and terrified, their actions impossible to predict. Something that should go without saying when it comes to wild animals roaming a metropolis. Novak understood this as well as anyone. He had been alone at the lake for weeks before the crews showed up to document this phenomenon. It started with a video camera. A few stands of lights. A man with a microphone. Soon there was a trailer parked along the lake to house cue cards and a man whose job it was to call out when it was a wrap. A television documentary crew had shown up with a modest budget, set up cameras on the rocks, and shot a special report on the rising number of coyote casualties recorded in conjunction with this stretch of land. The documented number of wild coyotes in Chicago was staggering by all accounts, but recently their bodies had begun showing up in the lake. Scientists were interviewed, along with eyewitnesses claiming to have seen coyotes jump. Novak was happy to have the company at the lake. He never saw a coyote jump, but he saw plenty of the crew, staging reenactments with life-size stuffed animals. When the stuffed animals were pitched into the water, they floated for a few minutes before sinking. Sometimes, there was the outline of a tail or snout resting just above the surface of the water. It was good to see something besides a stone sink. Gravity at work called to mind a larger world of momentum operating outside the laws of his own body and brain.

It seemed (lately, again) like the rest of the world was in on some enormous gag, so he could either resist or play along, and why not play along, at a time like this in which he was grateful for the diversion, willing to accept whatever followed. He was feeling as he had felt when he first came to Chicago, a much younger man. He had worked construction then, before he secured the job at the foundry, and that was another time in his life in which it seemed that the rules in operation in his own brain were not necessarily those generally accepted as law, as if he were looking up from a page in a book he had been plodding through for years, only to find that it was the wrong book, or the wrong sort of book, a dictionary, a cookbook.

He remembered riding the bus to various construction sites in the morning during those first months, before he could afford to buy his truck. Fellow commuters had carried their morning coffee in thermoses or paper cups beside him, whistling through the tiny hole with their tongues, slurping. It was obscene. Talking about the weather was out of the question. People here were militant about the weather. Novak thought he had put up with his fair share of turning seasons before coming to Chicago, but people here acted as if they were privy to a specific brand of seasonal severity with which those from the other parts of the country couldn't begin to sympathize. They squinted like martyrs into the sun during the summer months, martyrs who didn't own sunglasses. Their winters were unanimously agreed to be harsher, windier, worse than anything you'd seen. Also there was something here called lake effect.

"How about all this snow?" Novak had erroneously said to another commuter on the bus during his first Chicago winter.

"What, this? No, this is just lake effect!" Everyone had laughed, as if the wet white fact of it were an optical illusion, a trick up the lake's sleeve. Even now, with the merciful first taste of spring in the air, there was a persistent attitude of the city bracing itself for the soon-to-rise heat index.

And then there was the way that people in Chicago were defensive about the fact that their city was in the middle of the country. Novak always heard the question posed of the city's deserters, "You think you can do better on a coast?" Making something of yourself didn't mean as much if you had to go to New York or L.A. to do it. People spoke of it as if proximity to the ocean made any aspect of everyday life a big free-for-all. The thing to do was to be a success smack in the middle of the country. *Hey buddy, try doing that landlocked.* That got respect.

But Novak never felt landlocked. During his first year, he spent so much time near the lake it was enough to make him forget where he was. You couldn't see Michigan or Canada or any land to speak of, so it might as well have been an ocean. He might as well have been on the edge of the earth looking off it into the unknown and not in the center of what was verifiably nothing. Five nights a week, in the spring of his first year in Chicago, Novak sat on the lip of this great lake, skipping rocks, watching the quick shiver and plummet of every one he threw.

That had been a year of unimaginable loneliness. The feeling had slowly subsided, as he found a better wage at the foundry, one that he could reasonably live on, and he made a few friends to drink with on his nights off. There was even a woman — Carolyn — who worked in the pet shelter around the corner from the foundry, and she was (physically, conversationally) nothing spectacular, but she had a good heart, she loved those homeless animals in a way that Novak could appreciate — Jesus, how sometimes she would talk and talk about the obscure anguishes of some of these animals! — and sometimes, when they were both feeling festive, or lonely, or drunk, they slept together. It was never committed, or regular, but there was an enormous comfort in the arrangement, if only because it reminded him that there were others in the world for whom wants and desires and needs and schedules did not ultimately line up, and yes life was sad, but here was this small thing they could offer one another, some small kind act that sometimes looked a little like what one supposed love resembled. But after a while even Carolyn and her homeless cat stories and her pale thighs didn't bring him any relief. He worked through the days as if in a trance, and evenings he would find himself back at the lake, just staring at the surface of the water. The lake was a place he returned to every few years when he entered a period of solitude. But this was the first time the area was so populated at night. This was the first time there were packs of wild animals supposedly running around.

Perhaps his judgment was playing tricks on him again. It was like the eyes playing tricks, but with inflated conscience. It was like the explosions that had started up full force in the scrap yard again most nights. Yes, there was a logical explanation for the smoke and the sound: some poor junker trying to make an extra buck by throwing the weight of a gas tank into his pile. But just because you knew the cause of something didn't mean your body would learn how not to process this, how to sensibly react. The brain could know something to be harmless, but the body could not deny that the ground shook. The body knew better. Or, the body was gullible. Either way, things were not balanced. By day, Novak mitigated the stress of such delusions by melting metal, stirring evenly so that the pieces of broken things could be reconstituted. Old things became new things. A fender, a can-opener, the body of a bicycle. By night, he sat alone at the lake and watched the documentary men reconstruct a narrative for the benefit of the camera. Every day went like this. Novak woke up alone. He went to sleep alone. He drove his truck to the foundry. He put on his uniform and protective mask, and he stirred the melted metal closer to its newest forms. The cameras continued to roll. The cue cards dropped to the ground with every take. The trailer became lighter as its stuffed inhabitants drowned in dramatic reenactments of lived events, while later still, the real coyotes, remote and wandering, forgotten by their packs, abandoned their hiding places and continued to make the morning paper with their leaps.

He had a penchant for the lost and the missing, for rejects and runaways. In the last few months he had started taking care of a stray at the scrap yard. Novak had seen the dog before, rifling through the dumpsters in the alley behind Marcy Street, and it was a beautiful goddamn dog, fierce, the kind of dog you'd imagine pulling sleds across the arctic, with those intense gray eyes and sharp teeth. He took care of the poor thing, left out food and water, always in secret. He didn't tell anyone about it, and he couldn't say why exactly. He liked to think of himself akin to one of those anonymous donors you read about in the newspaper. Also he had the sense that maybe anyone else would find something to criticize about the act, like maybe you weren't supposed to feed a stray unless you were going to pay for her shots and vaccines and take her in to the vet and all this shit. But Novak wasn't looking for that much commitment. He was just trying to do the right thing. When he was smart enough to carry a piece of lunch meat in his pocket, the dog would practically jump into his lap, like he'd saved her life or something. Sometimes Novak thought of the dog as his dog, he referred to her with the name of this dog he used to have. The stray didn't mind. She'd answer to any name if it was in her best interest.

Novak went to the bathroom with a glass, filled it with water, swallowed a sedative, and placed himself back in front of the television. The footage from the girl's abduction was playing on a loop now, the few moments caught on a security camera. The kidnapper's face was obscured. He had a hat angled down over his face, and anyway he wasn't about to look in the direction of the camera. The girl, however, was staring straight into the eye of the thing. She exchanged a few words with the perpetrator, but the whole time she kept her gaze steady on the camera. She was a good-looking girl, as they usually were, but the interesting thing was there wasn't a hint of fear in her posture. She was talking to the camera as if she were delivering lines. Novak kicked his feet up on the sofa and clicked through the channels a few more times before he began to doze off. When he fell asleep in front of the television, he didn't dream as much.

SOMEONE HAD SWITCHED on the radio in the house while cleaning. It was background noise only; it was practice listening to spoken English. For this reason, Sheila alone looked up at the sound of her name in the context of a report on a forced abduction, robbery, and auto theft in Coralville, Iowa. The radio explained that Sheila Gower had been kidnapped nearly five weeks ago from her place of employment; Sheila Gower was thought to be alive and within the Chicago metropolitan area. The name of the crime's primary suspect had already been given; it was said moments before her own name, then repeated, but this name she barely heard, the way so many strange names on the news slip quickly out of mind a few moments after they are spoken. Sheila panicked to hear each fact and detail of their crime listed aloud and broadcast to listeners everywhere. She dropped a bottle of Windex into the sink of the master bathroom. She closed the door, and then she locked it as if some crazed kidnapper were truly on the loose, coming after her. She started to unbutton her jeans, as if to calmly use the bathroom. Instead, she removed them, followed by her shirt; she stood in front of the mirror in the master bathroom with her underwear at her ankles, and stared. The woman whose bathroom it was had a collection of perfumes on the counter. Sheila picked up one bottle in the shape of a pyramid and sprayed her wrists and neck with the scent inside. She thought she looked like someone else. Her hips were nonexistent. Her breasts, thin enough to scarcely raise the front of her T-shirt, seemed unremarkable at best. When she was with him she felt bigger, filled-out, more solid somehow. She couldn't imagine how this girl's body was the one people on the radio were looking for, the one that Peter saw in his dreams.

Last night, they had spoken about leaving the city. Peter was afraid for her safety because she wouldn't stop showing up in his dreams with the crazy suicidal man who, as it turned out, they happened to be searching for together — which was news to her. At first, Sheila had been concerned, to put it lightly, finding Peter in the bathroom, drinking water from the bathtub and the sink, calling her name. She had been concerned to learn that Peter's dreams had been what had initiated their entire acquaintance. But when presented with the alternative of, say, going back to Iowa, she understood, however irrationally, that she would rather chase a suicidal man from someone else's dream than go home.

Why? What was so bad about home? It was a question she was trying to work out. She wasn't abused or adopted, sexually molested or emotionally deranged in the way runaways always were in the magazines her parents kept in the bathroom. She had come from good stock, as people liked to say in Coralville.

There was an idiom in her French workbook and tape set — être sans histoire. It literally meant to be without story, but it was an expression you were supposed to use when talking about someone who was easygoing or unremarkable. Sheila had taught

Peter this expression while passing the time during the drive to Chicago. Technically idioms were for the advanced student, but Sheila liked to jump around.

"Repeat after me," she had directed him.

"Without story?" Peter had said, once she'd translated for him. "It doesn't make any sense."

She tried to explain to him the thing about idioms, how you couldn't take them literally, but he didn't get it.

Sheila remembered being in the gas station with Peter one night when a woman in stilettos and a leather dress came into the station and started talking to them.

"Hi honey," she greeted Sheila, then turned to Peter. "That your cab parked outside?"

It happened all the time. People with nothing better to do would kill time in the station, just long enough for a conversation. The woman was complaining; she had walked six blocks already from the club where she worked — here she'd gestured to her footwear as if to explain the utter impracticality of the six blocks — all because the taxi she called never showed. And this wasn't the first time either.

Peter lifted his hand and rubbed his thumb and two fingers together. "How's your tipping?"

"A couple bucks," the woman said. "It's late when I call. It's not a far drive."

Peter shook his head, gravely. "There's your problem, sweetheart."

"Okay, smartass," she said. She put her hand on her hip. "You tell me. How much do you tip a driver?"

Peter smiled. He opened his mouth slowly, as if searching for the best way to pose an answer. He said, "How much do you tip a stripper?"

Sheila had been shocked to hear that come out of his mouth. She didn't think the woman would warm to that kind of comment at all; but the woman started laughing. She had taken a step toward Peter and put her hand on the arm of his jacket. "You working now?"

Peter had opened the door and held out his hand, as if to lead the way. "Don't work too hard, sweetheart," he called to Sheila as the door closed behind him. It was the first time Peter had called her anything like that. It made her face flush to hear it, even though he'd just called the woman in the leather dress the same thing. From the glow of the fluorescent light inside the station, Sheila could just make out Peter opening the door for the woman. She saw the way that he looked at the woman's legs before he closed the back-seat door of the taxi, and she didn't like it.

But that was the way it was with Peter. It had everything to do with why Sheila had left with him. Before she'd met him, she didn't know that real people existed in the world who could walk around talking like that. Men in movies she'd seen could be that crass, certainly, but to be that crass and that odd at once, to be so confident and so strange. "Don't talk to strangers," her father had advised when Sheila told him she'd taken a job at the Sinclair station, as if she'd been a toddler impatient to cross the street. But Peter made her want to talk to strangers. He made her think that there was something worth talking about, even in Iowa — something she didn't need to go to France to find, if people could talk to one another in this way right on the Coralville strip. To learn that even her own language could allow for something like that. It worked the same way the night that she left with Peter. When Peter had called her that other name for the first time, there was the feeling that this too was partly true, and her heart raced at the sound of it, because here was an invitation. There was already this story that Peter had, he was living inside of it; here he was offering to share it with her, and all she had to do was agree to come along. The choice had been obvious.

But last night, for the first time, they had fought over this choice. Peter had tried to give up on her, to get her to go back home without him.

"If anything happens to you," he said, "I'll never forgive myself."

Sheila said, "Nothing is going to happen to me."

"Tomorrow," Peter said, "I'm going to buy you a bus ticket."

"Oh yeah?" said Sheila. "With whose money."

He had looked at her strangely. "With my money," he said.

"With *our* money," Sheila said. "With the money we took together from *my* gas station."

She looked at him for a second. They both knew that that money was long gone. It had barely lasted the first week of their cohabitation. They had already lived almost five weeks as fugitives together.

"Fine," Peter said, "With *our* money." And he continued. "I'll buy you a ticket with *our* money, you'll get on a bus, ride it home, and be with your family, who probably think you're dead by now. This isn't right that you're with me in another city when your family is thinking you're dead. Do you get that?"

Sheila felt all the heat building up in her face. She squeezed all her fingers together into a fist, as if to counter the feeling in her stomach of having been punched, but she waited; her fingers crouched against one another in that tight ball, but she was still. She made her voice small. She shook her head. "No," she said, "I want to be where you are."

"Well, sorry," Peter said. He shrugged his shoulders like he was the one making the rules and that was the end of it, like she was a child under his care. "It's not going to work that way. It's not safe anymore."

She wanted to lunge for him then. In that moment Sheila wanted to charge her whole self into his and push him into the window. She wanted to reach into his body, pull out a tibia or a femur and squeeze its proteins to dust. She felt like she had more strength concentrated in every muscle than she'd ever had in her life, and her joints were shifting around inside of her, her cells were multiplying, like the real living organism she supposed she had been all along, but also — and this was the strange thing — she felt helpless, she felt drained of every available energy, like all of this velocity building in her was a product of what he had given her and what she had done with it. She remembered Mr. Zorn, her sophomore-year physics teacher, stepping back from the chalkboard in admiration of an equation he had just written, saying how beautiful it was, how perfectly and essentially balanced, and Sheila had rolled her eyes sitting at her desk at how pathetic this had sounded, how devoid of beauty Mr. Zorn's life must have truly been for him to even think to say something so insane, but now she felt the weight of this truth sting in her somewhere. She and Peter had built this, they had built it together — that's where the velocity came from, that's where the force of the thing came from — and to remove one of the variables from the equation was to leave it unbalanced, and she was not going to let this happen. She stood several steps away from Peter in their bedroom. She continued to breathe steadily in and out. She said, "Okay, Peter Parker, now you listen to me."

She caught something shifting in his eye already, but he held his tongue.

"If you think you're dealing with a child, if you think you're dealing with someone who will let you call the shots from here on out, you robbed the wrong fucking gas station."

His eyes were filling now, but he said nothing still.

"I asked you to point the gun at me because I wanted to go with you. If you think that I would have asked any crazy person who showed up with a gun to do the same, you're an idiot, Parker, I really mean it, you're really an idiot. And if you're stupid enough to give up on everything now then you go ahead, really, but I want you to know that no one has ever let me down so bad in my life. I took a risk on you, Parker. Do you get that? I had nothing to run from. I had my own life, my own plans. Now if you're going to give up on me this fast, then you're a coward, then the whole thing's just been a game, a lot of bullshit, a lie from the start."

Peter held out his hand. He said her name.

But Sheila shook her head. "Don't lie to me," she said. "Don't lie to yourself. Don't ask me to keep this up if you don't really believe it."

Peter reached again for her hand and this time she let him take it, and it was only as she looked down at her hand inside of his that she realized it was shaking.

He said, "I have never believed in anything the way that I believe in this."

Sheila let her face fall into his chest. She breathed in the cotton collar of his shirt, gulping at the air there, greedily, unevenly. She inhaled the air closest to his jaw, his neck, his chest, his hair, his hands, as if this were the only oxygen in the room that her body would know how to use.

There was a knock at the door now, and Sheila jumped at the sound of it, her pants still slung around her ankles, her shirt crumpled in the sink.

"Yeah," she called out from the bathroom.

"C'est moi," Iva said. "Tout est fini?"

"Oh shit, sorry, Iva," Sheila said. It was their last house of the day. Petra and Lenka and the others would already be standing in the front yard smoking cigarettes and squeezing lotion into one another's dry hands, impatient to call it a day. "Gimme two minutes."

"Very good," said Iva. "We wait downstairs."

Sheila dressed, splashed water on her face, and rushed to the first floor. Sure enough, the others grimaced with impatience as they lit second cigarettes off the burning ends of someone's first.

Iva had a car that all the women piled into together, but they usually had more women than there were seats, and the last time Sheila had sat between two women arguing over her head in Czech for the duration of the car ride in rush-hour traffic.

"If it's cool, I think I'll just take the bus," she said to Iva, and though the bus was $2.25 to ride, and everyone knew this was wasteful when there was a car waiting to drive her right to her door, Iva said it was cool, gave Sheila her cut of the day's earnings, and slid in behind the wheel.

"À bientôt," Sheila waved from the driveway, and she passed the bucket and mop through the open window, as the others organized themselves into the open seats for the journey across town.

The first time she heard the howling from the scrap yard, it sounded almost human. The unmistakable sound of a living thing in pain or fear issuing from the same space as the clatter of machinery and metal crushing metal, metal folding back onto itself, folding itself into new forms. But it was not human; it was some animal lost in the industrial corridor, punctuating the steady pound and grind of men at work. It was a week ago that Sheila had climbed onto the roof deck of one of the houses she'd cleaned to shake debris from a set of matching bathroom rugs and spotted the sound for what it was: a cry for help. She had noticed the smoke rising from the scrap yard, and she'd asked Iva about it. "It is rubbish," Iva had answered. "Metal of no use." But one only needed to gaze at the tower of half-flattened cars to ascertain that while the metal pile might not have a use, it was a strange sight to behold in the middle of the city.

That night, she had described the place to Peter, and at the mention of the scrap yard, it was obvious that Peter was interested already. Whatever had happened that night, she was still trying to make sense of it. He had tried to save her from something, something obscure and benign, an empty sound, a false explosion. But even so, the way he fell over her, how he covered her face on the ground so she wouldn't breathe in the smoke. He had dived over her in a moment of crisis, but the moment was as if it were staged, the explosion wasn't real. Was he capable of orchestrating something of that magnitude? Clearly not. Then the man who was there seemed to know something, and in speaking to him, Sheila understood she would have to direct things, or let Peter give them away. She had kissed Peter to absolve him, to unframe him, to convince the man that there was nothing to suspect, nothing to uncover. And it had felt good to protect Peter, to rescue him, but it was also as if this moment marked the change in him, the moment when the dreams began in which she was showing up in the water.

Now she wandered around the scrap yard by daylight, alone, hoping to see something to help her make sense of what had happened there, but she saw nothing from that night with Peter, neither the man who had stopped them, nor the signs of another strange explosion. Only when she had all but ceased looking for it, did Sheila find the source of the howl that had called her attention to the scrap yard in the first place.

The animal was medium-sized and gray with a lighter patch around its eyes, and in her exhausted state, it looked like something from a dream, a fluffy, hazy suggestion of a dog, its silent approach, treading out a path on the concrete. When she spotted it, the animal was walking away from the piles of scrapped cars, parallel to Cortland Street, headed straight for her. When it reached the cement block where she stood, the dog stopped and sat beside her. She knelt down and began working her fingers into its coat where burrs were matted, speaking quietly in its ear. The dog allowed itself to be petted, arching its body against her hand as she stroked its back. "Where do you belong?" she asked. "What are you doing in the scrap yard?"

The dog was beautiful, its coat thick and gray, with a white undercoat, and its tail full and wavering slowly as Sheila spoke. It was only as she pulled the animal closer to her that she noticed something off in its eyes. The eyes were fierce and Sheila pulled her hand away fast. The animal continued to watch her, as if studying something.

It seemed too tame to be truly wild, but there was something about the eyes that didn't sit with her. There was something that reminded her of the mountain coyote in the case at Macbride Hall.

"You're one of the lost ones," she said. "What are you doing in the city?"

The animal regarded her with more distance. "Where is your pack?" Sheila asked. "You shouldn't be traveling alone."

Sheila should have been afraid to touch a wild animal, but the animal had become something else from its time in the city. The animal seemed confused about how to be something wild. Sheila took the ribbon out of her hair and fastened it around the coyote's neck. She was going to save this one, she decided.

The coyote gratefully licked the palm of Sheila's hand. "Where do you want to go, the forest preserve? The wilderness? The lake?" The possibilities were endless, each one more gratifying than the last to consider. Sheila's plans were interrupted by the call of a man approaching.

"There you are, girl!" the man cried. "I've been looking all over for you."

The coyote turned to the man, her tail wagging slowly, as if remembering something.

"Making friends, I see?" The man glanced in Sheila's direction for half a second, before returning his focus to the animal.

"May I help you?" asked Sheila, a little curtly, as if she were back in the gas station dealing with a problem customer.

"I think it's rather a matter of whether I can help you," the man said. "I've been looking after this dog for almost a week."

"Dog?" Sheila repeated.

"Hey girl," the man addressed the animal, seeming to ignore her. "Why did you run off on me like that? I brought you something." He began digging around in his pocket. Sheila looked up at the man for the first time. He looked to be about forty, but his voice was younger, the voice of a younger man.

"This is not a dog," Sheila said.

The man laughed, ignoring her. "Come on, Patch, girl. Get in the truck." Sheila could see the truck from the parking lot. It was white and covered in mud.

"I'm serious," Sheila said. "I'm pretty sure it's a felony to do mesticate a wild animal in this state." She didn't know this herself, but it sounded like it could be true.

"And what exactly were you doing putting a ribbon around the neck of a *wild* animal?" asked the man.

"And where exactly are the identification tags," asked Sheila, "proving this *dog* belongs to you?" She looked at the man again, and saw a name stitched into the pocket of his navy jumpsuit. She remembered Andrea saying you had to start from the middle and work to the ends to be sure it came out even. But this stitch looked like it had come from a machine. There was something familiar about the letters sewn there, but she at first couldn't place the reason. She gazed into the thread that had formed the first letter, an N; it seemed slightly larger than the rest of the script, almost an oversight, an error — there was something strange there. It took her another moment to understand the strange thing was that she had heard the same last name spoken aloud that morning when the radio had named her abductor: Seth Novak.

"Patch," the man repeated. "Get in the truck." But this time, he sounded tired when he said it. He sounded like he wouldn't have the strength for a fight if it came to that. He squatted on the cement and placed his hand on the animal's head, between her ears. The man was studying her, suddenly; she could feel his eyes on her. Sheila met his eyes and retracted her own hand from the animal with a start, as if a current had passed between them.

IT WAS OBVIOUS ENOUGH to make the heart feel sick and slow on the job. If you were deranged, if you were mindless enough to put all your efforts in one place, on one thing, it was only a matter of time before that thing would turn up missing. Peter sat alone in the kitchen with a beer in his hand. It was his second beer, and he tried not to drink it all at once. He had come home from work and made dinner; he had eaten dinner, he had cleaned up after dinner and put Gwen's untouched plate in the fridge, and she was still not home. He paced in a line from the bedroom to the kitchen. He crushed the beer can in his hand. It was nine o'clock before he allowed himself to walk down the narrow stairs that led to Iva's apartment and knock on the door.

Iva answered in a bathrobe. Her dark hair was gathered into a spout at the top of her head, and she was yelling in what he assumed to be Czech into a cell phone. Immediately, she seemed older than he first had guessed. He didn't know why he'd pegged her as Gwen's age. She opened the door wider for him to step inside. "Peter!" she said. She kissed his cheek and pulled him into the room. "This talk is finished soon," she said, indicating the telephone. She spoke quickly, cutting the other speaker off, then closed the phone and dropped it on the table.

"So many girls and so lazy!" she said.

Peter knew from Gwen that Iva had an entire brigade of Eastern European women whom she called when she had jobs. For her ability to set appointments in English, Iva took a 10 percent cut of the women's profits. She did not take this cut off Gwen's earnings.

"A glass of beer?" Iva said, making her way to the kitchen. "But where is your girlfriend?'

"I thought maybe you knew," Peter said.

Iva furrowed her brow. "But why should I know?" she said.

"You worked together today," Peter said.

"Yes," Iva said. "In the morning." She placed two pint glasses on the table and poured from bottles into the glasses. She sat across from him at the table and studied him. "You are worried?" she said.

"Yes," Peter said.

Iva frowned, then nodded as if understanding. "Yes, but she loves you." She said this slowly, delicately. She topped off their beers. "I know this."

"But where is she?" Peter said.

"The night is warm," Iva said. "She can be breathing in fresh air somewhere. It would be okay?"

"Yes," Peter said. But he thought if she was breathing in fresh air somewhere, she would have told him. She knew he had dreamed her drowned for four nights and counting. He had explained that last night. He had explained to her every dream of his she'd ever been in, as if to atone for not telling her from the start. He told her how pretty she looked in her underwear the first time he saw her in his sleep, how he thought of nothing else for weeks. He explained how he had dreamed she would get in the car with him and drive east on the interstate, how after a while, the fields would give way to skyscrapers rising up on either side of the highway like growing things; there would be crushed metal floating up a river despite its weight; there would be a man whose life would be spared for their effort.

Gwen had spoken quietly. "And everything so far has come true," she said. "Like with the girls in the car."

"Not yet," Peter said. "Not for sure."

"Who's the man?" she said.

"I don't know," Peter said. "I only see him in parts."

Gwen pushed her hands into her hair. "You don't know him," she repeated. "So why are we trying to save him?"

"He's trying to kill himself," Peter said quietly.

"And so are a million people," Gwen said. "Are we going to chase all of them down with a gun?"

"No," he said. "Just this one."

Gwen nodded. She looked at her nails.

"You need to go home, Gwen," he said.

She stiffened. "Forget it," she said. "I want to be where you are."

He wanted to kiss her and he wanted to push his hands into her hair. Also, he wanted to drag her out the door, put her in a cab, get her out of the city the way she came. It was undeniable that he needed her help. The night at the scrap yard proved that much. But if she were really in danger, he was ready to give up the search.

"Then we're both leaving," he decided.

Gwen shook her head. "Where would we go? Home? We can just ask for our old jobs back, right?" She let out a nervous laugh. "I'm not going back there, not yet. We're better off here than any-where else. You know that."

"If anything happens to you," Peter said.

"Nothing will," she said.

But certainly something had. This is what they had fought over last night. This was what he was afraid to say aloud to Iva as she poured more beer for him and tried to make him laugh. After they finished their beers, Iva explained the only thing to do now was go back upstairs and get some sleep. Peter walked back up the stairs that led to his apartment, but he did not sleep. He did not go near their bed. He was afraid to dream. Instead, he pulled a kitchen chair to the front window. He sat in the chair and turned out the lights. He faced the park. He thought he could make out the hind legs of animals running, rushing toward something, but they were always just in his periphery and never there when he turned his head. He watched the park until the sun abandoned the other side of the world and showed up in Chicago, and only then did Peter stand up from the chair and give up his watch with the understanding that Gwen was not coming back.

The next morning, the onslaught of spring rested heavy in the breathable air. Spring was hideous. It was a season of everything trying, relentlessly, to come back to life, and while there were always a few small victories, for the most part, the general effort was pathetic. In Chicago, as in Iowa, the first nice day, everyone wore shorts. Eventually, the frost would show up again and put any gesture toward renewal in its place. This, however, was one of the nice days. There was the smell of dew. There was the smell of cut grass. Skateboarders descended on the parks in packs, like another life form — the most inexperienced freshly hatched in kneepads that bulged about the delicate joints. Birds sang. Bikers signaled. Dogs sniffed up trees. Peter sat on a bench at the lakeshore and held his face in his hands.

He hadn't slept, and that choice was taking its toll. All that he perceived was bright and oversaturated. He saw shapes, colors, forms, but everything hurt to look at. After sitting upright all night to discourage dreaming, morning brought the decision to come to the lake. That was where Gwen had been when she eluded him in his dreams. He didn't know where else to begin. Then there was the fact of the comic books, a fact he was working hard to forget but was exceedingly aware of: in the Spider-Man comics, Gwen Stacy dies falling toward a body of water. In light of this fact, it now occurred to Peter that it was nothing short of irresponsible to use this name to address the woman he loved. What exactly had been wrong with her real name? Sheila was a lovely name, Peter thought now, and he began to repeat the name under his breath, as if to attract attention, so any bystander looking in on the situation would understand that in fact there had been a mistake. While the girl who was trapped underwater in his dreams may have been referred to as Gwen, the whole rest of the world called the girl a different name — her real name, and Sheila was wholly unlike Gwen Stacy. Did Gwen Stacy speak French in Spider-Man comics? No! Did she have very light freckles on her cheeks and across the bridge of her nose that could only be detected in sunlight, and even then, only if you were right beside her? Of course not! Gwen Stacy had a pasty complexion with no natural variation in skin tone whatsoever, and the more that he thought about it, the more Gwen Stacy's complexion made him feel a little sick to his stomach. Gwen Stacy was a fraud. She was stuck up and she wore hideous outfits to parties. She was nothing like Sheila. Really there was no way in which one could be confused for the other. You would be hard pressed to find two women who were more staggeringly different in every way, Peter decided. He sat on a bench and watched the waves make contact with the rocks along the shore until he convinced himself he had come to the wrong place. He wouldn't find her here, near the rocks or under the water as he had in his dream, and comforted by this knowledge, he made his way back home, where it was only a matter of time before she would show up.

Someone had been in the apartment. Someone had been searching for something quickly, violently, and left the place in ruin. Their drawers had been turned out, the contents spread onto the floor. The CD player and been removed from the wall, and Gwen's CD snatched from it. His duffle bag lay half empty on its side, but nothing of his seemed to be stolen. The kitchen cabinets were open, and their boxes of cereal and cans of soup sat sideways on the counter and in the sink. They had so little, it made Peter's eyes smart to see all they had accumulated together so easily upended.

When he turned from the mess in the apartment, he felt someone standing there in the hallway behind him before he heard her speak.

"Peter," she said.

He felt his stomach rise and fought to temper his breathing. "Jesus, Iva," he said. He held his hand to his chest.

"What is this?" she said.

Peter stepped back from the mess. He shook his head. "Did you see anyone come into the building?" he asked.

"I was working," she said. She looked at the floor, which Peter understood to mean that Gwen had not shown up at work. Iva would have said so if she had.

Iva took a step into the apartment and stared. "But why this?" she said. "Like COPS on television." She shook her head.

"Iva, you watch COPS?" Peter asked.

"Yes, sure," she said. "If there is nothing else to see."

He nearly laughed before it occurred to him that Iva was right. She meant nothing by it; she had no reason to think that her neighbors had done anything to attract such attention. But once she had said it, the thought took root in his brain and settled there, like a confirmed fact. Someone had been here poking around for a reason. It wasn't so unthinkable that a cluster of poor decisions made during their exit from Iowa had caught up with them by now. It wasn't safe to stay in the building anymore.

"I need your help," he said to Iva. "I need to find another place to sleep."

Iva nodded and asked no questions. She looked from the opened cabinets to Peter. She placed her hand on his arm. "No problem," she said.

NOVAK STRAINED TO HEAR the radio, but the kidnapper girl kept it so quiet in there, he could barely make out the words. He smelled nail polish again. The girl couldn't get enough of painting her nails he guessed. He was tied to a chair in his own kitchen. At first the whole situation felt vaguely erotic — though the girl seemed too naive to pick up on that kind of thing. She had a pair of tiny breasts, barely visible though her T-shirt, and a handgun that he knew she kept in her purse. But Novak had been tied to the chair for the past two hours, and all she'd done so far was paint her nails and listen to his radio in the other room.

He had just finished a shift at the foundry, and he was going to leave out a few scraps for the stray before he took off for the night. The dog had been hanging around all day, making a general nuisance of herself, but when the time came to actually seek her out, the dog was nowhere to be found. He had started calling for her when he noticed the dog was huddled up at the far end of the scrap yard, beside a girl. Novak noticed nothing about the girl at first, save for the fact that she was acting vaguely proprietary with the stray in a way that didn't suit him. He had started to call for the animal as if she were his pet. *Here, girl! Come, girl!* That kind of thing.

"This your dog?" the girl had asked in an odd way that, in retrospect, he identified as a test.

"Yes," Novak had responded tentatively.

"Ha, I'll bet," the girl said.

"Excuse me?" Novak asked

"This is a wild animal!" she had shouted. "You're trying to domesticate a wild animal?" But even as she was accusing him of this, he noticed that she was securing a ribbon around the dog's neck. It wasn't until she finished with the ribbon that she looked Novak straight in the face, and he recognized her from the security camera kidnapping on television he'd seen a few weeks before. She looked different, of course. Her mousy-colored hair from the photographs had been converted to a shocking blond, but there was no question that her face was the same. The strange thing was that, in that moment, something seemed to shift in the way she looked at him as well.

"Okay," he heard her say, and he noticed her voice had changed. Novak looked up to find the girl was now holding the gun. The girl was pointing the gun at his chest "Okay," she said again. "You and the dog, get in the truck."

The girl looked to weigh about a hundred pounds, it would have been easy to wrestle the thing from her hands, but as Novak was getting into his truck, as she raised the gun and ordered him to drive, he thought here was something he had never seen before, and that maybe there was a reason for it all, that a pretty young victim of kidnapping wanted to kidnap him. Perhaps there was a reward for finding her. Perhaps the girl needed rescuing. Either way, something was actually happening, and who was Novak to stop it? So he drove. She didn't tell him where to drive, so he drove to his apartment. He unlocked the door, checked the mail, and set it on the coffee table.

"Do you have any rope?" the girl asked.

He figured she meant for the dog, but once the dog was tethered in the yard, she asked Novak to sit in the kitchen chair with his hands behind him, and he understood that she had it in mind for him as well. When the girl had insisted on tying him to the chair, Novak offered his wrists to her. She had his attention.

"Let me know if this is tight enough," she had said. "Let me know if you could get out." This was strange, he thought; the girl seemed to assume, or understand, that Novak had no intention of breaking free of the shackles she'd fashioned.

"No, it's tight." Novak answered honestly. She had tied a good knot.

After another twenty minutes of sitting there in silence, Novak was starting to get annoyed. She had barely spoken to him. He yelled toward the front room. "Hey?" he called. "Miss?" He didn't know what to yell. She was the most nonthreatening captor one could possibly imagine; it was difficult to know how to address her.

The girl craned her neck around the corner of the kitchen. Her fingernails were the showy red of fake blood that you could buy at the drug store, confirming the smell wafting around the place. Her face looked even younger now than it had as she was tying him up. "Um, yeah?" she said.

Novak regarded her carefully. The gun was nowhere in sight — what the hell was there to say? Novak improvised his way toward confrontation. "Do you think I could get a glass of water or something? I get pretty dehydrated if I don't drink eight a day."

The girl looked at him hard, so at first Novak thought she was going to refuse him the water — a small titillation — but then she asked, "Do you really drink eight? That's really good for you."

Novak adjusted his wrists where they ached, a dull pain he had to work to freshen. "Sure," he said. "Keeps the doctor away, right?"

"No," said the girl, "you're thinking of apples."

She had turned from him by then and began randomly opening the cabinets. She guessed wrong twice, revealing first a shelf full of instant rice and ramen noodles, then his dishes. Novak was a little shy about the disorder of his cabinets, but then he remembered he was being held hostage and decided not to be embarrassed. "To your right," Novak said, just as her hand was hesitating before a third incorrect choice.

The girl pulled down a pint glass and placed it under the faucet. She set the glass in front of him on the table, not so much to be cruel he thought, as because she seemed to have forgotten she'd tied his hands together. Maybe all that nail polish was affecting her brain. Novak was about to direct her to the drawer where there might be straws, when she spoke again.

"Can I ask you something?" She seemed a little nervous suddenly, and it made Novak uneasy. He nodded.

When her voice came out again, it shook a little. "Is this some kind of trick, some joke between the two of you?" she asked.

Novak looked up at his captor. "Sweetheart, you're the one with the gun. You tell me what the trick is."

She studied his face. "You talk like him," she said quietly.

"I talk like him?" Novak repeated.

"I need to ask you something," she said again. "And I need you to answer honestly." She looked to the kitchen tiles, looked up again. She said, "You're Jake Novak." It didn't seem to be a question at all in her tone of voice, but in her forehead there was the perplexed wrinkle of insecurity that sometimes accompanies questions.

Novak was startled for only a second before remembering that the girl had obviously gone through all his things in the other room, bills or mail or whatever. "Great detective work," he said.

She smiled distractedly, not processing the insult. Then she spoke again. "I thought you were supposed to have died twenty years ago."

Novak stopped shifting in his chair.

"So what I want to know," she continued, "is who is lying to me. You or him?"

"Him who?"

"Are you from Iowa?" the girl asked.

A tiny fear was growing in his stomach now. He wanted the girl to stop talking. He wanted her to go back into the other room and put on another coat of nail polish.

"I'm from Iowa myself," said the girl, as if explaining all. She held out her hand, waited a moment, then let it drop. "I'm Gwen Stacy," she announced, but this time she said it like a question, as if awaiting his approval. "Ever heard of me?"

The name sounded vaguely familiar, but this was not the name that was given for the girl on the nightly news. He knew it from somewhere, but couldn't place it.

She made her voice low, almost flirty, as if she were delivering someone else's lines. "*Actually,*" the girl said, "*I never thought of you as the motorcycle type before, Pete!*"

She was quoting something, clearly. "Gwen Stacy," he repeated now, getting closer to the source. "Spider-Man's first love."

"So you do remember me," said the girl. "I thought so."

"But your real name is Sheila something," Novak said. "Isn't it?"

She turned on him sharply. "Why would you say that?" she asked.

"Honey, your face is all over television," he said. "Surely you know that much."

"Oh, her." She seemed to be the one getting nervous now. "You thought I was that girl who got kidnapped?"

"Of course," he said. "Why do you think I let you kidnap me?"

The girl stared.

Novak hadn't exactly worked out this connection himself. "I thought maybe I would help save you somehow."

"That's the stupidest thing I've ever heard. You were going to save me by getting kidnapped yourself?"

Novak shrugged. It did sound pretty unlikely, the way she said it.

"You are way out of line, Mr. Novak," she said sternly. "You have no idea how far out of line."

But her body began to shake and she went into the other room where Novak could hear her blowing her nose loudly, and then flushing his toilet.

He wanted to get out of the kitchen now. He thought maybe he could get her to untie him. But then, he thought better of it. As aloof as his captor seemed to be, she did seem to know something of his past, though a past so distant, there was no way she was old enough to have firsthand knowledge of it. He was from Iowa. He should have died twenty years ago; that had been his first attempt at it anyway. He had taken every pill in the family medicine cabinet — no small feat what with Mom's trouble sleeping — but he had failed embarrassingly, and when his mother came to see him in the county hospital, she had sat across the room from his bed while he slept it off, and it was only as he was waking up that she walked over to his bed and slapped him on the mouth. His mother retreated to the other side of the room and began to cry, though it wasn't clear whether she was crying for him or for herself. They had already been on their own for the past six years, he and Mom and Seth.

Two weeks after he was released, he woke in the middle of the night, filled a backpack, and walked to the Greyhound station in his slippers because his shoes were in the hall closet behind a squeaky door that would surely wake his mother. He could afford a ticket to Chicago or Detroit and chose Chicago because the bus was boarding in an hour. He'd lived there since. Once, and years later, he had written his mother a letter of apology; that had been eight years ago, and he never had heard anything back.

In another room in his apartment, he could hear the girl crying again, softly, but audibly. Novak placed his head down on the table beside his undisturbed glass of water and closed his eyes.

It hadn't always been his plan to try to destroy himself by the age of eighteen. There had been so much going on. By his junior year of high school, he had broken every record in the three-hundred-meter hurdles that the boys' track team had ever set. He had a driver's license and a Chevy Impala with a radio. Never mind that no one ever came to watch him run. Never mind that he was fatherless and friendless. His life was finally getting started. His coach had said there was even a chance of running for a small private college, if he was so inclined, and he might have been so inclined. There was really no saying the extent of his options then. He had reason to believe he would have some say in his future.

He had tried out for the track team on a fluke. No one had ever suggested to him that he was the least bit athletic. He had been sneaking cigarettes in the garage since he was fifteen. He had never played a sport in his life. He'd spent a good chunk of his childhood and most of early adolescence indoors with his face in a comic book. Exercise and fresh air were neither enforced nor encouraged by his mother. But these coaches, they couldn't get enough of him. They threw up their hands, bearing stopwatches, and cheered at the numbers reflected there as Novak crossed the slender white line painted on the track. They gave him a uniform, a number.

"Good for you, honey," his mother had said, when he'd shared the news. Then she'd sighed heavily and looked at the calendar beside the phone. He had been looking after his brother in the afternoons. With practice after school, his mother would now have to change around her shifts at the hospital so someone would be home with Seth.

One-hundred-meter dash, four-hundred-meter dash, three-hundred-meter hurdles, four-by-two-hundred-meter relay. Novak said the names of the races quietly to himself as he drove to school or walked through the halls, or waited to fall asleep at night. A world of hollow batons and narrow specialty shoes had revealed itself to him in all its complexity, so there was nothing else he wanted to do but run. It was only later that the running itself was no longer enough, that he needed an audience for it to mean something.

As a general rule, Novak didn't pay much notice to the other boys' mothers in the stands. For the most part, they seemed an embarrassing lot — cheering excessively, brandishing homemade signs praising the speed of their progeny — it seemed a faintly disgusting display of familial bias that made him a little glad that his own mother worked on Saturdays. Edith sat away from these mothers in the stands. She attended the track meets regularly, always the full four to six hours, always sitting in the top left corner of the stands in the same red raincoat, even on the sunny days. It was halfway into the season when Novak first noticed her, and after weeks of trying to determine whose mother she was, and never once seeing another boy approach her, he decided she was there for him. It was a crazy presumption; she could have been anyone. But before Novak knelt into starting position, he would look for the orange-red streak that was her at the top of the stands. He would focus on her raincoat until he bowed his head at the starting line and took a deep breath.

He was lacing up his racing spikes in the grass beside the track, getting ready for the three-hundred-meter hurdles, when he saw her up close for the first time. She was leaning over the fence by the concession stand with a hot dog in one hand and a cigarette in the other. Novak smiled at her, and she waved with the hand that held the cigarette. As he stood up from lacing his shoes and made his way toward the track, he was aware of her presence, so he knew it was her voice speaking when he heard someone address him.

"Think you'll win again?"

He turned. She had finished the cigarette, but she was still working on the hot dog. In addition to the raincoat, he now noticed she wore platform sandals that seemed to be made of straw, and sunglasses propped on top of her short hair. She was short even with the sandals, and small-boned, almost miniature. If it weren't for the tenor of her voice, Novak would have thought she was closer to his own age.

"Beg your pardon?" he said.

"You're pretty fast," she said. "Where were you last year?"

Novak smiled. "This is my first year on the team," he said. "Who are you here watching?" he asked.

She looked puzzled for a moment. She was looking out onto the track lanes behind him like there was someone else there. "Whoever wins," she said.

The announcement for his event was being called over the

loudspeaker then, and Novak made his way to the starting line. He already knew that he would win the three-hundred-meter hurdles, and when he approached the last hurdle, as he took a final leap, he felt just as sure that Edith's eyes were fixed on the finish line, waiting to see the red of his uniform pass.

Halfway into the season, he had broken three school records already. His coach said he was doing a hell of a job. Novak drove home from the meet with all the windows open. The sweat in his hair dried in the wind. When he saw her, she was standing at a stoplight, waiting to cross. Novak saw her before she saw him. He was still trying to figure out if he should acknowledge her, when she looked up from traffic and into his car.

"Do you need a lift?" he said.

"You again?" she said, as if annoyed. But he could see she was glad to have run into him. "I'm Edith," she said, as she got into the car.

"Jake Novak," he said.

"I know," she said. "I hear it announced."

"You'll let me know where we're heading," Novak said.

"Sure," she said.

But the place she directed him toward seemed much farther than she could have walked in her shoes made of straw. "You live all the way out here?" he asked.

"Oh no," she said. "There's a diner up ahead that I always stop by on my way."

Novak nodded.

The diner was a rest stop a mile out of town, the kind you pull up to for lunch when you're on the road all day. It stood alone on a frontage road. When he had pulled the car up to its entrance, Edith opened her door. "Well, thanks for the lift," she said.

"How do you plan on getting back?" Novak said.

Edith pointed to her feet. "They still work okay."

Novak looked at her ankles, crossed on the floor mat of his car. Then he looked at his own floor mat, as if for direction. "Maybe I'll join you?" he heard himself say.

"Sure, honey." Edith said. "Whatever you like."

She bought him a chocolate milk shake, and a coke for herself. She was on a first-name basis with all the waitresses and knew the jukebox as well as a personal collection, giving him a couple of quarters with specific requests for half of the songs she wanted played.

"Geez," Novak said, "Come here often?" which was supposed to be a joke, but she seemed to take it as an accusation. She stirred her straw around her coke, stabbing at ice cubes.

She smiled then, a little meanly. "You hear what Hank's singing over there about minding your own business?" she said, indicating the jukebox.

"Yeah," Novak said.

She raised her eyebrows and stabbed at her ice again.

Novak felt stupid for asking if he could join her then. For a moment, he had felt like an adult, someone who could speak plainly to a woman in a raincoat and make her laugh. Now he looked down at the red shorts of his uniform, the straw of his milk shake. Everyone probably thought she was his mother. Novak was hoping that the check would come soon, and he could drive back home and get in the shower, get out of these red shorts and sweat socks. They barely talked as he finished his milk shake. When she paid the check, she only lifted her chin to let him know it was time to go. So he was surprised when he got back behind the wheel of his car and asked her once again where they were heading, to feel, as if in reply, her small hand on his leg, her tongue inside his mouth.

* * *

"I thought the meets ended at one," his mother said when he walked in the door at a quarter to four. "I only had a sitter hired till one."

"I gave someone a ride home," he said. "And hung out for a while. I forgot," he said. "I'm sorry."

"I really need you home by one," his mother said. "Seth can't be alone with a sitter all day."

"Where is he?" he said.

"Upstairs."

Novak headed toward his room to take off his clothes and shower; he opened the door to find Seth inside.

Novak smiled. "What, are you lost or something? Aren't you in the wrong room?"

"No," Seth said. "I was looking for something."

"Looking for what?"

Seth pulled a comic book from behind his back. "I read this one already."

"And what? You want another one?"

Seth nodded.

"Too much reading rots the brain," Novak said.

Seth shrugged.

Novak pulled down one of the crates from the top shelf of his closet. He could see Seth's eyes widen at the stack, so he let him pick another one, then sent him back to his own room with it. He closed the door to undress, but first he sat down on the edge of his bed. He touched his hand to his leg; he touched his hand to his mouth.

They started meeting at night. After track meets was no good due to his family obligations, and anyway Novak wanted to keep his interaction with Edith to a minimum around the team. Whole Saturday mornings would go by in which he barely said a word to her. But at night, he was allowed to leave with the car, and he would pick up Edith and drive around. Sometimes they drove a long time on middle-of-nowhere dirt roads and tried to find their way back. But first they would roll up all the windows and climb into the back seat of his car. The first time Edith let him do with her whatever he liked. He pushed his hands under her raincoat, her skirt beneath it, and lifted her on top of him. He was surprised by how light she was. She felt as slight as a girl, which made it easier to forget she was older. Her raincoat was like a girl's. The way she laughed was like a girl. But in the back seat of his car, in the way she pressed her fingernails into his arm, in the way her mouth formed lines around her cigarettes as she lit them, Novak saw the habits of someone older, someone who hadn't been a girl for a while.

But Novak didn't mind this. Edith looked after him. In his car, she kissed his forehead and smoothed his hair from his face. She asked him about his upcoming races, and come Saturday, she was there in the stands, every week, silently taking in his victories.

One night, they pulled off one of the dirt roads and into a field. They were sitting in the car when she reached for his hand. She looked into his palm, like she was tracking down something misplaced, and traced her finger along the lines there.

"You're going to live a really long time," she said.

Novak shook his head. "I don't want to know."

But Edith didn't stop talking. "There's those people who live forever, longer than anyone would want to," she said. "But you're not one of those." She was looking out the window now, but she didn't let go of his hand. "I can only tell you a few things anyway."

"Where did you learn how to do it?" Novak said.

"California," she said. "I took a class."

"California?" Novak said. "What were you doing out there?"

"I used to live there. A long time ago," she said. "Before I was married." Now she was concentrating on his hand again. He was watching her nails move around his palm. She said, "You will never stray too far from home. You will love two women in your life, deeply, but you'll never commit." She dropped his hand. "That's probably enough," she said.

"You don't wear a ring," Novak said.

"No," she agreed.

"Why not?" Novak asked.

"I stopped wearing it last year," she said, as if this were a reason.

The next Saturday, Edith wasn't at the track meet. Novak waited before every event to find her in the stands, but she never showed. He drove to her house that night and knocked on the door. He had picked her up there before, but she was always outside waiting for him. He had never walked up to the door. She answered in sweatpants and a T-shirt that was twice her size. She answered the door without saying anything.

"Can I come in?" Novak asked.

She shook her head. She didn't apologize, or make an excuse. She looked just over his head into her front yard.

"You weren't at the meet today," he said.

"I'm moving," she said to the oak tree in her yard.

Novak looked behind her, into her house he'd never stepped foot inside. "None of your stuff is packed."

Edith shrugged. "I'm not taking any of it."

She had been crying, he noticed then. He could see it in her eyes. "Edith?" he said.

She looked at him. "Listen," she said. She squeezed his hand for what seemed like a long time. Her bottom lip shook, and he reached for it. Edith shook her head. She said, "Please don't come here again." Then she shut the door. Novak stood on her front stoop for another fifteen minutes and waited before driving home. He didn't know what else to do.

She wasn't there the next week either, and Novak started to lose races. At first, it happened from sheer lack of motivation. But once he had started to lose, he felt he was under less obligation to win, and he found himself stalled in starting position at the sound of the gunshot, rising a half-second after everyone else had taken off. His coaches did not agree.

"Novak!" they yelled. "What the hell's wrong with you? Get your head out of your ass!"

He said nothing. Or he promised to concentrate better, to train better.

He was in the locker room changing into his sweats when he heard the question put to him a different way. Larry Vlasnick was a high jump prodigy, a senior. He was tan with long hair, and he had a towel tied around his waist. When he approached, Novak took a step back.

"Decided to let Thompson keep some of his records, Novak?"

He blinked at the sound of the name. Jeremy Thompson was a boy who had died in a car wreck the year before. He had been popular and school had been cancelled for the day to allow students the necessary opportunity to grieve. He also held most of the school records for hurdles that Novak had broken. Novak had never known Jeremy Thompson; he had only known of him.

"I guess so," he said. He shut his locker.

A couple of boys were listening now.

"I didn't realize you were tight with him," Larry Vlasnick said.

"I wasn't," Novak said. "I didn't run last year."

Larry Vlasnick smiled, obviously already knowing this. "But you're tight with his mom."

There was some snickering between the lockers.

Novak shook his head. "No," he said. But as soon as he said it, he understood his error. Before Larry Vlasnick had described her raincoat, before someone else said how everyone knew his mom went a little wacko after Jeremy died, Novak understood that he had been sleeping with someone's mother. He had been sleeping with Jeremy Thompson's mother, weeks after breaking his three-hundred-meter hurdle record.

He quit the team Monday, and with it went any chance for a scholarship. His grades were low, and as long as he wasn't going to continue his education, he saw little reason to continue go-ing to class. Instead, he drove the Impala around during school hours, up and down the highway, until one day he ran out of gas near Atalissa and hitched a ride back to town.

"Where's the Impala?" his mom asked.

Novak shrugged.

His mother grabbed his arm and shook him, but Novak brushed past her and went upstairs to lie down. It was then that he decided he would prove Edith's premonition wrong; it would be an easy enough thing to do to steal a few pills. By then, every-thing he thought he cared about had been systematically stripped away until there was no reason not to try. If he had known he would fail so terribly, he wouldn't have put his mother through it. But once he had, he felt ashamed enough to leave town through any exit he could uncover.

He had fallen asleep with his forehead resting on the kitchen ta-ble, and when he woke up, it was with a stiff neck. It was starting to get dark, but it was hard to say what time it was. The girl had left a note on the table where he could read it.

Mr. Novak,
    You looked like you really needed the sleep, so I didn't want

to wake you. I'll be back before nine, and then I can make something for dinner if you're hungry. The "dog" is with me, if you're wondering. I've been doing a lot of thinking, and I think I've figured some things out which pertain to our conversation earlier. This is really important. Please don't try to get away!
Gwen
P.S. Even if you do free yourself, if you would please just stay there until I get back.

He wasn't sure how long it was until nine, but he wasn't the least bit hungry. He did, however, need to use the bathroom. He made no attempt to free himself. The rope was an annoyance now, but an annoyance he bore patiently. The girl promised she would return, and Novak believed her.

After an entire spring of solitude, it felt good to run his eyes over the letters the girl's hand had produced again and again. The girl's handwriting slanted down to the right, lopsided. Her letters were fat and lightly rendered. *You looked like you really needed the sleep*, the girl had written. She wrote, *Please just stay there until I get back.* Novak stared and he waited. He blinked at the page. It had been a long time since anyone had thought to write him a note.

THE COYOTE WAS HUDDLED over something in the yard when Sheila came for it. She approached with a map and a flashlight — courtesy of Jake Novak's coffee-table cabinet — and saw that there was some living thing in the grass there beside the coyote.

"Hey," Sheila said, "what do you have?"

It was difficult to say at first. It was a small rabbit, still alive just in the hind legs. It must have been very young, unable to run even from a tethered coyote. Its tiny eyes were flat and black though its leg continued to twitch in the animal's mouth. Well, that was the food chain for you — gruesome, unforgiving stuff. Sheila stepped back and allowed the coyote to finish with the rabbit, checking with the flashlight to be sure. Then she untied the coyote and began to walk toward the place where she planned to release it.

The coyote looked frightening with its blood-stained mouth, but Sheila supposed her ratty ponytail and her industrial-strength flashlight made them a fine pair. Besides, it wasn't more than an hour and a half walk to a decent-sized park with some forested areas. The two walked on in silence. Really she didn't need the flashlight to consult the map as she expected she would. She was still expecting Iowa. Here there were streetlights everywhere.

The radio in Jake's living room had used the word *wanted*. The radio said police were gathering an investigation team presently, that it was only a matter of time before Seth Novak would be located and apprehended. The radio listed his offenses: grand theft auto, larceny, the kidnapping of a minor — one Sheila Gower — and the crossing of state lines. She had tensed again upon hearing herself identified as the kidnapped minor, for it meant it was Peter they were coming for; Sheila Gower was only the victim who got caught up in this mess. But she had started to think of herself as Gwen Stacy, and Gwen Stacy operated on a wholly different set of rules.

A month ago, if she had seen a man who was supposed to be dead walking down the street, Sheila would have thought she'd seen a ghost and probably would have run. In other words, she wouldn't have, say, pointed a gun at the guy's chest and demanded answers. But even the gun was getting more comfortable in her hands. It had been in her handbag the whole time she had sat on the street and spoken to Jake and the coyote, so once she'd finally worked out just where she'd seen his face before, her first instinct was to believe she'd been lied to about his death for a reason, that she was in possible danger. So, yeah, she had pointed a gun at the guy. But Jake Novak was a very strange guy. In fact, at first he had given her the creeps.

It took a whole afternoon of interrogation and crossexamination in the kitchen to establish that Jake was as scared of her as she was of him. He appeared genuinely perplexed by her presence, by her knowledge of his past, so that it seemed pretty unlikely that she had walked into some sort of strange pact or scheme between brothers. She had to consider the possibility that she had discovered Jake on her own, independent of anything Peter had planned. How this related to the man who was the one they were searching for, she still couldn't say, but for the time being, it hardly seemed to matter. Back at the house, tied up in his kitchen, was the brother Peter thought he had lost twenty years ago; Sheila had found him without even looking. She considered all this as she walked. It was important to take it one thing at a time. The coyote was the first thing. It gave her time to be alone and think everything through.

The rope went taut and Sheila turned to find the coyote had paused to smell a tree.

"Don't stop," Sheila ordered. "We're very close now."

It was another ten minutes before they reached their destination. As they walked on, the lawns became better manicured; the cars parked along the street became larger, more menacing and tanklike. Then they approached the forested expanse of the park.

"Home sweet home," Sheila said to the coyote. She started to slip the rope away from the animal's neck.

But once free, the coyote made no attempt to wander from her.

"Love makes this house a home," she announced. "Home is where you hang your heart."

The coyote looked at Sheila strangely, showed some teeth.

"Sorry," Sheila said. "My sister always says that kind of thing. But anyway, this is where you belong, like it or not."

Not! the coyote's eyes seemed to protest.

"Come on," said Sheila. "Aren't you supposed to want to conquer new lands? You want to be somebody's pet? You want to be crazy Jake Novak's puppy?"

The coyote began sniffing around again, on the trail of something, she hoped. Sheila started to wander in the other direction, at first slowly, the way one is told to flee from bears and other wild things, but then with more speed. It was a matter of minutes before the coyote was back at her side, looking up at Sheila as if for a cue.

It was getting a little annoying. Here she was, trying to do the right thing, and the coyote was turning the attempt into a replica of one of those heartwarming scenes from the movies. Sheila remembered primarily two veins of movies about canine-human friendship. There was the kind where the human tries to reinstate the wild animal to its natural habitat only to be reduced to yelling the kinds of obscenities appropriate for children's programming ("Scram! Get lost! I never want to see you again!" the hero yells at the wild animal, holding back tears). There was also the variation where the canine-friend was domesticated at first, and the two were pals, but then the animal develops rabies and has to be shot, usually by the kid who raised it. What sort of stories were these to share with children anyway? And why for example was her entire fourth grade class forced to read *Where the Red Fern Grows* and watch *Old Yeller* back to back? Even the boys had sobbed.

Sheila turned around and sat down on a log. She counted the number of seconds it took the coyote to run from the patch of earth it was sniffing to the place where she sat. (Seven.)

"Scram!" She tried yelling, but the line fell flat.

The coyote cocked her head the way speakers of other languages sometimes do when you speak to them in English, the gesture of listening.

"Get lost!" It came out more like a question.

Then she tried something else.

"Patch?"

The coyote pounced beside her, quickly, half-violently, in a way that at first made Sheila gasp and draw away, but then the coyote rolled on her back, offering her belly.

"Seriously? You're going to respond to that, *Patch?*" Sheila said, giving the animal a few test pets. It was the name she had heard Jake use to address it. "Hey good girl, Patch, okay good girl," she continued mumbling, pushing her palm along the short fur of the animal's belly.

Could it be possible that the animal was part dog after all? Sheila wondered. One of those hybrids, the offspring of two species? Could it be two things at once, regardless of the genetic material in its cells that determined the expectation for how it should act, what it should want?

She thought of the coyote in Macbride Hall, who had faced death as bravely as any animal, and then the horrible embarrassment of the afterlife, to be stuffed and set up, expected to act alive. To be asked to play a regular breathing mammal again, with legs and a language: an ordinary organism, but to have crossed into this other world, where everything was almost as it should be — business as usual with a few slight variations. And Sheila thought it made sense that the best ones to talk to were always those who could make a home for themselves anywhere, the ones who could look at a glass case and couple of rogue predators they'd really never be caught dead with in the natural world and say, yes, I think I could make this work.

It was while she was walking toward Jake Novak's apartment, with the grateful animal beside her, that she decided maybe this was what mothers and therapists were trying to get at when they talked on idiotic television shows about finding "one's place in the world." The one part they had right was that it wasn't a real place, like Paris or Iowa or something you could point to on a map and say, "the beaches there are lovely," or "dead-end town."

She was becoming an ace at calling the shots and making up the rules. Peter was right. She hadn't seen that at first. When he'd made her try on the stupid dress, she had thought him dramatic, odd, obsessive. He had scared her with that ratty secondhand thing, the way he pressed his face into it. But when you understood things like that, like the plain fact that everyone was, by living in a body, completely alone — entering the world that way, leaving it that way — it made sense that it took little effort to know how to react to the will of another living thing.

She entered the apartment, turning the corner into the kitchen, and found Jake sitting at the table, exactly as she'd left him. He seemed genuinely happy to see her. "Hey," he said. He smiled.

"Hey," she said.

"Where'd you go?"

"I tried to release Patch into the wild," Sheila said.

"Oh?" He looked disappointed. "I was kind of looking after her."

"Well, she refused to go," Sheila said, "so I brought her back with me."

Patch walked into the kitchen, her nails tapping out a rhythm on the tile floor.

"Hey girl," Jake said, but he didn't make as if to pet her because his hands were still bound. Patch paused for a moment in front of Jake's chair before collapsing with a huff on the rug in front of the kitchen sink. Jake turned toward Sheila. "I got your note."

"Yes, good," Sheila said, remembering.

Jake shifted in his chair. "The thing is," he said, "I've been tied up here for hours now. It's late. I need to use the bathroom."

Sheila considered this. Of course the request was legitimate, but she couldn't risk letting him get away either. She said, "If I let you go into the bathroom alone, are you just going to use the toilet? Or are you going to try to jump out the window to escape or something?"

Jake looked at the ceiling. "I'd say just the toilet," he said.

Sheila stood behind the chair and began releasing the rope. The gun rested in the waistband of her jeans, and as Jake turned and touched the places on his wrists where the rope had bitten down, Sheila placed one hand on the gun. She said, "You have five minutes."

But he was out of the bathroom within two. Sheila was standing in the kitchen, listening to the sound of the toilet flush, when Jake walked into the room and sat back in the chair, offered his wrists again.

"Maybe it won't be necessary," she said.

Jake shrugged. "Whatever you think."

"Look me in the eye and tell me you won't try to get away," Sheila said.

Jake looked at her strangely. "This is my apartment. I live here. Also, in case you haven't noticed, I'm twice your size," he said. "If I wanted to get away, no offense, but it wouldn't be that difficult."

Sheila set the rope down on the kitchen counter. Jake Novak had a point.

In the cabinets she found a few boxes of macaroni and cheese, and she doubled the recipe, measuring twice the milk, twice the butter, to accommodate them both.

"Can I help with anything?" Jake asked. And sometimes Sheila would say, "Yeah, find me a measuring spoon," and "Where do you keep the bowls around here?" But mostly she found her way around the kitchen and preferred him to keep sitting where she could see him. When everything was mixed together in the pot, she put the pot at the center of the table on top of a kitchen towel, and doled out servings in each of their bowls.

It was Jake who spoke first. "Hey, this is really great," he said, tasting his dinner.

"It's just macaroni," she said. "It probably tastes the same when you make it yourself."

Jake shook his head. "It never tastes like this when I make it," he said.

"It seems like maybe you don't take very good care of yourself," Sheila said.

Jake shrugged.

He ate quickly, voraciously, like a stray unsure where its next meal would come from, and Sheila felt a little sad to imagine Peter's brother eating alone at this table other nights, every other night. She said, "Don't you ever miss your home?"

"This is my home," Jake said.

"Not this," Sheila said. "Iowa."

Jake swallowed. "Of course," he said.

"But you never went back."

"There are too many things I am ashamed of."

"Because everyone thinks you're dead?" Sheila said.

His lip began to tremble a little then. It was hard to say if he already assumed this, or whether it hurt to be reminded. He set his fork on the edge of the bowl on the table. She didn't know if she should continue, but he looked up at her now, eager to hear what other information she carried with her. Now that she had started to speak, it was clear the thing to do from here was not to stop.

"Your brother," Sheila said.

Jake waited.

She tried again to find the words, the correct way to begin.

"Your brother," she said again.

Jake reached across the table for her hand, and Sheila placed her small palm inside of his. She watched the way her tiny hand fit there, nested inside.

"He's here," she said. "In Chicago. He came here to find you."

But only in saying it aloud did she understand that this was true, that sitting across from her at the table, his hand trembling around her own, was the man whose life they had come to intercept from the start.

PETRA AND LENKA SPOKE no English. They lived further west of the park, in a one-room apartment with slanted floors. Iva had called them right away. She had explained that they owed her a favor, and it would inconvenience no one for Peter to sleep there a few nights. No one would think to look for him there. But Peter had his doubts. When Iva had knocked on the door, Lenka opened it only a crack to admit her, and Peter was instructed to wait in the hallway. He waited there for five minutes of audible negotiations before Iva opened the door and announced, "It is okay." Inside, there was one queen-size bed, which the women presumably shared, and there was a mattress pad, a bit thicker than a sleeping bag, stretched out on the floor of the kitchen, which Peter understood to be for him. Now Iva had gone back home, and Petra and Lenka were playing cards at the kitchen table, while Peter sat across the room in an armchair and pretended to watch television.

On the television, a group of people were living on a remote deserted island surrounded by sharks, and they had to try to get along or the sharks would eat them one at a time, one at the end of each episode. But they still couldn't do it. Every day they tried to get along; they tried team-building exercises like preparing food and going on scavenger hunts, but it just wasn't working out, they explained to the camera. "At the end of the day," one man said, "it's us against the sharks, and the sharks don't give a sh** about getting along. As far as the animal kingdom is concerned, getting along is a f***ing waste of time." The other people on the island agreed that this comment was bad for team morale before the show cut to commercial. Peter stood and switched off the television. He didn't think anyone had really been watching it, but instantly Lenka turned from the kitchen table and looked at the empty screen, as if confused.

"Is it okay?" Peter asked.

Petra scowled and mumbled something in Czech.

Peter retreated and turned the television on again.

He shifted in his chair and continued to wait. Every once in a while Lenka would say something to Petra that would make her laugh, and Petra would look at Peter, or at the television, it was hard to say which.

It was evening, nearly dinnertime, and Peter sat listening to the people on television trade insults before the next scheduled shark attack, thinking that if Gwen didn't show up soon, it would be too late. Iva had promised to continue to monitor the apartment for any further activity, but he couldn't help feeling helpless, sitting across town, waiting for something to happen. He had seen a bar at the corner when Iva dropped him off, and he thought this would be a better place to wait. If he was going to be trapped here, he at least was going to have a few drinks. He stood from his chair, and Petra and Lenka looked up from their cards.

"I'm going out for an hour," he said.

"An hour," Lenka repeated, trying on the words like a misfit sock or glove, and Petra smiled and hid her mouth behind her cards.

Peter took a step forward. "One drink," he said. He held up one finger, then tipped two fingers in front of his mouth to gesture toward the act. Petra and Lenka stared at him, like a painful game of charades in which no one had seen any of the same movies, read any of the same books. *Two words, two syllables. Sounds like* . . . "One beer," Peter said slowly.

Petra's eyes widened at Lenka, as she made the same tipping gesture in front of her small pink mouth. Lenka rolled her eyes. "Pivo," she said. Then both women threw down their cards and began to laugh.

"I'm coming right back," Peter continued, emboldened by this tiny success in communication. "Please don't lock the door." He opened the door and pointed to the lock. "Please," he said again. Why hadn't he asked Iva the word for *please*? But finally Petra nodded. Lenka said, "Door, okay," and she waved him off. Peter decided to take this as confirmation that he would find his way back inside, and so he smiled, in a way he hoped looked sincere, and felt confident enough to step through the door and let it shut behind him.

"What're you having?" The bartender hobbled from her seat at the end of the bar and threw a coaster in front of him.

He ordered a scotch, then another. The televisions were on here too. There were several of them; there was no escaping them. But the volume was muted so Peter kept his eyes close to the ground. Even now, late in the day, the weather was temperate, and the back door was propped open with a phone book. Without the distraction of communication, Peter's thoughts reorganized themselves toward contemplating the many errors that needed his attention. He sat at the bar and thought only of Sheila. Sheila lost, Sheila drowned, Sheila missing. Sheila's eyelashes, her neck, the perfect spaces between the tiny bones along her spine.

He was staring at the bottom of the jukebox across the bar

when he saw something slink in through the door. Out of the corner of his eye, whatever it was passed for a dog, but it was a strange-looking dog. This was confirmed by two men playing pool across the bar.

"Will you goddamn look what we've got here," one said to the other.

His partner straightened up from his shot at the table and leaned into his cue.

Then everyone was looking. The animal seemed to shy from the extra attention, and settled quietly near a cooler at the front of the bar, looked the other way, as if mesmerized by all the different colored bottles of beer.

The animal looked perfectly harmless. One woman cooed, "Hey, pup pup puppy," and announced she was going to pet it. But the man she was with grabbed her wrist and said it was actually time to get going.

"Settle down," the bartender chided. She clapped her hands above her head. The bartender announced that yes, there was a coyote in the bar, and that Animal Control had been called. Everyone was free to take off or stick around. "If you're leaving," she advised, "don't forget to close your tab." A few people walked away from half-full beers with an exaggerated tiptoe by the animal. But most picked up their conversations after a few minutes of taking pictures of the animal with their cell phones. The coyote didn't even look up. It had curled into a ball in front of the cooler and closed its eyes. Peter wondered if this was such a strange occurrence really. Stranger things, it seemed — more absurd and unthinkable things — happened all the time. The bartender turned the televisions up as a means of distraction. It was the people on the island again, organizing their ranks before the attack everyone knew would come at the end of the hour.

Peter ordered another scotch.

He drank it slowly to balance the pace in his brain. Peter was sitting in an unknown bar on an unknown street in a city he had no business being in. He had come here to save a stranger for no good reason. But now, none of it mattered. The whole natural world felt skewed, its order difficult to anticipate, to penetrate in a way that made any sense to him now. Coyotes walked into bars. Sharks attacked on schedules set by television executives. Sheila was gone. He dreamed her disappeared, floating or trapped, and in doing so, he had put her in danger, and now she was lost. He was irresponsible. He was afraid. He was alone again.

A woman with long dark hair sat on the stool beside him watching the televisions, but she was muttering something about the animal. "Third one found alive in the city this month alone," she said. "It's not a good sign."

"What do you mean?" Peter said.

"Look around!" the woman grumbled. "The whole world's fucked. Starting with the food chain and working its way on up the line."

"Keep it down," the bartender said. "You're freaking everyone out."

But the woman would not stop talking. "You know what they say about coyotes," she said, laughing. "Wily? Pranksters? Right?" the woman said.

Some of the people at the bar nodded their heads.

"Well," the woman said, "that's all bullshit. They're messengers. They move between the living and the dead and they carry messages."

"Keep it down over there!" The bartender was becoming more insistent.

Peter felt his body slide off his stool. He lifted his eyeglasses from his face, propped them on his head, and crouched to the ground to get a better look. He remembered Iva saying how the animals ran along the lake in packs. Peter looked at the coyote, and the coyote opened its eye closest to Peter. He didn't know what he was thinking, but he was thinking the animal had information.

The coyote looked away from Peter, at the bottles of beer in the cooler. But it knew. The woman was right; animals don't walk into bars for no reason at all. They carry messages.

"Get away from the animal," the bartender advised. "You've got about three seconds to move."

Peter moved a step closer to the coyote and leaned into it, his body asking the animal to confirm or deny it carried information. His body asking the animal if Sheila was living or dead.

The coyote turned to Peter. Its ears were sharp and, when it looked up, its eyes, translucent yellow. Four uniformed men appeared in the bar then, with instruments in their hands — a metal glove, prod and a lasso, and tranquilizer darts just in case. The coyote showed its teeth but — messenger or not — the animal was little match for four men with a strategy and the tools to implement it.

Messengers take on all different sorts of forms, so sometimes it's difficult to predict their arrivals. When Peter walked back into the apartment, he found Iva was there again, sitting at the kitchen table with Petra and Lenka, drinking tea. The cards had been put away. Iva stood when Peter entered the room and pushed an envelope in his hand. "It was beneath my door," she said. "But it is for you." She indicated the name scrawled on the front of the envelope: *Peter.* He reached for the envelope and took a step back from the kitchen table. All three women watched as he read.

Peter, I found him. Where are you? I found him. Near the scrap yard, like you dreamed. I came home for you but you aren't here and I don't want to leave him alone again and you know why! But there is nothing to worry about because we're both safe and I am looking after him until you get here. So I guess the plan is working, just like you said it would and we're doing fine love. I mean it. His address is 1534 W. Walton. Get over here fast, I need you and so does he.

Love,

Gwen

P.S. Also stay away from our apartment — it isn't safe.

"From Sheila?" Iva said. "Yes?"

"Yes," Peter said. He breathed out and then in again. "It's her," he said.

Iva nodded. "I knew it must be," she said. "You will make up with her?"

Lenka asked something in Czech, and Iva pointed to Peter, smiling, and answered.

"I say to her that now you found your love again," Iva explained. "And Lenka says this is good."

Petra was smiling now too. "Dávej si pozor," she said. She clucked her tongue like a grandmother giving counsel.

"Yes," Iva agreed. "Also to be careful."

Peter nodded in assent to all of it. He would be careful; he would find her again; he would set everything right. He would find the man and the dreams would stop and he would get them all out of the city. Sheila had done her part, and now he was needed; he had a function, a purpose, a power, just as he'd been promised. He felt he had to move quickly and he felt he could barely move. He kissed Iva on the cheek, mumbling his gratitude for the message, and started to make his way to the door. Then, he turned back and kissed Petra and then Lenka, before running into the street to find a taxi that would take him to the address in his hand.

HIS CAPTOR, THE KIDNAP victim, the messenger, the angel, the girl with the gun, the girl with the name of Spider-Man's first love, Gwen Stacy, sitting across the table from him, her hand in his.

He had heard it said that when human beings screw things up beyond repair, make a complete mess of what they've been given, sometimes there is need for intervention from elsewhere, help from the next world, but really, who would believe such outrageous claims, but the weakest, the most desperate and dependent. But perhaps he was one of these. What else could explain it? And what sort of next world could it be that would send an angel down looking like this? With a handgun tucked in the waistband of her jeans, with interrogation tactics and the stray dog as her sidekick. To imagine an angel wearing no bra and a shirt so thin you could see everything. And now she was leaning into the table across from him; she was trying to get his attention.

"Your brother," she said.

She had made him macaroni and cheese for dinner, and they were eating it together when she started again with the things that she knew, the past he was always already working to forget, and

Novak put down his fork to listen, to hear her better and accept the news she had clearly come to deliver.

"Your brother," the angel-kidnapper repeated.

For all his stubbornness, it could take so little to shift the will. For months he could think only of his errors, his oversights, his solitary work and meals and bed and bathroom. But at the sound of the girl's voice acknowledging that he had a past, Novak found he wanted to be in the place where he was, to be in his kitchen, at his table, to be a man with his past and his slowly shifting present that was now, he could see, starting to become something different already.

"He's in Chicago," the girl said.

He felt his heart shift in his chest to conjure it: Seth, as a boy of six, with his dark, sly smile and nine-thirty bedtime.

"He's come here to find you."

Novak closed his eyes. He held the girl's hand inside his own. To imagine that decades after disappearing, so long after a clumsy exit from his prior life, his brother would seek him out. Novak raised the girl's hand to his face and pressed the thin bones of her knuckles across his mouth. There was no way to compare the feeling of being forgiven to anything else in this world.

Novak knew what it was to disappear, and he knew what it was to be on the opposite side of it, the receiving end of the act, to be the one at home, sitting on his hands, waiting for word. His father disappeared when he was eleven. This meant that for eleven years, Novak had felt like he had a normal life, before he had nothing but an overworked mother and a baby brother who he had to look after. His father had been in the Marines for many years, even before Novak was born. He knew how to sail, and all the different parts of a ship. He knew how to read a compass. He had given Novak a compass of his on an old gold chain. As long as the arrow points north, he explained, you can never get lost. Exact co-ordinates could always be determined. It was tricky, because this sort of thing could allow you to feel safe, at home in the world. When his father was away, in some unimaginable sea that was impossible to conjure up from his Iowa bedroom, it helped to think these spaces existed somewhere — there were numbers, degrees of longitude and latitude that corresponded to the places his father went. But even within the most precise coordinates on earth, it's possible to lose one's way: say, at night, say, in a storm, tropical winds cutting across the south Pacific all that summer with little regard for even the most able and well-equipped vessels, to say nothing of the men inside; it is possible to exist in a space that can be found on a map, but to eventually breathe in water and sink to the ocean floor.

It was only a few months after his father didn't return that his mother started to show, low in the belly, but she was eight weeks away from delivery before she would sit Novak down and explain to him that he would soon have a brother. From then on, his mother threw herself into the business of preparing for this baby, and when the baby came, no one talked about the father. Novak knew for a fact that his mother never told Seth anything of his father, for Seth had come to assume that his father was different than Novak's. Novak never told his brother differently, because he had never been completely sure. Also, there was the fact that it was easier not to think about him. This skill he had learned from his mother. The more time went by without speaking of his father, the easier it became to live without him. If the fact of Seth's birth was a reminder of the man who had brought him into being, then it was better to imagine that he had come into this world by alternative means, through the act of another man, a stranger, or without any father at all. The only thing that suggested that Seth had come from any common origin was his name; when he was born, the baby was given the name of Novak's father, the man whose return, not six months before, he and his mother had given up on.

Now, standing at the kitchen sink, washing the dishes from the meal the girl had made, Novak tried to run over what he could still remember of Seth, but it was difficult. It had been so long that Novak found that in his memory, the image of his brother had conflated with a thousand images of home.

Doing pull-ups on the bar in the garage while Seth counted, his voice still like a girl's, always speeding up the litany of numbers to try to get Novak to pull his chin onto the bar faster.

Beyond the garage was the field where the lake would freeze in the winter and Novak had taught Seth how to find the weak spots in the water, and how to find the tough spots that could resist the weight of them both, sliding in boots across the width of it, taking turns.

"You're not scared of falling in?" he asked Seth.

Seth shook his head.

"Think there's any fish down there still?"

"If I fall through and see any fish, I'll bring them back up with me," he said.

In his memory of home, he and Seth were always on their own. His mother was always at work, though it wasn't her fault; she had to raise them. Novak understood that he was supposed to take care of Seth when his mother was at work; he was supposed to fill the areas where a father would have been. He tried. He told Seth stories at night to help him get to sleep. He passed on his comic books when he finished reading them. The spring he left home, the spring he tried to leave the world for good but then settled on Chicago as an alternative, he had felt he couldn't keep up with all the ways he was expected to fill in for absences left in the lives of others. His mother thought it was selfishness that prompted him to swallow so many of her sleeping pills; she'd said as much at his bedside in the hospital where he woke up, and maybe she was right. But after playing father to Seth, after trying to be a confidant and support to his mother for too long, and then learning that he had also been standing in as a surrogate son and lover and — he couldn't say what else — to Edith; he had come to understand, finally, that he wasn't doing anyone any good as himself. It was around this time that the only thing that settled him was imagining the exact coordinates of this pitch-dark place in the pit of the sea. Chicago was supposed to be temporary, a neutral territory, a place to stay while he processed the shame of his failed attempt to abandon his family. But weeks passed, then months, and the longer he stayed away, the more the shame grew, the more difficult it became to imagine a way to return.

The night he left home, Novak had poked his head around the corner into Seth's room. It was late and his brother was asleep, but for a second he saw Seth's eyes flicker open, his head on his pillow, without moving. He waited for a moment longer, but Seth didn't stir. His body still had been so tiny at six he barely filled half the twin bed. Though it seemed impossible, Seth would be nearly thirty now, ten years older than Novak had been when he left the boy alone with their mother.

He made the girl a bed on the sofa. She insisted this would be more comfortable than his bed, and Novak didn't argue. He unrolled the sleeping bag that he had bought for camping but never used, and offered her his own pillow, the only one in the house. It was late, and they both needed sleep. The dog was already asleep in the corner under the kitchen table. She was accustomed to seeking shelter from the elements, burrowed inside or under whatever structure was available. He showed the girl where the switch for the overhead light was, and where she could place her glass of water so it wouldn't spill if she got up in the night. The girl sat on the couch and began to unlace her shoes. "Thanks a lot," she said.

Together, they had devised a plan. At first the girl had wanted to go to Seth right then, but it was the middle of the night, and that wasn't the way Novak wanted to meet his brother after so long, waking him from a dead sleep. He convinced Gwen that they should get some sleep themselves; then, first thing tomorrow she would go to Seth and she would bring him to Novak, and there would be time to talk, time to start to explain. They had discussed exactly how it would happen. Novak smoothed the sleeping bag at the foot of the couch and began to walk back to his bedroom. Before he turned out the light, he looked back over his shoulder again at the girl, who now was removing her socks and fitting them neatly into each of her sneakers. He paused.

"Where did you come from?" he asked the girl.

"Iowa," the girl said. "I told you already. Anyway, you didn't need me to tell you. You said my face was all over television."

"Yeah," he said, "but what were you doing in Iowa?" He was embarrassed to admit that her presence conjured the supernatural, that he only could imagine otherworldly messengers barging in unannounced and bearing the type of news she carried around. But, clearly, this was just a girl; he could see it in the way she folded her socks and the way she ran her fingers through the knotted ends of her hair.

"Nothing really," the girl said. "I went to high school. I was working in a gas station when I met your brother."

The footage from the security camera flashed in his brain for a second. He remembered the unidentified man with the black hat, his posture, his shoulders. There must be some mistake. He felt he was losing the thread of all the facts he had accumulated; he was starting to feel confused again. He saw the footage weeks ago. It was possible the police had named their prime suspect by now.

"Just this little nothing gas station on the Coralville strip," the girl said, and she smiled a little in the corner of her mouth, like her brain was stuck on the tail end of remembering something.

Novak said, "My brother kidnapped you, didn't he? Is he the one the cops are looking for?"

The girl was stretched out on her back, staring up. The half smile disappeared from her mouth's corner, and her voice went hushed. She said, "Your brother's the one who rescued me. He's the one who got me out of there."

Novak added this new piece of information to the story. "You're his girlfriend," he asked. "Something like that?"

Gwen smiled.

Novak looked at the girl and tried to imagine his brother with her. He tried to imagine his brother at all. Standing beside the girl in his sleeping bag was the closest he'd been to his brother in years. Here in his sleeping bag, on his couch, was the girl Seth loved. He said, "What's he like?"

"Peter?" She bit her bottom lip.

Novak blinked. He swallowed. He said, "Is that what you call him?"

Gwen looked at the ceiling.

Novak nodded, beginning to understand the rules in operation here. He said, "Gwen Stacy is kind of an unusual name for a gas station attendant."

The girl continued staring up. She spoke to a crack in the ceiling. "Can I ask you something then?" she said.

"Yeah," Novak said.

"You've read all those comic books too, right?"

"They were mine," Novak said. "A long time ago."

The girl nodded. "In the comic books," she began, "when

Gwen Stacy dies," she said, "why doesn't Spider-Man save her? I mean if he saves everyone else?"

Novak looked at the girl in his sleeping bag, this sweet little twig of a whisper of a woman who looked after his brother, and he felt sorry then that Seth had to be the one to seek him out, that he hadn't had the fortitude or the balls to do it himself. "I don't know, honey," he said to the girl. "It's sometimes harder with the ones you love."

Novak went into the bathroom to get ready for bed. In the medicine cabinet were the vials of pills, still lined up in a single row. There were different colors for different prescribed uses; some calmed and deadened the nerves, some helped you get to sleep. Novak regarded the tiny white ones, the ones that he took in the evening. He poured a pile of them into his hand and traced a path through the uneven heap with his fingers. They looked strange in his hand, like a palm full of sugar or sand, a pile of something better housed elsewhere. There was always something in their color and uniform size that calmed him, like tiny waves in the narrow ditch of his hand. It called to mind the place at the pit of the sea, the way he had felt when he had swallowed enough of them to return to the place his father was. But this was the problem with thinking that way, preferring to hobnob with the dead, to snub the living, and then to think of Seth, alive and nearly thirty now, and practically on his way. There was the toilet. He had a strange impulse to flush the entire vial of pills down it, how he wouldn't want his brother to come and see so many of the same sorts of pills he had swallowed so many years ago. But this was unreasonable, of course; they presented no threat to anyone now.

There was a knock on the door then, and Novak was startled. He started to guide the pile of pills back into the narrow mouth of the bottle, but before he had finished, the door was opening and the girl was pushing her way inside.

"I need to brush my teeth," she said. "I forgot." Her eyes were sleepy and slowly scanned the room. "I guess you don't have an extra toothbrush?"

"No," Novak said. He capped the bottle and pushed it back into the cabinet without comment.

"I'll just use my finger then," she said. "Even though it's a little gross."

"You could use mine if you want," Novak said.

Gwen made a face. "No thanks."

"Toothpaste is on the top shelf," he said, and he started to step aside to make space for her in front of the mirror.

"Jake," she said, just as he was leaving, and he paused at the door.

"Yes," he said.

She looked him in the eye for several seconds, saying nothing, but Novak understood in this look that, yes, she had seen the pills on the shelf already, and she knew full well what his history of swallowing such things was, but she was going to trust him, she was going to trust this was something that was already part of the past.

"See you in the morning," she said.

He didn't see her in the morning. He slept late into the day, and it was early afternoon when Novak opened the door to his room and found she was already gone. Still, there was nothing to worry about; Gwen knew what to do. The plan had already been devised.

"When he gets here," Novak had asked last night, "can we have some time alone?"

"Of course," she said. "I'll get out of your way."

"It's been a long time," he said.

The girl looked at her shoes. She said, "I know it."

So now there was nothing to do but wait. The rope was on the kitchen counter leftover from yesterday's interrogation. Patch was missing again; Gwen probably took her along. Novak sat in the same kitchen chair, this time with his hands free, or with his hands fidgeting or straightening the kitchen, organizing the dishes and the boxes there, because all there was to do now was wait. Wait for the sound of the door, when he could stand up, when he could walk through the kitchen and onto the landing, when he could open the door and invite in the past that he had given up and that he always believed had given up on him.

THE GIRL IN THE MISSING person poster looked young. Sheila was walking home from Jake's apartment when she saw the poster stapled to a telephone pole. It was past midday, and she was walking fast with Patch beside her, barely pausing at crosswalks. By now it was clear that Patch didn't need the encouragement of a ribbon and a rope. The animal had no intention of wandering off, and the two walked swiftly down the sidewalk, side by side. She had been thinking only that she had to hurry, that Peter would be worried by now. She had spent the night at Jake's without calling home — she and Peter didn't have their phones, so it wasn't that easy, though she might have called Iva to deliver the message — and now she felt guilty for keeping him waiting so long. She had been walking fast and only stopped momentarily in front of the poster, mustering up a half second of sympathy for the kidnapped teenager, when she recognized the photograph.

She had been sitting in the backyard with her father last summer, keeping an eye on the meat on the grill while he ran inside to check the baseball scores. It had been just before the Fourth of July; her mother was in the kitchen, frosting a cake fashioned after an American flag, with rows of strawberries for the stripes and blueberries for the negative spaces between the fifty stars. Sheila had been examining the underside of a hamburger when her father came outside with the camera slung around his neck, his face pressed up against the viewfinder, framing her there, though this kind of thing wasn't really his strength. Her mother was always the one who took pictures, the person who organized and cataloged every family event — birthdays, graduations — by date and by album. These photographs everyone was prepared for, dressed appropriately, animated according to the occasion. But for her father to snap an unexpected photograph of only Sheila on a nothing summer night was something strange. It had reminded her that in a number of years she would be the one taking care of her parents, instead of the other way around. Between she and her sister, Sheila had always been the more sentimental, the more prone to tears. Watching her father behind the camera, squinting into the last bit of sun in the yard, Sheila felt her face become warm.

"The light's no good," she'd said to her father. "It won't turn out."

"Shows how much you know," he mumbled, snapping the shutter.

But the girl in the poster didn't look like someone who had a father; her eyes were fearful, feral, the eyes of an animal lingering by the shoulder of the road before running headlong into traffic. She ripped the poster down from the telephone pole where it was stapled. Under the photograph, she read:

MISSING PERSON: Sheila Gower
Age: 18. Height: 5 feet, 6 inches. Weight: 115 pounds. Hair: light brown. Eyes: light brown. Last seen: March 20, Sinclair Gas Station, Highway 6, Coralville, Iowa. She is thought to be residing in the Chicago metropolitan area. Anyone with information about

the whereabouts of Sheila Gower should contact the Special Victims Unit of the Chicago Police Department.

You would think that the cops in a major U.S. metropolis would have something better to worry about than the disappearance of a girl from a gas station three hundred miles away. This was a city full of crime and criminals; you had to wonder how the cops found the time to even bother. According to the poster, Sheila Gower had been kidnapped and taken from her home against her will. According to the poster, someone was responsible; someone was going to have to atone for all this trouble they caused Sheila Gower and her family. Looking at the poster she understood that there was still a way she could return to Iowa, to her father and mother, to Andrea and Donny; she could find another job, find a new lunch table in the cafeteria, or take up eating with Anthony again. All this could be nothing but a brief wandering off from the regular course of her life. A misstep, a mistake.

She imagined herself in her parents' backyard. Her mother would dab at her eyes with a tissue and her father would pace in awkward circles around her for weeks, like something in orbit. There would be a party with corn on the cob and mashed potatoes and a seven-layer cake. Andrea would give her some cross-stitched thing, and Donny would be there in one of his undershirts, telling dirty jokes. His jokes were so dumb, sometimes you had to laugh a little. But it would mean saying she was kidnapped. It would mean betraying Peter and giving up Gwen Stacy.

She thought of all those long lunch periods spent with Anthony in the cafeteria when she had been waiting for something like this to come and interrupt the regular plodding course of her days. With Anthony, she had taken comfort at first in having someone to sit with, but the fact was the only reason they sat together was because they had no one else. Yes, maybe after a while they had developed a little more affection or appreciation for one another, but from the start the arrangement was practical, and in essence this was the problem as well. The thing about Peter was there wasn't a single good reason for her to leave with him. But he made her feel like she was the only one in the world who could help him, the only one in the world who would do.

As a child, Sheila had spent all her time alone on the front stoop of the house with chalk or a jump rope, daydreaming of some weary, self-possessed foreigner showing up in the yard, a cross between Mary Poppins and Marie Curie. The person would show up with a suitcase and a strange manner of dress because she had traveled from so far away to get to Sheila. She would be an illusionist, or a fortune-teller, a figure skater, a Russian ballet teacher, a gypsy street musician with a saw and a bow peeking out of her rucksack — the details didn't matter. *So you've been here all along!* the woman would gasp through her thick accent. *I've been searching the world for you,* she would say to Sheila. *And finally I have found you here.* Sheila would step away from the front stoop of her parents' house, and the woman would take the shawl from her own shoulders and wrap Sheila in it like an infant and lead her away toward some hazy destiny. Of course, whatever the woman had come to teach her would take work and dedication, many long hours of practice at a tedious and very specific skill, and she would have to leave her family behind for a time, but it would all be worth it.

Sheila looked at the girl in the poster again, steering her brain away from the words below her picture, and in it she could see the yard at her parents' house, the smell of freshly cut grass belly up on the lawn, smoke rising off the grill, the noise of the baseball scores on the radio, Cubs up 4–3 in the seventh, summer night heat, the moths and mosquitoes. Her father. She could think of

Andrea or of her mother without much guilt, but her father was different. Now, in her mind, he was sitting at the desk in the corner of the living room with his thinning hair and his high blood pressure, muttering the initials of cusswords at the television, and it made her heart hurt to think of him red-faced and fuming and ignorant of her whereabouts. He sat at the desk in the corner of the living room when he was watching baseball on TV while doing the family's finances — balancing the checkbook, filing bank statements. Above her father's desk was a little plaque that said COURAGE: ACTION CURES FEAR, but there was a time when she was still learning how to read when she asked her father what the sign said, and he had told her to sound it out for herself and she had come up with *Action Curious Fear.*

Her father had laughed. "*Action curious fear* doesn't make any sense, honey. A sentence needs a verb."

But there was a way in which, even years later, when looking at her father sitting at the desk with the ball game on in the background, if she glanced quickly in that direction, the sign said both things. It said that the way to overcome fear was to challenge it with decisive momentum. But it also said something murkier that she could never quite work out. Something about the still moment just before an action in which curiosity and fear crouched closely against one another, sharing so much of the same breath and breathlessness, it was hard to tell them apart. She missed her dad. Her eyes started to sting, but she blinked the feeling away.

"Let's get out of here," she said aloud: to Patch, to nobody.

Sheila stuffed the poster in her handbag and continued walking home to Peter.

The apartment was empty. The bed was unmade. There were several cans of beer in the sink. Sheila sat on the edge of their mattress and stared at the wall on the other side of the room. She had counted on finding Peter in the apartment. She had counted on him waiting there for her until she returned. What if the cops had taken him away? What if they had found him here alone and had taken him, were questioning him, and she didn't get back in time? Don't be an idiot, she told herself. He's working. He's on a walk. He's out looking for you. Fine, good, Sheila thought, but also she thought that it was time to clear out. She had to find a way to get him to Jake's apartment, and she couldn't wait around. She realized then that she had never been alone in the apartment in the late afternoon, and it felt eerie in the hazy sunshine, no curtains on the windows, the dirty mattress in the corner of the opposite end of the loft. This wasn't living. This was squatting. They had found what they had come to Chicago to find; now it was time for them to get out of there.

Sheila knocked on Iva's door, but there was no answer. She would be working of course. Sheila would be working with her if it were any other afternoon. So she would leave something in writing. She didn't have any paper, but all the mail for the building's residents was collected in a bin at the bottom of the stairs. Sheila opened a bill addressed to a name she didn't recognize, scratched out the name with her pencil, and wrote "Peter" on the envelope. Then, on the backside of the bill she wrote Jake's address. She wrote as fast as she could. She explained how she had found the man from his dream by the scrap yard, how she needed Peter to come as soon as he could, that he should stay out of the apartment. Then she stole another piece of mail from the bottom of the stairs and wrote a second note.

Iva —
C'est moi — Sheila. Je suis désolée pour — (Here she paused for
a second before switching to English. The thing was she was in a
hurry, and Iva spoke English perfectly, or in any case just as well,

and anyway, she would understand!) — skipping work again. I wanted to call, but we will talk soon, and I'll explain everything. Could you make sure you get this to Peter for me? Merci!

Then she slipped the note under Iva's door where she was sure to see it. She turned from the door, walked back across the hallway and up the stairs, and it was only in walking away from the note that she considered that she, in all likelihood, wouldn't see Iva again. She should have at least written the whole note in French, or added some pleasantries at the end, or learned some Czech, but it was too late, and it didn't matter now. She had bigger problems to sort out, so she tried to put Iva out of her mind as she turned the knob of her front door, stepped inside, and proceeded to trash her own apartment.

She started with the cabinets. She pulled the few boxes and cans from the shelves and let them land in the sink and on the counter. Patch eyed her with a look of panic, beginning to pant heavily and pace around the apartment, but Sheila didn't stop. If the cops were to show up, it would look like they had fled. She pulled all the sheets off the bed and threw them in the middle of the floor in a heap. She unplugged the CD player Peter had bought her for her birthday and shoved the CD in her handbag. Her movements were practiced, methodical, erasing their habits and routines from the place. She went to the closet where they each had two sets of clothes. She pulled each item of clothing from its hanger, until she got to the secondhand dress that Peter loved. She kicked off her jeans and T-shirt and slipped the dress over her head. She pulled her hair out of its ponytail, so the blond mass of it rested long against her back. In the bathroom mirror, she decided she could pass for someone else.

She placed a hand on her hip. Name? she demanded of the girl in the bathroom mirror.

Gwendolyn Stacy, she replied.

Then she practiced pulling the ID from her wallet to back it up, because everyone knew Gwen Stacy didn't stutter when giving a straight answer, and she didn't have any trouble dealing with the cops. Her father was a cop.

She arrived at the comic book store just before closing, and this time she didn't waste her energy riffling through the issues along the walls or worrying about the etiquette of the place. She parted with Patch on the sidewalk outside the store. "Stay," she said. Patch growled slightly, but seemed ready to comply. Then she walked straight to the checkout and placed her hands on the counter.

"Can I help you?" the boy behind the counter asked.

"Hope so," Sheila said. "I'm looking for *The Amazing Spider-Man* #121."

The boy squared her up. "Is that right?"

Sheila dug in the bottom of her handbag and produced several hundred-dollar bills, placing them one at a time on the counter. "That's right," she said.

"Hold please," said the boy slowly, and he went off into the back. After several moments, he reappeared with another boy, slightly taller, who seemed to be in charge.

"I'm looking for a particular Spider-Man comic book," Sheila said again. *"The Night Gwen Stacy Died."*

"Issue 121," the boy who was in charge said. "I'm familiar. You know it's not the kind of thing you can just walk into a shop and expect to pick up. What you're asking for is something of a collector's item."

"I understand that," Sheila said. "You're telling me you don't have it." She started to put her money away.

"Hang on a second," said the boy in charge. "I said it wasn't the sort of thing that's usually just going to be sitting in a shop, collecting dust. I didn't say I don't have it."

"How much?" Sheila said.

"Look," the boy in charge said slowly, looking her up and down, "you're obviously not a collector. What do you want with it?"

Sheila paused and consulted the ceiling. "It's a gift for my boyfriend," she said.

"Try again."

"It's a gift for my brother?" She hadn't planned on the need for constructing an elaborate story.

The first boy piped up from behind the counter. He smiled at his coworker. "Well which one is it?"

The boy in charge chuckled.

Sheila said, "It's important."

Just then Patch began to howl from her post on the sidewalk. A fierce long howl that commanded the attention of the boys in the comic book store. "What the hell was that?" one boy said to the other.

"It's my dog," Sheila said. "She's getting sick of waiting out there. I really can't stay too much longer."

The first boy she had spoken to peered through the front window. "Jesus," he said. "Some dog. What do you feed that thing?"

Sheila glared. "Do you harass all your customers like this? Or just me?"

"Okay," the boy in charge said slowly, putting up his hands as if establishing order again, "Tell you what. You're obviously in a hurry. You name me three of Spider-Man's most important archenemies from 1962 to 1973 and issue 121 is yours."

"The Green Goblin," Sheila said. It was the only one she knew. It would have to be good enough. The boy continued to stare at her, as he waited for the names of two other villains. She looked down at the corner of this boy's T-shirt where it was torn, and wondered if he had bought it that way, or if he had gotten it caught on a fence, or a tree. She looked back up at his face and noticed that he was older than she first had estimated. He was at least thirty, older even, but his clothes were of someone who jumps fences.

"Your shirt's ripped," Sheila said.

"Don't change the subject," the boy said in mock, or genuine, disgust, "You got one of the biggies and I'll give it to you, but you're two enemies short of a sale," he said. He paused, and when he noticed Sheila had exhausted her repertoire of enemies, he opened his mouth as if to prompt, "Doc . . . ? Doc . . . ? No? Doesn't ring a bell? Doctor Octopus? Doc Ock?"

Sheila glared.

"Try again?" he said. "I'll make it easy. Green tail? Scientist and friend to Spidey in his saner moments, when he also cares for his wife and son — boy's name's Billy. The Liz, the . . . Lizzzz. . . . The Lizard? No, don't know that one either, huh?"

"Forget it," said Sheila, and she turned to leave.

But the boy raised his hand in truce. "Hey, come on! I'm playing. You want the issue, you can have it. It's not doing me any good sitting here." He went into the back and produced the issue and placed it on the counter in front of Sheila. It was in a thick Mylar sleeve as she expected it would be, and at first glance, the cover was not nearly as terrible as she had imagined it.

On it, there were pictures of everyone in Spider-Man's life. Each person close to him was represented in a self-contained black frame, and Spider-Man hung from a bit of webbing before each of their portraits, frantically looking between them. In the little bubbles of speech by his head, his thoughts raced: *Someone CLOSE to me is about to DIE! Someone I cannot save! My Spider sense is never wrong! But who? WHO?*

The cover promised a *Turning Point*, promised a moment after which things would never look the same again. Sheila ran her hand along the wrapped edge of the pages, fingering the price tag in the corner.

"That'll be three fifty and change," one of the boys said. Sheila counted out the money to pay them, flattening each bill onto the counter under her palm. On the cover, you couldn't see Spider-Man's face, only the back of his costume, but he was clearly frantic, swinging between all the illustrations of these people he loved, looking for the one he was going to lose.

"Thanks," Sheila mumbled.

"Hey, no sweat."

She was still looking at the cover when one of the boys started to put her purchase into a plastic bag.

My Spider sense is never wrong! Spider-Man insisted from inside.

"Wait!" Sheila said. It came out in a shout, louder than she meant it. It was the comic books, with their block letters and their interjections; they were mixing with the order in her head. The boys looked startled. "I'm sorry," she said. "How does he know someone is going to die?"

"I'm not sure I'm following," the boy in charge said.

Sheila swallowed a knot in her throat. "Spider sense," she said. "What exactly does it do?"

The first boy looked at his manager, as if asking for permission to explain something so basic to the customer to whom they'd just sold a collector's item. The manager nodded, and the first boy looked back at Sheila. "It warns Spider-Man of danger," he said. "It tells him when something bad is going to happen so he can try to avoid it in time."

"And it's always right?" Sheila asked.

Both boys nodded. "But it sucks," the boy in charge said. "It's a lot of heavy shit to have to deal with."

225

"I mean, that's the thing about his enemies," the other boy continued. "There's a ton of them, way more than three, and most of them reappear too, but everything that goes on in his mind, the stuff that keeps him up at night, it's worse than all of them combined, you know? I mean you feel bad for the guy, genuinely bad."

"Which is sort of the genius of Parker as a superhero," said the other boy. "I mean he's tough and everything. He fights some badass villains and wins, but I don't envy the guy. Not for a second."

"He's his own worst enemy," the other boy translated.

"And then they went and killed the girl he loved."

"*They?*" Sheila repeated. "They who? I thought it was the Green Goblin who killed her."

"Who?" both boys boomed, "Conway and Romita, of course. The writers!"

Both boys shook their heads at the thought of it. "It gets worse. The way it's drawn you can't tell if it's the fault of the Goblin or whether it's Spidey himself who's responsible. The Goblin pushes her off the bridge, sure, Spidey's trying to save her, he flings out his webbing, it catches her leg . . . SNAP! . . . but not in time, right? Which means — "

" — it could have been that her neck snapped from the impact of being caught by his webbing."

"The way they write it, it could have been Spidey's fault."

"The fans were outraged! Some stopped reading after that issue, boycotted, because the writers just couldn't give the poor guy a break."

"But that's terrible!" Sheila cut in. "He was in love with Gwen Stacy," she insisted. "Everyone knows that." She understood now that she was pleading — to whom, it wasn't clear. These stories had been written forty years ago. There was nothing the boys could do.

The boys exchanged glances. The boy in charge said, "You're preaching to the choir, babe."

Then the other boy ran into the back and produced a second comic book, *ASM* #124, three issues later, and opened it to the back page where there were letters to the writers. He placed the open issue in front of Sheila on the counter. Both boys leaned back and waited, gave her the reading space to see for herself. Sheila leaned in and began to read the letters printed there.

Gentlemen,

How much more agony must Parker live through? This issue, #121, has a certain finality to it. I know that Gwen is really dead. So I have the right to cry. I have the right to mourn her death. I have the right to know that I will not feel absurd three issues later when she is suddenly brought back to life by some super-alien life ray. The rest of "The Night Gwen Stacy Died" completes one of the most heart-rending, magnificently scripted and laid out sagas to date.

After a dramatic, typical Spidey rescue . . . BLAM! It hits you! "I saved you, honey . . . I saved you." He didn't save her. Fantasy? Reality? Where is the dividing line? Gentlemen, you have succeeded in placing the comic book, SPIDER-MAN, onto a newly defined aesthetic plane of realism. But Lord, you have also succeeded in touching my soul.

Salvatore M. Trento

Dept. of Anthropology, S.U.N.Y.

Buffalo, N.Y.

Marvel,

How DARE you kill Gwendolyn Stacy!? You are a pack of soulless, mercenary sadists. I am no longer a True Believer.

J. M. Black

Alamedam, Calif.

To whoever had the idea of killing off Gwen Stacy,

You rattlesnake, you buzzard, you large red insect, you worm, you cockroach, you lizard, you skunk, you tapeworm in the digestive system of humanity: Why is it when a superhero and his girl finally seem to be getting it together, you kill off the girl? May you lose every tooth in your head but one, and in that one may you have a toothache; may someone put arsenic in your midnight cocoa; may you be struck down by a spirit of justice and be reincarnated as an amoeba!

RFO Sergio J. Andrade

Roselle, N.J.

Gentlemen,

As you said, SPIDER-MAN #121 was a shocker. Frankly, I wonder what kind of home life you people must have, or had as children.

Donald Shinners

Wauwatosa, Wisc.

Sheila blinked and backed away from the page. The readers were right; the writers were sadists. When she looked up, both boys were huddled behind the counter. They had been watching her read, waiting for her to react. The boy in charge and the boy who worked under him nodded sympathetically in her direction. "Bastards," one of them mumbled, and everyone agreed, the things that the superhero was made to stomach were shameful. After sticking it out for years watching Parker survive so many disappointments, you couldn't help imagining some other life for him and his girl where things work out.

THE TAXI COULD NOT drive fast enough, and he thought he was never going to get there, that perhaps the driver was taking a circuitous route only to let the meter run, which was something you had to watch out for even in Iowa — Peter should know — and certainly here it was more common. Peter sat in the back seat of the taxi, staring into the address in his hand. Since turning the corner away from the street that housed Lenka and Petra's apartment, he recognized nothing in the dark — each time he managed to catch the name of a cross street in the taxi's headlights, the intersections seemed absurd, unlikely: Hermitage and Armitage, Hoyne and LeMoyne. What sort of city planners would make rhymes of so many intersections? — so all he could do was trust the driver, put his faith in the route they traveled. But when the taxi finally rounded the corner onto Walton Street and stopped in front of an apartment, Peter felt he had arrived too soon. He stood before the front door with his hands stuffed in his pockets and waited for a long time before he pressed his fingers into a fist and began to knock. His heart shook at the thought of Sheila on the other side of it, walking toward him now, and how he would hold her, how he would inhale the citrus smell of her hair.

Within a few seconds he heard the sound of the deadbolt and chain unlocking. "Coming," he heard a man's voice say, "coming."

Then the door was opened and the man who had spoken stood beside it. The man continued to hold the door open, but he didn't get out of the way for Peter to pass, and Peter made no attempt to advance into the apartment. He remained rooted to the spot in the hallway, a mirror opposite to the man inside, who stood exactly eye-level at Peter's height. So it was the eyes he saw first. The eyes of the man were dark, but clear. They were the same as those that he had dreamed every night for a week in Iowa. He felt his stomach drop in confirmation of this fact. He and Sheila had done it; they had done this thing together. It was as he was moving away from the man's eyes to take in the rest of him that he took a step backward, his foot caught on the mat in the hallway, and he stumbled slightly, he looked down at his shoe, and then looked up again and saw that the man's mouth now was beginning to open, as if to address him. There was something about the mouth too that Peter recognized.

The man was saying something now, and then he said it again. This time more quietly, more like a whisper.

Seth.

There was that saying, he had heard it said before: as far as the human ear is concerned, there's no equal comfort to the sound of one's name. People were always saying this, narcissists it seemed. But there was something else to it, he was now remembering; it had to do with the mouth of the other person, the one that was doing the speaking. Because it was rare for a mouth to be able to perform this trick, to offer asylum in a familiar sound, shelter in a syllable.

* * *

Peter stepped quickly through the doorway of the apartment so the man was close enough to touch. He pushed the palm of his hand against the man's shoulder; it was solid. He touched the top of the man's forearm where his shirt met his skin, and there was muscle there, and bone. He pulled together each one of his fingers into a fist and he landed the fist in the pit of the man's stomach, between his ribs. The man reeled backward for a second, coughed, touched the place where Peter's fist had made contact. He said nothing.

Peter took another step forward into the apartment, closing the distance between them. "It hurt?" he asked.

"Not bad," the man said, taking a quick breath, releasing it. "Yeah, a little."

Peter nodded. He spoke slowly to keep his voice from shaking. "You died twenty years ago." He said this plainly, neither question nor accusation.

The man looked at the floor. "I tried to, yes," he said. "I wanted to."

Peter's throat tasted of salt. He swallowed the taste. He had come here to save a man who died the way his brother had. Now, to find Jake standing before him in place of the stranger, alive, healthy, Peter thought he would kill him himself. He shook his head. "I tried to?" he repeated. He felt dizzy now, standing so close to the man, his brother, or some version of Jake, some vision of him.

"How long," he said.

"How long what?" asked his brother.

"Have you been here?"

Jake said nothing for a minute. Then he said, "Twenty years."

Peter was nodding now. He was trying to get his head on a single thought, he couldn't focus on the place, this definite place all along, never dead, never not eating or sleeping or washing his hair like anyone else, all this time, one state away. "Chicago," is what he said finally. Then, "Chicago, Illinois." Then he felt the room start to get hot, the heat under his fingernails again, as it had happened when he dreamed this place, and he felt like he needed to sit down, like his legs could not support his weight, and his brain was running the name of this place through its reels like the even sound of a passing train — Chicago, Illinois, Chicago, Illinois — and then the room started to go funny, dark spots, all of them fuzzy, like after looking at the sun, the white wall behind his brother's head was full of these dark pools, portals, negative spaces you had to watch not to fall into, he remembered thinking, which was the last thing he remembered thinking before he fell into one.

How to adjust the story you'd followed all your life to allow for the details that were continuously accumulating, piling on top of one another, until there was no sense in looking the other way? Always a new telling, a revision, had to be crafted to deal with the worst of it. He learned this from his mother. Jake was dead to them for twenty years because this seemed the only way to accommodate the reality of his abandoning them. But this had been his mother's imposition, her organization of the latest details into something they could live with.

That night again at the kitchen table: his mother, the dominos.

You and me, honey. How she wouldn't stop repeating it. How about you and me?

Where's Jake? he'd asked her. And for a long time she hadn't answered him, until finally she said, He's gone.

Gone where?

How she had started with the truth. How Jake had gotten on a

232

bus that crossed from Iowa into another place, this nearby city, in the middle of the night. In towns like theirs people talk; even outside of daylight, there are witnesses to everything.

He had started to cry, and his mother had pushed all the dominos to the side of the table. A few had clattered against the kitchen tiles. His mother had opened her arms and he'd crawled across the table and into her lap. And his mother had smoothed her hands against his hair and said, baby, I'm so sorry.

Because in a way wasn't it worse? To have helped to bring someone back to life, into the life you had all maintained together, and then to have to hear secondhand, from neighbors, from spies, that your effort wasn't worth anything. To not know whether he would ever come back, or whether he would always come back, and always they would be abandoned again and again.

His mother rubbing his back, rocking him back and forth in the kitchen chair. The white dots of the dominos on the kitchen floor winking up at him like faraway constellations.

Listen, his mother said. And Peter knew he would listen to anything. Whatever she said, he would believe her. He's gone, she said. Do you understand?

Peter nodded.

He went to sleep again, his mother said. Asleep, the way we found him in the closet.

How he'd howled, how he'd bit down into the wool of her sweater. But his mother didn't tell him this for nothing: it was better that he know, that he understand the bounds of their shared grief and his own place in it, understand irrefutably that they had only one another to care for from now on.

A pillow stuffed beneath his neck, a damp kitchen towel folded across his forehead. He blinked; he looked around. A kitchen chair had been pulled to the side of the couch, his bedside, and sitting on the chair was his brother. Jake was pushing his hair away from his face, away from the towel, like his mother used to do when he'd been down with a fever. Peter sat up with a start.

"It's okay," Jake said. He pushed him back to the pillow. "You passed out."

Peter nodded. "For how long?"

"A few hours," he said.

"I haven't been sleeping," Peter said. He felt the impulse to defend himself. "I've been having these dreams."

"It's okay," Jake said again.

Peter began remembering then. "I punched you," he said.

Jake nodded. His mouth tightened.

"I came here to rescue someone else," Peter admitted. "I dreamed someone who was trying to kill himself the same way you did."

"You rescue a lot of people?" Jake said quietly.

Peter shook his head. "No one," he said. "I have never done it right yet."

"You rescued Gwen," Jake said. "She said so."

Peter blinked. "From what?" he asked. But before his brother could answer, he said, "I got her in trouble is all I've done. I've done her more harm than anyone." But then he remembered: she was supposed to be here. "She was here in the apartment?" he asked. "You saw her here?"

Jake nodded.

Peter felt his stomach fold in his chest. "Where is she?"

"She's coming," Jake said. "She'll be here soon."

Peter stared into the ceiling. She was coming. She would be here. He exhaled hours of worry. He said, "How did she find you?"

Jake looked away for a minute into the other room. He said, "She kidnapped me."

Peter felt the tiny hairs on the back of his neck rise.

"What?" he said. "I don't understand."

"She was angry with me, I guess. There was this stray dog I was looking after, and Gwen thought it was a wild animal I was trying to unlawfully domesticate, and she pulled a gun on me, tied me up and everything."

"She tied you up?"

"Yeah, the dog and me both," Jake said. "She must have taken the dog with her 'cause she's not around, but you'll have to see her when she comes back. Beautiful dog," Jake continued. "I started calling her Patch, you know, after our old dog. Remember, you know how Patch was, real smart and the way his ears — "

Peter cut him off. "Patch is dead."

"Well, I figured," Jake said quietly. "It's been twenty years. The best ones don't make it past fourteen."

"No, not like you think," Peter said. "It was right after you left. I watched him run from our property into the field behind the house."

"How do you mean?"

"I mean he didn't stick around either," Peter said roughly, frustrated by the need to translate for his brother. Wolves lived in the woods behind the house. Foxes were sighted. Jake knew this as well as he did.

It was quiet for a minute. They were taking turns, asking questions, trying to fill in the gaping holes of all that had happened with facts they could trade.

Jake spoke then, a whisper. He said, "Why did you kidnap her?"

Peter raised his voice. "Did she say that?" The thought of

Gwen betraying him in this way made his stomach churn. He had offered this to her, this story as a possible alibi, but he didn't think she'd use it.

"Relax," Jake said. "She didn't have to say it. She's all over the news."

"We were only pretending," Peter said. "Gwen asked me to point the gun at her."

"Gwen's her real name?"

Peter considered this. He could feel his brother testing him. "It's the name I gave her," he said. But that sounded wrong, conceited, as if he thought he could walk around handing out new names to everyone, so he said, "It's more like a nickname."

Jake nodded. Then he said, "She called you Peter."

Peter swallowed.

"You found my comic books," Jake said.

"Yeah, I found them," Peter said. "I snuck them out of your room when Mom started throwing all your stuff away. I pretended that you had left them there for me to find."

"You read them all?" Jake said. "I had quite a collection."

Peter stared off into the kitchen. "I was lonely," he said, as if in defense. "I had just learned to read."

He wanted to explain about the dreams, this apartment, about Gwen and their journey, all of it, but Jake was talking over him then, saying, "Shhh, later Seth. Tell me later." Jake was folding the towel over his forehead again, he was telling him to go back to sleep. Peter allowed himself to close his eyes again; it was quiet for a long time. Then he started to hear Jake's voice speaking to him, speaking quietly while he slept, like his brother wanted to be the first to explain. He could feel Jake by his bedside the whole time, and sometimes he heard bits of things he said, like a car radio passing in and out of range. He heard Jake speaking, but couldn't pull all the words together. He felt the pressure of his brother's hands fold the towel again and again over his forehead. He heard him speak the names of familiar things. The name of their dog, the name of the park near the house, people they had known in Iowa. He heard him speak the name of their mother.

The lake. The way he dreamed it was the same as always: there are tiny tremors of waves touching the rocks close to shore, retreating. Always the water there is black and full of living things: things with gills and spores; things with lungs must keep treading water.

A crowd is gathered around. A crowd is waiting for word. There is the camera. There is the microphone.

Algae, garbage, pieces of silt.

Sheila, her hair drenched and floating. Her eyes open wide as a swimmer's.

It was late when Peter woke up alone in the living room with a glass of water in his hand. He stood from the couch quickly and started making his way from room to room. "Sheila," he said aloud. Jake had said she was coming; hours ago she had been on her way. He started looking through the rooms. "Sheila?" he said into every dark room of his brother's apartment. The door to Jake's bedroom had been closed. It was late now; the sun had gone down long ago. He reached for the doorknob of his brother's room but thought better of it. He reached for the switch on the television. He needed something else to look at to stop seeing the way her eyes had looked in the water. He needed to watch something moving for a while until morning came. He turned on the television and sat back down on the couch. The couch smelled of Sheila, and for a moment it settled him to find a trace of her.

On the television, it was difficult at first to say what he was seeing, except to say it was the lake. It was the lake as he'd dreamed it.

A crowd had gathered. There was the man with the microphone. He was speaking to the camera, and behind him was a crowd, a stretcher, a searchlight trawling slowly through the water and settling on a place close to shore, the shallow parts, where the rocks stood up at odd angles like the ends of sunken boats. There was a swarm of orange vests, circling a bit of land like hurried animals, gathered around the water as if they were trying to pull something out of it. Peter stood in front of the television and waited for the camera to settle on the thing in the water. He felt a warm pulse move from his head out to each of his extremities.

NOVAK AWOKE TO THE uneasy feeling that he was being watched. He had left Seth sleeping on the couch with a pillow and a blanket hours ago, but as Novak forced his eyes open, he was startled to find his brother standing over his own bed.

"Jesus Christ," Novak said. "What are you doing?"

"I need a ride to the hospital," Seth said.

"What are you talking about?"

"I'm dying," Seth said.

"You're not dying," Novak said. "Go back to sleep."

"Okay," Seth said. "You would know better than me. I just swallowed everything in the cabinet in your bathroom."

Novak sat up in bed.

"So am I dying?" Seth asked.

Novak was looking for his pants. He was looking for the light switch to find his pants. He said, "Get in the truck."

Seth didn't say another word. He walked to the passenger side of the truck parked on the street and was already sitting in it a few minutes later when Novak found the keys and made his way toward it.

Novak started the engine. He began to drive fast. He said, "Don't put your fucking head down. Talk to me," he said. "Start talking."

At first Seth didn't say anything, and Novak thought he was already losing him. He thought he was starting to go to sleep. He reached over and slapped his brother's face. He said, "Talk to me."

Seth's eyes watered but would not focus. He said, "They're looking for her body in the lake."

So the drugs were working quick. His brother was already talking nonsense, but he had to keep him talking. Novak spoke quietly. He said, "Whose body, Seth?"

"Sheila," Seth said. "Gwen."

Novak tightened his hands on the wheel. He said, "How do you know that?"

"The cameras there," said Seth. "I dreamed it. I saw it on TV."

Seth's voice had started to drone. His head was shifting with the road. Novak said, "Keep talking."

"They're coming for me," Seth said.

"Jesus, Seth, no one's coming for you," Novak said. "We're getting you some help."

Seth started to laugh then, a quiet laugh.

Novak pulled up to the hospital and called to two orderlies standing around. He needed their help to lift Seth from the truck; his body had become heavy. Novak pulled at his brother's hair. He slapped his face.

Seth's eyes were rolling back and forth in his head. "I've changed my mind," he said softly. He sounded like a child again, the way he spoke to Novak. "Is that okay?"

"It's okay," Novak said. He started to think of his mother then. The thought came quickly and landed hard in his chest: he wanted to see his mother. As he watched the men push Seth's body flat onto the stretcher and wheel him through the sliding glass doors, he thought back to his mother, no older than Novak was now, with her hands hard on his face. Novak hadn't wanted to be found. He had shut himself inside his closet for half a day, curled still beneath a pile of dirty laundry. He hadn't wanted to be found, and he hadn't changed his mind when he woke up in the hospital to his mother's hands on his face — two days after she'd dug him up from the linens and dragged him into the living world of his childhood bedroom.

The night before, he had tried to ask Seth about their mother. Between his brother's long bouts of sleep, Novak had gone to the refrigerator and pulled out two beers. He thought a cold drink would do them both good. He walked into the living room and offered Seth one of the cans. Seth propped his head up slowly onto the arm of the couch, like a kid home from school preparing to swallow a spoonful of some sort of antibiotic. Novak tried to offer Seth the glasses that had fallen from his face when he passed out, but Seth waved them away. "I don't really need those to see," he said.

"No?"

"They're more like a disguise."

Novak nodded. Coming from his brother, this somehow wasn't entirely surprising. It was hard to see Seth as an adult, despite his size, despite the tenor of his voice; his mannerisms were the same as they had been at six. He had a tendency to blink too much when nervous. His posture was atrocious. But Novak felt like it was time; he had been explaining his side of things up until this point, and now he had questions whose answers he wanted to hear.

"How's mom?"

Seth shrugged his shoulders. He took a sip from his can. "Fantastic," he said flatly and looked at the ceiling. "She's starting to act like an old lady already."

"She's sixty-two."

Seth raised his eyebrows. "You've been keeping track of birthdays all the way out here, but never bothered to write home for one of them."

Novak looked at the floor. The truth was he wrote a letter almost every year. He had a shoebox full of handwritten letters beneath his bed, addressed to his mother.

"When's mom's birthday?" Seth asked.

"November seventh," Novak said.

"When's mine?" Seth asked.

"January eighteenth. You turned twenty-six this year." Ask me anything, he wanted to say to his brother, as if a few minutes of trivia could make up for so many years of absent acknowledgement. It was only that acknowledging the passing years at all became increasingly difficult as so many began to pile up on one another, that his handwritten notes seemed pathetic, unwarranted, a selfish desire to dredge up a past that everyone else had already ceased thinking about. He was beginning to understand only now that wasn't really the way it was.

Seth said, "Sixty-two is young. Her brain is young, but it's getting lazy. She's eating almonds and berries for meals like a squirrel or some kind of scavenger animal that hordes things." Novak smiled, but Seth wasn't smiling. He wasn't making eye contact at all anymore. He spoke to the carpet in the living room. "She stopped working at the hospital three years ago already, and so much time alone isn't good for her, you know, and I'm trying, I mean, I'm trying to be there as much as I can." He looked up now and met Novak's eyes, and Novak could see Seth's eyes were glazed and blinking like crazy. "I never should have left her,"

Seth said. "I never should have left her alone, but I thought I had to do it."

Novak said, "She's an adult. It's okay."

And Seth said, "No, it isn't." His voice shook, but his point, his accusation, was made regardless. Novak had already freed himself of such obligations long ago. If anything happened to their mother, it was Seth who would consider himself responsible. Novak was a wildcard, an extra, an other, beside the point. There was no one who depended on him anymore. He had done what he had done in Iowa because he wanted to be free of so many obligations, and he'd gotten what he wanted. He was free. It was a terrible feeling.

He was in the waiting room, waiting again. He was waiting for the doctor, but when finally a man stood over him, Novak looked up to find a police officer in plain clothes flashing his badge.

"Jake Novak?" the man said.

Novak stood up.

"Your relation to the patient?"

"He's my brother," Novak said.

"This way please, Mr. Novak," the man said. He began to walk, and it seemed the man would take him to Seth, but he led Novak into a vacant hospital room and closed the door.

Novak looked to each of the room's empty beds. He said, "Is he going to make it?"

The officer produced a notepad and flipped it open. "I'm not a doctor, Mr. Novak. The doctors are doing what they can. In the meantime, I need to ask you about your relation to Seth Novak."

"I thought I just told you he's my brother."

"Mr. Novak," he said again, "are you aware that your brother is wanted by the police?"

Novak had to make a split-second decision. There were two sides to every story, and in that moment he decided he would stick with one version and plead innocent to the other. "What for?" he asked.

"Armed robbery," the man said. "Illegal possession of a fire-arm. Abduction of a minor. Grand theft auto."

"It's a mistake," Novak said. "You've got the wrong guy."

"Oh, it's no mistake, I can assure you of that," the officer said. "Did you know anything of your brother's plans to abduct this woman?" The officer produced a photograph of Sheila and placed it in Novak's hands.

Novak lifted the photograph. "Gwen Stacy," he said. "That's his girlfriend."

The officer shook his head. "This woman's name is Sheila Gower. She was abducted from her place of employment in Coralville, Iowa, five weeks ago. Did your brother ever speak to you about this woman?"

"Yeah, just yesterday," Novak said. "He told me he was in love with her."

The officer wrote something down in his notepad.

When Seth woke up, Novak was allowed into the room. The police officer was already standing in the hallway, waiting, when Novak approached. The doctor opened the door, and together Novak and the officer advanced toward Seth.

Seth was in bed, propped up with pillows. He didn't watch either of them walk into the room. He stared straight ahead at the wall directly across from him.

"Seth Novak," the officer spoke first. "I need to advise you that you're under arrest."

Seth said nothing. He stared at the wall. Then he said, "I confess."

"Confess?" Novak shouted. "Confess to what? You were with me all last night." Novak turned to the officer. "He was with me all night. What happened to Sheila Gower has nothing to do with him. My brother is confused."

"Mr. Novak," the officer interrupted, "I'm going to have to ask you to either settle down or leave the room."

Seth continued speaking to the wall as if he'd heard nothing. He said, "Gwen Stacy died because of my negligence. I accept culpability for my error."

Novak walked to his brother's bedside. He pushed his hand into Seth's hand. He began speaking low. "Listen to me, Seth," he said. "Shut up and listen. Peter Parker is a good man. He did the best he could to save Gwen Stacy. You know he didn't kill her. There was somebody else on the bridge that night, remember?"

Seth continued staring at the wall, but he nodded his head. He looked up at Novak.

"Mr. Novak," the officer was saying again, but this time it was unclear which of them he'd meant to address.

"Who else was on the bridge, Seth?"

"The Green Goblin," Seth said quietly. He closed his eyes.

"That's right," Novak said. "The Green Goblin killed Gwen Stacy." Novak was making headway. He felt it in his chest. A small victory, a matter of simple, sound logic, and he would prove his brother innocent. Somewhere in the city, there was a green goblin on whose presence all of this could be blamed, some alternate evil force or deed that could explain these false accusations. Novak turned to the officer who again had taken up his notepad. "I hope you're getting all this."

PART THREE

COURAGE IS A SLIPPERY thing, difficult to grasp, and the more she caught a look at it full on lately, the more it had a tendency to resemble running in the other direction. Sheila hailed a cab. In Iowa you had to call ahead if you wanted a taxi. They weren't just driving around aimlessly, waiting for you to throw up your arm. Sheila started to settle into the back seat.

"Where to?" asked the driver.

How easy it would have been to give the address of Jake's apartment. Peter was surely there by now, and to think how he would push his face into her shoulder and breathe in her hair. She fingered the edge of the comic book she held to her chest and hesitated.

"Where you going?" the driver asked again. He sounded like he wasn't from around here.

"To the lake," she said.

The man caught her eyes in the rearview mirror. "Cross street?"

Sheila blinked. She hadn't counted on this. In her mind, the lake had become a mythical thing, not a place with cross streets one could give precise directions to get to. She was going there to look around, confront this place Peter had dreamed for her.

"Doesn't matter," she said. "Whatever's closest."

The man nodded, but when Sheila opened the door wider for Patch to jump into the back seat beside her, the driver shook his head. "Whoa, uh-uh, easy there," he said slowly. His voice turned more aggressive then, shouting: "Get back, get back." He had a folded newspaper in his hand and he began to swat it around the back seat in Patch's direction.

"Come on," said Sheila. "Just one ride."

The man growled. "Lady, get that thing away from my taxi!"

"We're tired," Sheila said. "Please."

But the man began yelling at her in another language, pointing at Patch, reaching for his dispatch radio, and Sheila climbed out of the cab and slammed the door; she decided they would be fine walking after all.

The sun was already starting to set, the wind was picking up. She heard a homeless man sitting on a bus stop bench shouting *windy city! windy city!* as if he'd just coined the epithet to compete with the sound.

You sometimes heard about how all names are false, that's the whole problem with language, having to refer to things somehow. You sometimes heard how there are names that only dogs can know, at the frequency of whistles and earthquakes. How there are names that make themselves heard only to broken bones.

Sheila was surprised by how calm she felt at dusk in the city. She felt strangely confident in their route. She paused briefly to consult the numbers below each street name on the signs she passed to confirm they were heading east, and from there Patch seemed to know the way. The animal walked just ahead of Sheila, a guide or a guardian of some kind. It made her feel less lost.

Windy city, windy city!

Sheila remembered hearing her mother say that when things are misplaced there is a prayer to Saint Anthony that sometimes works, the bulk of which is: *Saint Anthony, Saint Anthony, look around, something's lost that can't be found.* In this case you don't have to name what's lost, but you've already named the saint to whom your prayer is directed. Even in this case, you need to be specific. There is another saint who is the patron of lost causes. Holy men and women are not above this kind of bureaucracy.

Jude, John, Peter, Paul, Sebastian.

Michigan, Huron, Ontario, Erie, Superior.

Anthony. Not the saint. The boy in the cafeteria.

Her mother. At the sink washing dishes while her father dries.

The temperature was dropping. Mothers were cleaning up from dinner while upstairs, girls learned their bodies in beds or in bathwater. Families concentrated themselves, huddled around the television. Lost things waited silently in mines and wells. Everywhere people were speaking aloud the names of loved ones and strangers.

Sheila started walking to the place where the tide was coming in. The lake was shaking from the wind. It looked dark and uninhabitable, but certainly there were scores of living things making a home there under the tide. A large swath of grass separated the lake from the traffic of the highway, an expanse wide enough to resemble a park if you could forget about the chaos of Lake Shore Drive behind it. A concrete walkway hugged the shoreline, where the waves occasionally lapped up onto the pavement. Sheila found a flattened patch of grass near the water and made a seat for herself there. The tide was loud and the traffic was loud, and it surprised Sheila that there could be so much noise in a place where she was alone. She had been sitting for a while when she started to make out a new sound in all of the racket. It was a call, long and low, a faraway cry, but when she looked around her she only saw a thin man, standing on the shoulder of the road, walking with a strange gait, walking slowly, looking now either at the traffic or at the lake, she couldn't say which. Sheila turned to the water. Patch chose a nearby spot to sit for a while; Sheila folded her legs beneath her and opened the comic book in her lap.

And there she was, alive in the pages. Gwen Stacy was as pretty a girl as everyone said — remarkably tall and thin and delicate in bone structure — and Sheila felt strange but also a little sad, as if she were spying on another woman's private life, the way she imagined a man must feel each time the most beautiful woman he's ever seen walks into a room, how it stifled the breath for a second and how it made you want to give her hair a little tug, to take the woman and press her firmly down under your thumb, like the corner of a page in a book. But Gwen does not make Peter starve for her attention. These are the facts at the start of the *ASM* #121: It has been a while since Gwen and Peter have spent any time together. Peter's been in Montreal, taking pictures for the newspaper. And to see how Gwen adored him, how she watched him from the corner of every frame they shared. It isn't long before she is captured. This is how it happens. She is sitting in Peter's apartment waiting for him to show up. She is standing by the window with her black velvet headband and her impossibly long black eyelashes, clutching her handbag, waiting. Impatient, she turns from the window and cradles her chin in the palm of her hand. Her eyes are closed, her back is to the window. So it is the reader who first observes the outline of a flying green form approaching.

Sheila looked up from the comic book. There was that sound again, that low calling. It sounded more definitively human now, and as Sheila turned, she recognized that it was indeed the man, the thin one from the road's shoulder, but he had closed the distance between himself and the lake, he had crossed Lake Shore Drive; he was closer to the water now. Sheila continued reading; she fingered the pages, turning them fast.

By the time Spider-Man finds his love collapsed in a heap at the height of the George Washington Bridge — in fact, the art portrayed the Brooklyn Bridge, the boys at the comic book store had explained; you can't trust the writers to tell it to you straight! — Gwen Stacy is already unconscious. She will stay unconscious for the rest of her story. So she doesn't hear Spider-Man approach and tell the Goblin he'll pay for threatening the life of the woman he loves, she doesn't hear the Goblin call Spider-Man by her own boyfriend's name — his true identity all along — because the poor girl sleeps through everything.

The fight continues, villain and hero taunt each other from either side of her, and the push comes before Sheila anticipates it. The Goblin zooms by on his remote-controlled flyer, and it looks like it's the rush of wind trailing behind him that knocks the sleeping Gwen Stacy from her perch off the bridge's shelf. Everything that follows happens as the boys described, but it's always more terrible to read it for oneself.

It starts with a *WHAK!* The *WHAK!* of the Goblin's shove and is followed by that frantic cry of Peter's.

GWEN!

NO!

FFFFTT! His webbing gasps, flung over the edge of the bridge, which catches the girl's thigh with a *SWIK!* and offers a moment of relief.

But there is also a *SNAP!* and it is this *SNAP!* that breaks the hearts of disbelieving readers, the smallest, the quietest of the sounds, lightly drawn near the corner of her neck where her long blond hair still chases the length of her body in its flight, and you want to push your hands into her hair and feel for where you imagine the tiny shell of her ear is waiting for word of whether she is going to survive this. And when Spider-Man approaches the same ear, after pulling her slowly up from the fall with his webbing, when he crouches before her ear and says *Hey kid, what's wrong? Don't you understand? I saved you* — and he pushes his hands into her hair, you try to forget about that *SNAP!*, and wait for the sound of Peter's voice to reach her ear and her eyes to flutter open and then for the kiss. Of course this never happens. Gwen Stacy is dead. The cause of death is uncertain. She was asleep or unconscious or poisoned or dead throughout the entire conflict, and now you're left at the edge of the Brooklyn Bridge with a crazed and desperate superhero clutching the body of the woman he loves in his arms, slurring insults in the open air at a goblin who you have to assume is hovering there still, just out of frame.

Sheila stared at the final page for only a moment longer before closing the comic book. She felt sick to her stomach. Gwen Stacy never had a chance. She had been out like a light for the entire issue. She could do nothing to react to the elements of the story that befell her. Even with her long hair and lovely bone structure and quick tongue, even with her extraordinary boyfriend — none of it made a bit of difference; she was a victim of circumstance, of accident, of fate — helpless to the sway of the story that had already started happening around her.

There was the sound again. This time Patch's ear gave a slight twitch in the direction of the call and she stood up quickly. The man who was making the sound was fully visible to Sheila now just on the other side of the grass. He wore a leather jacket, a jacket too warm for the weather. Sheila stood as well; she and Patch began to walk out of the way of his path, but the man seemed to be heading right for them. He was still yelling some-thing she could almost place. It might have been another lan-guage, but he was looking at Sheila when he said it like she would understand the words. She was just starting to run when she was able to make out the man's call. "Hey, wait a minute," he was say-ing. The man had something to ask her. He was asking her not to run. Sheila set the comic book down in the grass, dead weight, and picked up speed. Patch began growling under her breath, foaming a little at the mouth; she started to angle her path toward the lake where the water was spilling over onto the pavement. Sheila followed.

She thought, *So this is how it starts when the goblin comes for you.*

Sheila had run off the grass and was fully on the concrete walk-way, along the lake, when the man caught up with her. He closed his hand around her wrist.

"Let go of me," Sheila said. She tried to wrestle her arm free of him, but his grip was firm.

They were closer now to the edge of the walkway. The man's hair was blowing all over the place, into his eyes, away from his eyes. His eyes were watery, rimmed in red. He looked half-crazy, but when he spoke again his voice was quiet and pleading, almost a whisper. He looked her in the eye, and Sheila looked back at him. He said, "Stop yelling." He said, "I won't hurt you. I want to talk to you."

Sheila felt dizzy. It was dark, and she couldn't see well. They were very close to the water now. She heard a sharp bark, a low howl, but she couldn't see anything. She spoke slowly. She did not cry. "I'm not who you think," she said to the man, but her voice sounded wrong and raw, not at all like her own. The man looked back at her with his red-rimmed child's eyes and tightened his grip. Her wrist ached and she was afraid, but he was afraid too, and then she saw him for what he was: an unfortunate, a drunk perhaps, a lonely man in green pants by the lake at night.

The scuffle came sooner than she expected it, but it felt more like a temporary imbalance than a certain shove. She dug her nails deep into the flesh of the man's forearm in an effort to free herself, but his grip was firm. He was going to hurt her if she didn't hurt him first. That much was obvious, an old trope from the comic books even a non-reader like Sheila could recognize. She had to think fast to save herself. There would be no outside intervention. She had lost track of Patch in the struggle. She heard a nearby splash. "Patch?" she shouted, but it was quiet again. There were loose rocks beneath their feet on the edge of pavement closest to the water there, and Sheila struggled to keep her grip firm. The sound of their shoes in the gravel was all she heard for a moment, and her breath and the man's breath heaving around her, and then the other sound came up to Sheila on the concrete all at once. It sounded like shallow bubbles coming up from the water. It sounded like a howling under the tide. Sheila looked down — straight down now into the water — and she saw them then. There were hundreds of them and their fur was wet and slick and they were moving their bodies in different directions like carp. There, the hollowed pink of an ear. There, the whisper of a tail flapping at the water. Down here, the coyotes were saying, they were calling to her. Here we are, here we've been all along, our girl, our own cub, here we are, always here. The water there was shallow, and she could see the rocks too — sharp in spaces, alternately pushing up, breaking the tide with their surfaces, and Sheila felt her chest quiver as she thrust every bit of her weight over the edge of the rocks, as she broke her hand free of his, and she smiled as she plummeted down into the water, how they had come for her like this, and how could it be any other way. Even here in an unknown city, at the edge of all that dark water, there were choices to be made, there were things one could do to break free of the thread of a familiar story and fall headlong into something else.

FOR HIS BENEFIT ALONE, his brother was telling the story.

The cops were there too, they were saying Mr. Novak, I'm going to have to ask you to be quiet or leave the room, but Jake was not being quiet, and he was not leaving the room. He was telling the story. Peter had forgotten how good at this his brother had been. Jake perched at the foot of Peter's bed, and in the inches between them there was a space taking shape that had nothing to do with the cops, with the law, the hospital regulations, the day of the week it was, the city they happened to be in. Jake knew the story scene by scene. He started at the beginning.

"There was once a boy who was bit by a spider," his brother said.

"An orphan," said Peter.

"A recluse," Jake nodded. "An absolute nobody." His weight shifted the bed. A fly buzzed in circles around the ceiling tiles. The television weatherman predicted strong winds and rain. The new day would not come for hours.

UNDERWATER IS ALWAYS the reverse of the world above. The coyotes know it as well as anyone. They understand, there are places where all worlds collide. The known world and the world of other things, underlings, alternates, substrata, substitutes.

It sometimes seems to outsiders like the coyotes are just listing every word they've ever heard of, reading aloud from some secret underwater dictionaries.

The coyotes surround the floating girl in the water, say, *sweetheart*, we've been meaning to have a word. Take a load off. Let your guard down. Make yourself at home.

A house, a home, thinks Sheila.

Let bygones be bygones, continue the coyotes. Let sleeping dogs lie.

You're not dogs, Sheila says, you're coyotes. She's grabbing for loose ends of the story here, like she's lost her place in a long and lonely book. Now where was I? she wonders.

Oh dear, the coyotes roll their giant watery eyes, this one is going to need an education.

THE REST WOULD COME later. The scholarship to study science. The attention of the two prettiest girls in school. The villains who give up at the end of each issue but always return. The way he would shout, "Spider powers, I love you," before he knew better, and how he would hold the limp body of the girl he loved more in his arms. But his brother was starting at the beginning. His brother was trying to prove something.

The cops were repeating the names *Parker, Stacy,* writing them down in their notebooks as aliases for the perpetrator and his victim. You could see them thinking *copycat crime.* You could see them thinking *get all this bullshit down now and hand it off to the prosecution later.*

The cops were telling a different story.

They were saying, "Abduction, kidnapping, larceny." Also: "Grand theft auto, false imprisonment, willful endangerment of a minor."

Peter looked at Jake.

Jake said, "When his uncle Ben is killed, Peter is raised by his aunt May alone. She is like a mother to him. He has no father."

"And he feels responsible," Peter said.

His brother nodded. "And he feels responsible — " he repeated, but he trailed off, paused in his telling, and he looked to the black surface of glass that was the window in the room. Peter looked at Jake, feeling the shared terrain of the story start to shift into something else, to wander off course, and Peter was going to fill in the gaps, to help his brother along with the detail that followed which might have slipped between the cracks of memory, when his brother said, "Seth." Peter looked up in recognition as if to say, *yes, I'm here, I'm listening,* but Jake was still looking at the flat black plane of the window when he said it, like there was someone else out there listening as well.

THE COYOTES CONTINUE in their underwater interrogation. You were trying to steal someone else's story and pass it off as your own? You were borrowing something that didn't belong to you? They drop hints.

I was not, the girl stammers.

Oh yeah? What's your name? the coyotes ask her.

The girl pauses. She feels around for her wallet for evidence, identification, a clue, but it isn't anywhere around. *NO!* She thinks, *WAIT!* She thinks, *POW! ZAP!*

Wrong! shout the coyotes as if they can read her thoughts. Imposter! You think an ID would prove anything? The coyotes are laughing at her now, it seems. Official documents, ha! Stories too, just a different kind. They mean nothing here. But don't play around with us — you know this much already. Now, try again, the coyotes demand. Who are you? To what do we owe this visit?

The girl waits, she is thinking. *Être sans histoire* — again. How awful it feels to be without a story, to exist between stories, in this terrible netherworld where she isn't one thing or another.

Look, the coyotes explain, gentler now. We don't have all day. They eye one another nervously, and it's clear that they do have all day. They are always down here treading water. It is Sheila who doesn't have all day, is what they mean by this. It is Sheila who has been underwater for longer than would be advisable already and who is running out of stored air from above.

Then they lean into her ear and Sheila can feel the tough wiry fur around their snouts scrape the edges of her face when they whisper. She is trying with everything she has to concentrate on what they are going to tell her.

AND JAKE SAID, "It was our father's name first."

Peter felt his throat tighten, and he felt the impulse to swallow but could not. He said, "Our — "

" — father." Jake nodded. "You have his name. Mom didn't know how to talk about him after he died," he said, "but someone should have told you."

Peter could feel all the air in the room behind his ears, building pressure there, like tunnels under water. He said, "How did it happen?"

Jake shook his head. "I know it was an accident. I know he was in a boat. There was a storm and no one survived it."

Peter was thinking of water. He was thinking of swallowing water, of the enormous and awful bodies of water that always exist in dreams.

On the television, the weatherman was chatting with the anchorman. The five-day forecast evaporated from the screen as they went live to local coverage. The water of the lake continued to float behind them, black and giant as a piece of carbon paper.

EXPLAIN IT, IT starts simple and gathers speed fast. There are always entire worlds that exist alongside the one you think you've chosen to live in. Sometimes you chose the worlds, and sometimes they chose you. Here is Paris. Here is Iowa. Here is a story you couldn't stop reading as a child about a girl who cut off all her hair into the kitchen sink in the middle of the night and ran away from home. Here is a list of all the dirty words you knew at twelve. Here is the same list at fifteen. Here is the first boy you ever kissed. Here is the one who wants to become your family. Here is your family, same as always: your mother, your sister, your father with a hold on you so firm your feet start to lift off the linoleum of the kitchen floor.

Slow down, Sheila implores of her underwater lecturers. I can't keep up.

You want to keep up? ask the coyotes. So these things matter to you?

There's no more time left to be anything but honest.

Yes, Sheila says. Please.

The coyotes are speaking slowly now for her benefit. One at

a time, they're listing the names of places where stories begin, places where choices start to make landscapes appear one way, or another.

Welcome to Paris, the coyotes begin again. Welcome to Iowa. Welcome to Chicago. Welcome to Montreal. Welcome to Kathmandu.

Kath-man-what?

But it seems the places are irrelevant, their names arbitrary. They all exist. Flights can be purchased between them. This is evidence enough.

Enough!

Sweetheart, the coyotes conclude, there's nothing stable about it. If you're reading the signs, you're writing the signs — they say what you see in them.

Wait, thinks Sheila. Like *action curious fear?*

Duh, say the coyotes, but they say it sweetly. Of course, action curious fear. Isn't it obvious? When action curious fear, *être san histoire* isn't an option.

Please, says Sheila. In plain English!

Congratulations, say the coyotes, it's your life. You can do what you want with it. This sounds suspiciously like something her father said to her once, and it's difficult to say whether the coyotes have selected these words to produce this effect, or whether it is her own brain forging tunnels to make meaning where none exists, but as her foot makes contact with a stone at the bottom of the lake, she bends her knees and pushes off against it, and already she is looking up to the surface of the water now, and her body is rising to meet a light that seems to float there. For a moment, she sees into the next world and what is waiting in it. It's not that she sees a place, the details of the life that she'll construct of little odds and ends. What she sees in the moment is this. There will be consequences to every action. Also spoils.

Then there is the prodding and pulling and a strong light moving over the surface of the water. Helicopters drone above. Search lights and voices. The impossible prodding and pulling. The harsh taste of air.

THEN PETER SAID, "Jake?"

"Yes," Jake said.

"What was he like?"

Jake was quiet for a while, and Peter repeated the question. Finally Jake said, "He had a beard that was every color at once when he let it grow in the summer. He knew how to tie a hundred different kinds of knots. He loved our mother." Then he felt his brother push something into his hand and when he looked down there was a gold round thing sitting there, smooth as a pebble and on a long weathered chain.

"He used to show me how to use it," Jake said.

Peter closed his hand around the thing.

"It always points north so you know how to keep moving even when everything looks the same."

Behind his brother's head was the lake on the television. He was thinking of his father, the man he was named for but never would meet, when he saw the same cameras, the same microphones, the searchlights.

One of the cops said, "Well, I'll be damned," and everyone turned at the same time to witness the place that was being lit up in the water.

SHE WAS STILL COUGHING to adjust to the difference, blinking away the din of the light, when she felt someone lean in close to her ear and begin to speak.

There were news crews and cameras. There were reporters and microphones.

The paramedics were yelling, "Clear a path! A little space here!"

To her, they spoke quietly, so only she could hear. They asked her to answer things they thought she should know, answers to questions that would be important if they were going to let her back into the known world outside the water. They asked for her name and for the names of her parents, the day and the year, they asked her the name of the city where she was born, and what was the last thing she remembered. She could see she was doing well, she was answering all their questions correctly, because they were smiling as they were strapping her down to the stretcher, they were saying yes, good, very good, as they were fastening the tiny needle to her wrist with white tape and moving something cool and steel around where her lungs would be waiting beneath the skin of her soaked dress.

PETER SAT UP in bed and leaned into the television. He looked at the water and watched the same sequence of events he'd seen a thousand times in his sleep. There was the footage of the men in orange vests diving in the water. It seemed impossible that there could be more to witness. It seemed impossible that he should have to witness it again.

"The story is still unfolding hours later," the man with the microphone explained. "Details are beginning to surface since the Coralville, Iowa, abduction victim, Sheila Gower, was correctly identified by a witness who recognized her from a photo being circulated by the Chicago Police Department. The witness claims to have tried to approach Ms. Gower upon identifying her, but a struggle ensued — which ended abruptly with Ms. Gower, according to the witness, 'jumping into the lake.' The witness's allegation is still under investigation as police continue in their efforts to determine how exactly Sheila Gower ended up in the water."

Peter closed his eyes against the rest of the story, against the part he knew was coming, where her prone body would be pulled up from the rocks. He took his brother's hand inside his own. He waited for it to get quiet, the respect that was due. But the quiet didn't come. It started with a question, and then another, and then there was a cacophony of them, questions that came so fast they started interrupting those that came before, gathering speed.

Did you lose hope you would be found?

What do you want to say to your family?

What message would you send to your former captors?

He looked at the television then, and he saw her. She was in the center of all of it, the fixed object around which all the cameras and questions were rotating, and her long hair was still half-wet like a hundred small ropes that hung around her face. But her eyes were open. Her eyes were following the lights of their cameras.

Could you describe the feeling of being rescued?

Any words for the witness who identified you?

Any words for your rescuers?

Sheila blinked at the camera.

Their cameras hovered between her and the viewers at home who waited to hear her say something.

Sheila coughed. She leaned into the microphone.

SHE TRIED ONCE TO SAY IT, and it surprised her how difficult it was to say anything, how her lungs stung to make herself heard to all the things that flashed around her. She breathed in and out and heard the air pull and whistle into the microphone.

She looked into the eye of one of their cameras for the place where he would be, where she understood he would be waiting for word of what they were going to do now that they had survived this thing together. She said his name slowly, loud enough so he could hear it, and then she closed her eyes again against the noise of so much light.

"SETH."

At first it was only a whisper. It was gravelly and dull as a stone underwater, but there could be no mistake: now she was speaking to him alone. He began to laugh, loud and full and from the pit of his stomach. He laughed like a crazy person — this observation did not escape him, surrounded as he was by city authorities in his hospital bed — but a crazy person at the moment in which desperation became something else, something more akin to hope, and the laugh grew fat and fast, picking up speed, and still he did not stop. Even as the cops grew short-tempered, as he watched them escort his brother from the room, as they advised him to lose the grin, as he was read his rights — to remain silent among them — and handcuffed to the guardrails of his hospital bed, he felt the laugh grow in his stomach and spread to every expanse of his body, until it filled him like the first fully formed truth; and how good it felt to accept this fate as it was offered: to be an ordinary man — a criminal perhaps, a madman maybe — but a man like any other, with a certain past and the rest unwritten, trying with what he is and what he is given to deserve the love of an ordinary woman.

SHEILA CONTINUED TO CLOSE her eyes against all of it. She felt the air shift from the wind to the still and steady circulation of the ambulance, and their voices began to trail off and get quieter until she could hear only the regular beep and blink of the machines around her. She allowed herself to drift off and be carried across town to the hospital room somewhere that was waiting, a room she had never seen, a room toward which her father and mother would also begin to navigate now, this place where she would open her eyes, confront this living world again and start to forge her place in it. The machines continued to mark the time; they monitored the fluids that moved around inside her, even as she was so still, they advised her of the general stability of things that continued on course, things that knew what to keep doing even when you paused at an impasse and looked up for help from elsewhere, they kept moving for you, around you, inside you, they knew how to exist in any home you could fathom, how to get you to the next thing without your even knowing it.

ACKNOWLEDGMENTS

This book was written over many years in many cities. The list of those whose influence was necessary to its writing has been growing for a while.

I am indebted to my mentors during my time in the MFA program at Washington University in St. Louis: Kathryn Davis, Marshall Klimasewiski, and Kellie Wells, as well as my talented peers and readers. Thank you to Anton DiSclafani, Tim Mullaney, and Eileen G'Sell; to Eric Lundgren, who helped me find a way to begin again; and to Teddy Wayne, who read this book more times than anyone.

Thank you to my agent, Susan Golomb, for her belief in this book in all its various forms; to my editor, Jenna Johnson, whose direction restored energy and sanity to the revision process; to Anne McPeak for her meticulousness.

Marvel's CD-ROM collection *40 Years of the Amazing Spider-Man* provided an introduction to the first decade of Spider-Man comic books. Digital scans of each original two-page spread, including readers' letters and advertisements, simulated a tactile reading experience and helped situate each comic book within a larger social and historical context.

Many of the French lessons that appear in fragments throughout are modified from the Living Language *All-Audio French* series. Thank you Gaia Bihr for extra help with the French. Thank you Kateřina Meza Breña for help with the Czech.

For assistance and asylum, thank you friends and readers: Brian Gilman for always believing; Scott Polach for his faith in me during the toughest year; Claudio Gancedo Guerra for being a closer reader in his second language than I am in my first; Rob White for making lists with me; Stefan Merrill Block for his steadfast enthusiasm and advice; Isidoro Duarte for his solidarity and patience. Thank you Luther Moss, still one of the best storytellers I know; Christine Mladic for countless readings and for her insight as a photographer and designer; Sarah Ferone for her artistic collaboration and for allowing me to include her illustrations in this book.

Thank you Tim White and Leslie Wiedder for early encouragement. Thank you Tom Simmons, whose classes were an incredible refuge my first years writing in Iowa.

I'm grateful to my family for invaluable guidance, confidence, and love, especially my grandmothers, Rosemary Buishas and Eleanor Pignotti; my brothers, David and Michael, allies and really smart readers; my parents, Jeanine and James, without whose constant conviction and support this book would not exist.